I0629301

THE METHODIST BOBCAT
AND OTHER TALES

Borgo Press Books by ARDATH MAYHAR

The Absolutely Perfect Horse: A Novel of East Texas (with Marylois Dunn) * *The Body in the Swamp: A Washington Shipp Mystery* [Wash Shipp #2] * *Carrots and Miggle: A Novel of East Texas* * *The Clarrington Heritage: A Gothic Tale of Terror* * *Closely Knit in Scarlatt: A Novel of Suspense* * *Crazy Quilt: The Best Short Stories of Ardath Mayhar* * *Deadly Memoir: A Novel of Suspense* * *Death in the Square: A Washington Shipp Mystery* [Wash Shipp #1] * *The Door in the Hill: A Tale of the Turnipins* * *The Dropouts: A Tale of Growing Up in East Texas* * *The Exiles of Damaria: A Novel of Fantasy* * *Feud at Sweetwater Creek: A Novel of the Old West* * *The Fugitives: A Tale of Prehistoric Times* * *The Guns of Livingston Frost: Three Short Novels* * *The Heirs of Three Oaks: A Novel of the Old West* * *High Mountain Winter: A Novel of the Old West* * *How the Gods Wove in Kyrannon: Tales of the Triple Moons* * *Hunters of the Plains: A Novel of Prehistoric America* * *Island in the Lake: A Novel of Native America* * *Khi to Freedom: A Science Fiction Novel* * *The Lintons of Skillet Bend: A Novel of East Texas* * *Lone Runner: A Novel of the Old West* * *Lords of the Triple Moons: A Science Fantasy Novel: Tales of the Triple Moons* * *The Loquat Eyes: More Tall Tales from Cotton County, Texas* * *Makra Choria: A Novel of High Fantasy* * *Medicine Dream: Being the Further Adventures of Burr Henderson* * *Messengers in White: A Science Fantasy Novel* * *The Methodist Bobcat and Other Tales* * *Monkey Station: A Novel of the Future* (Macaque Cycle #1; with Ron Fortier) * *People of the Mesa: A Novel of Native America* * *A Planet Called Heaven: A Science Fiction Novel* * *Prescription for Danger: A Novel of the Old West* * *Reflections; & Journey to an Ending: Collected Poems* * *A Road of Stars: A Fantasy of Life, Death, Love, and Art* * *Runes of the Lyre: A Science Fantasy Novel* * *The Saga of Grittel Sundotha: A Science Fantasy Novel* * *The Seekers of Shar-Nuhn: Tales of the Triple Moons* * *Shock Treatment: An Account of Granary's War: A Science Fiction Novel* * *Slewfoot Sally and the Flying Mule: Tall Tales from Cotton County, Texas* * *Soul-Singer of Tyrnos: A Fantasy Novel* * *Strange Doin's in the Pine Hills: Stories of Fantasy and Mystery in East Texas* * *Strange View from a Skewed Orbit: An Oddball Memoir* * *Through a Stone Wall: Lessons from Thirty Years of Writing* * *Timber Pirates: A Novel of East Texas* (with Marylois Dunn) * *Towers of the Earth: A Novel of Native America* * *Trail of the Seahawks: A Novel of the Future* (Macaque Cycle #2; with R. Fortier) * *The Tulpa: A Novel of Fantasy* * *Two-Moons and the Black Tower: A Novel of Fantasy* * *Vendetta: A Novel of the Old West* * *Warlock's Gift: Tales of the Triple Moons* * *The World Ends in Hickory Hollow: A Novel of the Future* * *A World of Weirdities: Tales to Shiver By*

THE METHODIST BOBCAT AND OTHER TALES

by

Ardath Mayhar

THE BORGO PRESS

An Imprint of Wildside Press LLC

MMX

Copyright © 1993, 2003, 2010 by Ardath Mayhar

All rights reserved.
No part of this book may be reproduced in any form
without the expressed written consent
of the author and publisher.

www.wildsidebooks.com

FIRST EDITION

CONTENTS

DEDICATION

FOR CHARLES SHADDEN, WHO OWNED THAT BOBCAT

PROLOGUE

Although I pretty much stopped writing novels around 1999, I still find short stories breaking out from time to time, and some of these are new—or newish. Some, as well, are old ones that got put back in the files and either never were published or never were submitted to magazine. "Welcome to Shiara" is one of the oldest tales I found, one of my very early ones.

All of these were fun to write, and I hope you will have as much fun reading them as I did putting these together.

—Ardath Mayhar
Chireno, Texas
June 2010

Acknowledgments

"Night Song" was previously published in *Midnight Zoo* in 1993.
"The Face in the Fog" was previously published in *Hardboiled*, September, 2003.

From time to time, Solomon Peat revisits me with another tale from the past. As he speaks in my father's voice and with his inimitable style, I am always ready to listen! However, my friend and classmate Charles Shadden (who else?) was the one who had a pet bobcat and a visiting preacher....

THE METHODIST BOBCAT

Solomon Peat was sitting on the front porch of Mrs. Bragg's store, his hickory splint chair leaned back against the wall, his bare feet stretched out to catch the breeze wafting over miles of pine forest from the river. For once, he and the five small boys who were his usual audience were quiet, all being occupied with sipping sweating bottles of strawberry pop.

From inside the store there came a voice, gruff and firm. "Sol, put on your shoes! It may be spring, but going barefoot is for children, not old duffers. You'll put off customers!"

"My Lord, woman, can you see through walls now?" Sol complained.

Nevertheless, he shuffled on his worn canvas scuffs, just in time. A car was pulling up in front of the store, and he recognized the driver. Lucy Finner would definitely have been offended by bare feet. She even glanced disapprovingly at the unshod toes of the line of small boys swinging their legs off the edge of the porch.

Still, she greeted them as she passed. "Morning, Chuck, Will Henry. Hi there, Les, Tim, Fane. Tell your folks hello for me." The boys nodded back solemnly without missing a sip.

She glanced up at Sol as she climbed the steps. "And Solomon! Not telling tales today?"

He took a last sip. "Now, Lucy, you know it's not polite to talk while you're drinkin' pop."

Will Henry made sure his last gulp had gone down. Then he piped up, "Miz Finner, did you hear about our bobcat kitten? Daddy found it in a den with its dead mother. It's big enough to drink milk out of a bowl. We're goin' to raise it. You ever hear about anybody raisin' a bobcat?"

Lucy Finner plopped into one of the other chairs and began to laugh. When she caught her breath, she gasped, "Yes, indeed, Will Henry. My folks and I got pretty well acquainted with that cat, too. I've never been so scared in all my life...." She went off into another gale of laughter.

Sol thumped the front legs of his chair onto the porch and put his hands on his knees. "Now you know you have a story to tell, Lucy. Sit back and tell us. Your husband'll expect you to shoot the breeze with Mrs. Bragg, so he won't worry if you're a bit late getting home."

Although Mrs. Bragg pretended to scorn the tall tales spun on her porch, she came stumping out and dropped into the wicker rocking chair kept for her personal use. "Getting warm inside," she said, fanning her face with a handkerchief. "It's cooler out here."

Lucy Finner looked down the porch at the waiting audience. "You want to know about that bobcat, I see. Sol, you know my husband about as well as anybody. Did you ever hear him tell about Bobby?"

Sol squinted, thinking hard. Then he began to grin. His belly began to quiver with chuckles beneath his faded blue overalls. "You bet," he rumbled. "But he never said that you and your folks ever knew that cat."

"I met Bobby the same day I met Lawrence," she said. "Let me put this in order for you, or you'll get all confused.

"You see, Larry's Uncle Edward was a hunter. When Larry was about six, Ed shot a bobcat and then found she had a kitten in her den. He managed to catch it, and he decided it would be a nice pet for his nephew. So Larry and his mother and dad spent several weeks getting up at night to bottle feed that bobcat kitten, and once it decided to live, it settled down and was just like a house cat, though it got to be about four times as big."

"That's what we want to do with ours," Will Henry said. "Have a great big cat that can lick the fur off any tomcat anywhere."

Sol made a shushing gesture. "Let her tell her tale, boy," he said. "Lucy, how did your family get involved?"

"Mrs. Finner, Larry's mother, was a devoted Methodist. The church was just up the street from their home, and the Finners always put up visiting preachers and their families. Of course, the only room available was Larry's—nobody thought anything of turning over his room to visitors. That was the way things were done, back in the Thirties.

"Papa was a Methodist minister, and he was called to Templeton for an interview. Of course, the Finners put us up and shoved Larry onto a pallet in their room. What nobody thought of was the fact that Bobby had a habit of roaming in the evenings and coming home after midnight to jump into bed with Larry. I never noticed the cat flap in the screen door, and if I had, it wouldn't have meant anything to me."

Will Henry began to grin. Chuck looked sideways at him and his lips curved. Tim nudged Les, who elbowed Fane, and all three had wide white grins in their black faces.

Lucy glanced at Letitia Bragg and went on. "We had ridden the train all day and were tired before supper was over. I went to bed right afterward, and by the time Mama and Papa crawled in on either side of me I was pretty well out of it. We all slept like logs. Then in the middle of the night there came a sharp flap!—and a heavy weight came plopping down right in the middle of the bed, which was mostly me. Nearly knocked all the breath out of me.

"I screamed like a train whistle and sat up straight, right along with Mama and Papa. There was a dim light in the hall, enough to show a big round cat-face the size of a plate, its green eyes glaring at us. The thing snarled, and its teeth looked like a tiger's.

"I don't remember getting out of bed. Papa never remembered running out right through the screen door and onto the street. Mama was behind him and I was behind her, and every time I looked back that huge cat was directly behind me, bouncing along as if he intended to eat us all alive."

The boys were bent double, heads on knees, shaking with laughter. Sol was rumbling with chuckles, and even Mrs. Bragg couldn't quite manage to look grim. Lucy sighed deeply, but laugh wrinkles deepened around her mouth.

"We ran as hard as we could, all the way up the street, which was totally empty at that time of night, until we got to the corner, where a big power pole was set. It had L-shaped rods set into its sides, and Papa caught hold of the lowest one, swung me up above him, and pulled Mama along behind him as we climbed it almost to the top.

"The cat sat at the bottom, staring up at us as if it wondered what on earth we were doing. After a bit, we began to wonder, too, but we didn't really consider coming down. Every time one of us would move, the cat would reach up and bury its claws in the pole, as if it might come up after us, and we'd go still as a bunch of mice."

This time Mrs. Bragg couldn't quite smother her chuckle. That set Sol and the boys off, so Lucy had to wait for them to stop before she went on, "That was the longest night I ever spent, before or since. It was summer, but the breeze up that pole was pretty brisk, particularly with us in our night clothes.

"When it finally started to come daylight, Papa looked down and heaved a sigh. 'That beast's moving away,' he said.

"Mama gave a groan and began to climb down. Papa started down, too, and I could hear his joints popping as he went. He guided me down, too, and lifted me to the ground at last."

She rose and straightened her back, with a few pops of her own. "When we crept back to the Finner house, we felt mighty sheepish, because the first thing we saw was that bobcat, sitting in the entry hall waiting for us. Larry was calling it to get its breakfast, and it trotted back to the kitchen and settled down just like any tabby cat.

"Mama wanted to pretend we never left the house at all, but between the busted screen door with a Papa-sized hole in it and the state of our nighties, which had creosote from that pole all over them, there was no hiding it. Anyway, Papa was a minister and he thought a lie was next door to murder."

She stared down at her feet and looked sheepish. "Of course, poor Larry got blamed for the whole thing, though if he'd been in his own bed, as he should have been, nothing would have happened at all. Nobody fussed at Bobby, of course. When you're a forty-pound bobcat, not much of anything or anybody is going to tangle with you."

"How old were you and Larry then?" asked Solomon Peat.

"I was five and Larry was almost six. Fourteen years later we got married, and Bobby lived long enough to be at our wedding. He was pretty stove up by then, but he watched the ceremony in the Finner parlor as if he knew what was happening. A few weeks later he didn't come back from his nightly ramble, and we hoped he'd just gone to sleep in the woods, where he belonged."

Will Henry's eyes were wide and bright. Weddings were not his thing, but one with a bobcat in attendance fired up his imagination. "My sister...," he began, but Sol shook his head and the boy stopped.

"Don't often find one the caliber of old Bobby, I expect. How many years ago was that, Miz Finner?" Sol asked.

She gazed off over the pines, silent for a long moment. "Forty-seven years ago, Sol Peat," she said. "And Larry says he never missed his bobcat, because he had me to take his place."

Letitia Bragg snorted and rose in one great heave. "Come in and get your catfish, Lucy. Larry's going to be wondering about you."

With a sigh, Lucy Finner turned to follow the storekeeper into the grocery store, while the line of small boys and Sol Peat filled their minds with visions of three terrified people fleeing through the night with an interested bobcat at their heels.

They were still laughing quietly when the Finner Plymouth pulled away down the dusty road.

While researching something else entirely, I ran across the information about the church requiring people to be buried in the churchyards of their original home places. Given the lack of roads at that time and the terrible weather in the British Isles, that struck me as being totally inhumane.

THE LYCH ROAD

Rowall woke, as usual, to the pain of his chilblains and the crowing of the scraggly cock in the hen-run. For a long moment, while nerving himself for the icy plunge from his scanty covers into the frozen morning, he forgot what this day would hold.

When he remembered, he went even colder, and as he climbed out of his pallet bed he shivered with worse things than the early frost. Father was dead.

That was bad enough, in all conscience, but the thought of the effort and the danger involved in getting him to his grave was even worse. Why couldn't the Bishop sit warm in his palace and let poor folk be? What good was served by having men buried only in their home churchyards, when they had lived for sixty years without ever visiting the place of their birth?

Rowall was no coward. Had he not stood fast while hearing the Wish-Hounds coursing over the moors? And had he not even heard, above the whine of the wind and the voices of the spectral hounds, the shrill horn of their master, long dead and held down in his own grave by a great slab of stone?

To travel the Corpse Road was a thing he did not like, but he had done it before, with his Grandsir and his uncle and his mother. And now he must take that way to carry his father, too, the long way to his waiting tomb. The Lych Road had no bridges, no post houses, no aids to the traveler. It had only the cold dank miles of moor and the rushing rivers, unbridged and dangerous, and the lurking mists and the mire that lay at a distance, and yet near enough to trap those who went astray in the fogs.

The others had died in summer. That was the difference. Now it was fall, and an early winter was in the nip of the air and the crackle of the frost. If he waited, the ground would be frozen hard, and his father would have to be salted down, as others had been in the past, to wait for spring. That was a thing that edged toward sacrilege in Rowall's mind, and he was determined to get the old man decently underground, if it could be done.

He yelled as he stepped on the flagstone floor. His woolen stockings did little to shut out the chill. Margret thrust her tousled head around the corner from the kitchen, where she slept warm before the hearth, and frowned at him. Then she remembered, too, and her eyes grew round as she stared up at her brother.

"Today? It will snow, Gram says. A bad day to be out, at best. And on the moors, it will be terrible cold."

"He must go, else we will have to bide with him in pickle until thaw. The men have given their words to be here by dawn. Go and build up the kitchen fire. They will be wanting something hot in their bellies before we set out. Mull some of the last of the ale...it's little enough we can do to cheer them." Rowall pulled on his awkward hide boots and stood, stamping his feet well down.

The procession set out with first light, under a sky that hung low, in rolls like carded wool. The weather was not, Rowall suspected, going to hold. Not all the way. But at least the rivers might be frozen a bit upstream, holding back some of the flood that had washed away more than one funeral party as it tried to cross the stream.

The wind knifed across the moorland, wailing among the stones, shrieking around the shoulders of Keg Tor, as they drew even with its dwarfish shape. A spit of snow touched Rowall's face, from time to time, and the moor itself seemed to dissolve into the gray light of the sky. Even the occasional tree or standing stone was ghostlike in the tenuous light, and the creak of the wagon, toiling away behind, added a shivery note to the day.

Aln, just behind him, touched his shoulder, and he turned. The men pulling the wagon were changing shifts, fresh backs being put to the ordeal of hauling the heavy burden over the stony track. The way ran slightly uphill now, and the box holding his father's body was, he well knew, heavy with its own weight and that of the big bones and loose flesh within it.

He went back and took his place, bending to pull, while others alongside did the same and others pushed from behind. The effort warmed him a bit, though his feet were wet and almost frozen in the ill-made boots. They moved along, the axles groaning, the wind slicing their ears from their skulls and tossing wisps of their long hair about their faces. The day moved, too, and it was noon when they reached the worst of the streams.

The Wend had been low enough to cross without trouble. The Pharr was a bit worse, yet passable. Now they neared the Skeg, and they could hear the roar of its waters before they arrived at the high embankment and looked down at the turbulence below. This time, Rowall knew, they must carry the coffin by hand along the water's edge, seeking a way to cross.

The wagon could go at the ford, but it was more likely than not to overturn in the flood. If that happened, the body would be lost, and he had no intention of letting that occur. They would bear it to a crossing, and up the other side, staggering in mud and over icy patches, almost falling back into the stream. He had been there before with the kin of those now helping him. It was a terrible burden for human flesh to accomplish.

It was dark down in the shadow of the banks. The overcast day did nothing to lighten the shadows, and the footing was perilous. But they persevered, resting the coffin on a stone from time to time in order to catch their breaths and go on. When they found a spot studded with boulders and manhandled the casket across it, they were all weary, and Rowall felt as if he would like to join his parent in the box. His was by far the easiest task.

The farther climb was miles high, it seemed, and the wind, when they reached the top, struck through their rough clothing to freeze the sweat of effort on their hides. But to their dismay, it was blowing snow as well. The way to the road again was covered over, and the moors lay dim and featureless before them.

Aln stood, shoulders hunched, staring toward their goal, still miles away. Rowall knew that he was thinking with dread of the mire below Dredden Tor, which might well lie hidden beneath the light blanket of snow. It had swallowed men and beasts for generations, without returning so much as a rag or a bone of them to their owners and kin.

He sighed. "I will go ahead and sound out the way," he shouted above the moan of the wind. "Keep coming...there is the wagon now, just coming up from the crossing. Load him onto it, and travel onward. I will stop and wait for you if I come to the mire."

In some ways, it was a relief to trudge away by himself, into the teeth of the wind, and leave the wagon behind. It had reached a point at which he felt that it was his father himself groaning, instead of the axles and the men. The wind sang a cleaner note into his ears as he forged ahead.

Rowall thought of his grandmother and Margret, worrying in the kitchen as they spun wool and knitted hose and shirts. They might be safe, but he knew they were following him every step of the way. He didn't envy them; at least he knew what was happening when it happened. He thought with longing of his older brother, gone with a drover for a bit of coin to help them through the winter.

He sighed, feeling the chill pull deep into his lungs. It set him to coughing, another of those troublesome fits that had been the bane of his life since fall. He stopped and leaned against a standing stone until he could breathe again. Then he went forward, half blinded by the increasing snowfall.

Something moved in the white blur to his right. He paused and put his hands over his eyes, trying to see. A goat, he thought, or one of the moorland ponies, running from the blast.

He put his head down and went on again, setting one foot carefully ahead of the other, stabbing at the snow with his staff to make sure of the footing. It would not do to stumble into Dredden Mire.

The world went away for a time, as he forced himself onward. He found himself lying flat, once, and pushed himself up again, wondering how long he had been lying there. He passed a stone that he thought looked too much like the one he had leaned on, hours before. But he was strangely warm now, with effort, he supposed. Nothing troubled his mind, and he walked as if on a summer day, crossing the moors to see his Merry again, forgetting that she had been lost in Dredden Mire months before.

Then he came suddenly to his senses. The ground trembled faintly beneath his boots, as if he stood upon a vast pudding. His breath stopped in his throat, and he clutched the staff in hands that were numb.

He turned cautiously in his tracks. The ominous shape of Dredden Tor loomed to his left and slightly behind him.

"God ha' mercy!" he cried, his voice mingling with the wind.

He turned right around and tried to see his own tracks. He could follow them out of the mire again, he thought, but the snow had covered them over, and behind him was only the regular pattern of windblown drift that lay on every hand.

He thrust the staff at the ground. It sank too easily. He stabbed to right and left, front and back, but there was no difference at all. He stood deep in the mire. Too deep to hope for deliverance. He must have followed one of the meandering strips of solid ground that criss-crossed it aimlessly.

Suddenly Rowall laughed aloud, the wind snatching the sound from his lips. He was relieved of this day's duty, and if death be the price, it was cheap. Merry was gone. His life loomed ahead, labor and cold, cold and labor, until he lay down and died as his father had done.

It was against the law of the Church to die willfully, but accident was another thing entirely. He had been delivered from his fate by his own father's death, it seemed, and he no longer shuddered at his long trek on the Lych Road.

He laughed harder and harder. He plumped down in the powdery snow and lifted his face to the howling sky.

"Bishop!" he shouted, "You cannot say I must return to my own parish for burial! My bones will never be found, Bishop! And my curse upon you for bringing many well men to their deaths in serving those already dead!"

The wind moaned about Dredden Tor, and the mire lay hidden under the snow. The men who hauled his father's lych to its tomb would do their task and some would even grieve for him, he knew. But Rowall did not grieve for himself.

He was growing quite warm, now. And Merry...Merry was coming through the mire in her summer dress, her hands filled with wild daisies....

I love inventing alien landscapes and critters. Unfortunately, my alien critters tend to be pretty wicked.

THE VEAULES

They came out of the trees by night, hopping along the edge of the meadow like pale feather-dusters or perched on branches of the few bushes growing amid the grass. In the light of the green moon they looked eerie but harmless. By that of the silver moon they seemed spectral.

When the scarlet moon shone, their diamond-bright eyes shone with hungry fires, and their pale plumage was tinged with red. Even their shadows, cast by that rusty light, seemed menacing, edged with purple against the gray grass. We did not go outside the permaplast domes while the red moon shone.

Catterly learned the hard way. He was a big man, afraid of nothing, curious about everything. When the sensors proclaimed this world to be livable for human beings, he charged outside, wearing his protective gear but resenting its bulk, and checked out everything in sight.

"Nothing but birds, small creatures analogous to hares and squirrels and prairie dogs, as far as I can tell," he panted when he was inside the shuttle again. "Some insects, but I could find no stingers or mandibles capable of inflicting painful wounds. Looks like an ideal world for colonists. We need to set up the domes as soon as possible and begin cataloguing life-forms and analyzing the soil."

He was looking straight at me, knowing that the final decision would be mine. As the head of Alien Ecology on this expedition, my task was to assimilate the findings of everyone else, put together the puzzle pieces, and to come up with some pattern that would guide us in our cautious assessment of this world.

We were forbidden to damage any other world as our ancestors had done to old Earth. I had to make certain we remained within the law. Catterly, I had realized as we began our examination, was of the old breed that had ravaged Terra generations ago. Left to his own devices, he would have jumped into this new ecosystem and stamped it flat.

"Eco-Tech Dale!" he said roughly. "Pay attention! Do we put up the domes now?"

I stared him down. "We locate a better spot for the shuttle, farther from the trees. We examine every inch of ground before we inflate the permaplast. We take our time, Analyst Catterly, before we make any move that might damage this system." It was all I could do to keep from calling him "Anal" Catterly, which was the term my associates coined for him.

I heard him muttering his usual expletives aimed at female techs who had arrived at superior positions via exercises performed flat on their backs, which he knew to be false. As usual, I ignored him. This was my fourth mission, and he was my third impossible exploration and analysis tech. Somehow, that position seemed to attract a certain kind of unlikable male.

We did the job by the book, finding a spot suitable for the shuttle, and another, very nearby, where the domes would not damage either flora or fauna. We inflated the domes with care, watching the effect of their presence upon the prevailing breeze across the meadow we chose. Catterly was beside himself with impatience before we were set up.

The moons had been cycling, each holding the sky for many solitary days and nights, their orbits succeeding each other regularly. overlapping as they leisurely crossed the scantily starred sky. First the green, then the silver, then the scarlet moons made their transits, while we labored to locate, assess, and assign a name to every kind of plant, animal, bird, and insect we could find.

We went down the alphabet, trying to avoid, for our own convenience, having more than two or three species listed under any single letter. By the time the green moon was again overhead, we had come to v, and the creatures we named the veaules first appeared at the edge of the forest.

Catterly saw them first. "Yo, Dale!" he called softly from the instrument dome. "Look there, will you?"

In the greenish glow, the veaules hopped soberly into the meadow and sat staring at us. Those in the trees huddled their heads down into their neck-feathers and stared, too. They looked like poufs of silvery-green feathers atop stilt-like legs. Their long beaks shone in the moonlight, gleaming with metallic luster.

Only when Catterly moved toward them, despite my warning to

be cautious, did I see tall crests of feathers rise along their skulls; it seemed to happen only when they were disturbed. I whistled imperatively, and the big man bumbled back to my side, cursing softly.

"Leave them alone," I warned him. "Analyst, we are here to assess, not to upset, the local life-forms."

He grumbled but obeyed. Then we were very busy indeed, cataloguing and analyzing and fitting together pieces of the puzzle that was G-307, fourth planet in the Doura System.

It looked quite promising, by the time the silver moon came around for the second time; we had found no life-form that seemed sentient, although there were several that showed extremely sophisticated evolutionary patterns of survival. It was strictly against the rules to continue investigating, much less to colonize, any world holding an intelligent life-form.

When we finished our work in the late evening, we usually looked out at the staring veaules, enjoying the moon-colored feathers and the glinting brightness of their eyes. Although Catterly had wanted desperately to dissect at least one of everything, so far I had withstood his pleadings. Only insects had fallen victim to his voracious scanner so far.

I had particularly warned him not to bother the veaules. They were close to us. They had not threatened us in any way. I wanted no problem with any creature, large or small, no matter how dreadfully the colonists who would follow us might trouble them.

The red moon appeared for the second time some fifty days after our touchdown. The Assistant Eco-techs were helping me assemble our body of data, which was about as complete as we could get it in this limited area. It was time to deflate our domes and move the shuttle to another area in a distant and climatically different part of this world.

That was when Catterly went outside in the light of the red moon and brought down a veaule with his shock-rifle. The first I knew of it was when he stalked into the dome where I was working, a limp bundle of silvery feathers in his hand.

Something about the veaule physique was terribly vulnerable to shock, I found when I examined the creature. It was dead, its eyes dimmed to gray, its plumage reduced to a handful of smoke-dull wisps. I was angry—so angry I drove Catterly outside with the force of my fury.

When I heard his scream, I couldn't imagine how he had come to grief in the bare area where the domes sat. Once I stepped outside I realized what had happened.

There, ringing us in the red light, stood ranks of veaules, their eyes scarlet, their crests raised. Catterly lay sprawled on the grass, blood trails shining along multiple wounds in his scalp and on his neck and wrists. As I moved into view, those many beaks opened wide and clacked shut, and I saw that they were lined with saw-like edges, capable of doing the damage Catterly's skin revealed.

"Get him inside!" I whispered, and Jooss and Henri drew sharp breaths before following me toward our fallen companion.

A stir moved among the veaules, as if a wind had risen. Still, they allowed us to retrieve him; fortunately, he was still breathing. As we went again into the dome, I could hear a clattering of beaks, as if the creatures were signaling among themselves. My skin goose-pimpled while I stripped back Catterly's garments and examined his wounds.

Antiseptic and a few stitches were all I could do, for the doctor was aboard the orbiting ship. We had to get Catterly there, for he seemed to be developing a fever. Who knew what venom or enzyme could be in those alien beaks that might be deadly to our kind?

We could not leave the dome, even to go to the shuttle, for when we looked out again we were surrounded by veaules. Hundreds, thousands, possibly millions of the birds sat on the bushes, on the grass, even on the domes themselves, watching us with those scarlet-tinted eyes, waiting for a chance to serve us as they had served Catterly. The meadow and the treetops in the distance were a sea of veaules, shifting with red-tinted ripples as the creatures moved about.

Jooss signaled the ship, but his message seemed to go unheard. Philippe Henri and Joan Falville and the rest of the analysts and eco-techs huddled with me in the shelter of the big dome, wondering if our besiegers would leave when daylight came again. Wondering, indeed, if we would be able to get to the orbiting ship, and even if we would be able to reach the shuttle.

Henri kept peering out of the door-slot, watching the moon sink over the distant horizon. "They're backing off," he said at last, and I went to stand beside him.

The sky was growing pale with dawn. As the light increased, the moon set, and the waiting veaules began a slow and orderly retreat toward the trees. We had to move quickly now, or be trapped here for another night. Just as the sun rose, about half of the creatures took wing, and the sky was completely filled with flying shapes, which became a cloud as they sped away toward the west.

We left too much of our work in the domes when we ran for the shuttle, but even then we heard an ominous rustling in the leaves behind us. We gained the port, pulled everyone inside, and sealed the craft. Even as Jooss began the ignition sequence, pale shapes composed of fluff and long, transparently fragile legs began battering themselves against the permaplast of the viewports.

We moved upward amid a swirl of feathers and croaks and occasional splotches of coppery blood. I hoped desperately that the creatures would not find a way into the sealed domes and destroy the work of so many months. Although the location we first chose was beginning to seem unusable, surely our accumulation of data might help us with another, as far from the last as possible.

The veaules were, after all, not intelligent, and if colonists avoided their habitat there should be no problem with them. I was busy preparing a verbal report, with suggestions for alternative sites, all the while we shot toward the signal marking the present position of the ship.

We met the vessel inside the orbit of the green moon and locked the shuttle into its waiting socket. When the pressure seals whispered open, I felt a sense of relief that seemed too intense for the relatively slight danger we had faced below. We had, after all, only had a crew member injured by birds. We had met far worse enemies in our tour of duty.

My superiors were not happy. "We selected your position with utmost care," Commander Howell said in his old-maidish voice. "A forest for wood, fertile soil, plentiful small game—it was no accident that we sent you there. Catterly is not dangerously injured, as surely you must know.

"We cannot imagine why you and your associates were so disturbed by what is a fairly normal reaction from indigenous species when some of their number come to grief at our hands." He looked at me over the bridge of his nose, and I could almost see the glasses that were no longer used to augment sight. He had a face that needed to be garnished by frames and lenses, in order to possess any character at all.

I had, of course, no excuse. The unreasoning terror we had all felt while besieged by the throngs of veaules was nothing I could offer as an explanation. So we were, perforce, returned to the surface as a unit, although thankfully not to the precise spot we had left.

Howell and his staff chose a similar meadow some thousand kilometers from the first. That should, they felt, leave behind the disturbed birds and give us a fresh start. The group sent after our earlier work and equipment delivered it all to us in orbit, and we took it back down with us.

Again we chose a location and inflated the domes. Again we gathered information about local plants and living creatures. The silver moon waned, for we had missed the transit of the green one by the time we were reassigned and re-equipped.

When the red moon rose, the veaules crept out of the forest, stalking along on those glass-rod legs or hopping, with much flapping of wings, into the meadow. A few daring ones took to the air and swept above the domes, as if scouting out the situation.

Jooss decided to see if it would be safe to go outside. We were almost unable to drag him back to shelter before we would have been sliced and skewered by claws and beaks. Then, breathless and horrified, we watched them hurl themselves at the distant shuttle, shattering the almost unbreakable permaplast, stopping the vents with their bodies, freezing the guidance vanes with a dreadful glue of flesh and blood and feathers.

They trapped us here. We believe they assessed our situation in that earlier encounter and designed a strategy to counteract our escape. Where they had numbered in the millions, before, now the entire world seemed filled with veaules, crowding close in the light of the red moon and retreating to the forest by day.

They have not attacked the domes, as yet, although I suspect those saw-edged beaks could rip them to shreds, given the time. Jooss cannot get through to the ship, for the creatures seem to have jammed our frequency with signals of their own.

Do they have some kind of technology? We cannot know, and the days are not long enough for us to do any long-distance exploring to find some center of activity that might hold such matters.

The red moon has begun to wane. Surely when the green moon rises again we will be safe and can find some way in which to get a signal to our ship. We cling to that hope, though we all have similar fears. What if the veaules come inside after us? I shudder at the thought.

We do not go outside while the red moon shines.

*I was a middle-aged woman myself before I realized that few, if any,
sf or fantasy stories involved a middle-aged woman as protagonist.
Yet I also realized that I was only just beginning to have the understanding and the skills to deal with almost any situation, be it life-
threatening or otherwise.*

MAY BANKED FIRES RISE ANEW

Yarusha drew her fingers down Jarob's face, closing the eyelids
over his staring eyes; that familiar angular jaw, with its stubble of
unmanageable beard, had become cold and distant, infinitely with-
drawn in death. She took a new sheet from the chest beside the bed
they had shared for fifteen years and spread it over him. The children were pale with terror, as they saw their father lying still and
bloody in his own bedroom.

Outside the impenetrable stone walls of the fortress, she could
hear dim shouts, the crackling of flames. Kenir's men were firing
the village. She hoped the survivors there would have the wit to run
into the forest, where even Kenir could not track them down. And if
the invader should venture into the forbidden wood—she smiled
grimly. Shapes of hideous fear would find him there, for she had set
them in place herself, over her husband's protests.

That had been her sole use of the Gift, after her marriage. Jarob
had been strongly opposed to such practices, and she had foregone
them for his sake. But now he was dead, the stone of his house
dented and scorched, the fields about fired and ravaged. The men
who defended the House were scattered...or dead. Their children
huddled, crying, in the corner of the great room where the family
had slept. Because her man was too proud to ask for help, his people
faced the sword or starvation.

She sighed and turned toward her offspring. Elisse, the youngest, ran to her; she caught the child up in her strong arms. The other
three followed her, Rebesh slowly, his adolescent face pale and taut.
She could see that he longed for the comfort of her arms too, but at

fourteen he felt himself too old to indulge in childish needs. She reached to draw him, with his siblings, within her embrace.

"Your father is dead," she said, her words stark. "We are left to hold to what is ours, though we are surrounded by danger and death. I must find aid, or everything will be lost, not only for us but for our neighbors. Rebesh, your task is to care for your sisters. See to the defense of the House and gather what food can be salvaged from the crops, when the invaders withdraw.

"As soon as they are out of sight, blow the great horn to summon any villagers nearby into the walls. This is a hard task for one so young, but you are the only Halonath left to do what must be done. Your sisters are small, but you must make them help as well. There are things they can manage to do, and you must find them and set them to work."

Her son stared at her, eye-to-eye, he had grown so tall. Behind his grief, she could see excitement begin to dawn in his eyes. "Will the people obey me?" he asked her.

She drew herself up, gently loosing the hands of her children. "I will see to it." Her rawboned body held both promise and threat. She was a Kellen born, a Halonath by marriage, and when she spoke, those in her care listened.

"I will send for my mother, and she will come, through battle if need be, to your aid. Blind she may be, but she will be here. It will take time, however, and I have no time to wait. I must find those perilous allies in the wood and rally forces against Kenir. Every fort stead this side of the mountains will fall, and no man will walk free between the highlands and the sea, if I cannot gather a force to stop him," she said.

But Rebesh looked stubborn. "Father would not ally himself with those rebels in the wood," he said. "It will bring dishonor."

"The dead have no honor," she said. "Do you want to die with your sisters? I must go, and I will."

Elisse put her lips close to her mother's ear. "Will you take the not-men who seem to guard the keep with you?" she whispered.

Yarusha shook her head. "You know they are illusion," she said. "All they can do is to keep Kenir from storming the House, for they seem to be a strong force waiting to defend it. They will thin to mist slowly, after I am gone, but when Mother comes she will reinforce them. No, I go alone, but I hope that I will return with help. From the forest."

Rebesh reached to touch her shoulder. "The League of the Clanless!" He still looked rebellious.

She nodded. "When you see me again, you will not recognize

me. My graying hair will be black again; my face will seem young and smooth, for those who flee the steadings have no respect for the old or even the middle-aged. I must seem young, in order to gain a hearing from them. They would kill me at once otherwise."

She hugged them again, fiercely. "You will know me by this scar," she said, drawing her finger down the side of her chin, tracing the silvery streak that remained from her warrior days. "Now, go to Marilda and help her ready your father for his pyre. When I come again, I will be changed."

She felt a fierce pride as they turned obediently and went. Her children had been nurtured to be strong and capable people. Even so young, they showed the result of that rearing. If she could stop Kenir, they would have a chance to live; if she could not, they would surely die.

She turned to her brass mirror. Her harness and mail hung beside it, with her sword. She had wielded it only in practice for many years, but her muscles still held their old strength, though not, alas, the enduring elasticity of youth.

She took them down and let out straps, for her shape was larger now. The sword hooked onto the belt with accustomed ease. When she looked into the mirror, she saw a formidable warrior, grim and forbidding—and middle-aged. She must change that image now.

She closed her eyes and crossed her hands on her belt. "Goddess, grant me illusion. Grant me the semblance of youth. Grant me the ability to return to my hard-won self when I choose. I, Yarusha, ask it."

She felt the surge that signified the rising of the Gift, the kindling of fires that had been banked for fifteen years. Flame walked up her body, invaded her skull, bloomed outward through her flesh. She opened her eyes again and looked into the mirror. A tall, raw-boned young woman stood there, clad in mail, blade at her side. The black eyes burned and the unveined hands grasped the sword-hilt.

Yarusha smiled and saluted. "If I truly held all that young energy! But I do not truly regret it." She turned to meet the children in the hallway.

"Is it you, Mother?" asked Rebesh, staring. "Yes, there is the scar. But you seem so strange...."

"I am strange," she replied, feeling the Gift raging below her skin. "I cannot stay to light your father's pyre. Send my love with him into ashes. And pray that I return with Kenir vanquished and our home made safe again."

She strode down the long flights of stairs to the guard-bay, where Hameth, the Master at Arms, was busy among the wounded. He was on his knees, slicing expertly at the base of a shaft. Without speaking, she knelt on the other side of the wounded man and held the cut apart as Hameth pried the metal bolt from the bloody socket. When they were done, she stood.

"Hameth, I go to gain grim allies. While I am at that, be certain that all obey my son. Only in matters of war will he defer to you. Whatever you feel against me, do not let it temper your loyalty to Jarob's heir. He will listen to you."

The Master stared at her, his hostility, as always, plain in his gaze. He had never approved of his lord's choice of a wife. There had been tension between the two of them for fifteen years, but now he looked at the change in her, the notched blade, the mail, and he nodded. Respect stood between them now, if no liking.

"It is just. If Jarob had listened to me...." He shook his head. "You will leave those Seemings on guard here? There are few to defend the House, if Kenir should decide to return."

"They will stay, and my mother will come, for I loosed a pigeon to summon her. I go now to rally the Clanless Ones."

"Then go. I will do as you say. I have not been your friend, Lady, but I am not your enemy. Believe that."

"I do." She nodded. "Be blessed, Hameth."

She slipped from the sally-port and crawled up the trench in the shelter of a hedgerow, to emerge in the forest beyond. Turning, she looked toward the village, where smoke still rose. She smelled ash, but she could see no glint of armor. Kenir and his men were moving again, toward the fortress to the north. Rostath's house was now in danger, and Kenir would fall upon it without warning as he had done the House of Jarob. She must bring help in time!

She moved into the wood swiftly, picturing in her mind the terrible illusions she had placed there to guard the rear approach to the House and the village. The fanged fog she called, summoning that image. It slipped through dark boles toward her, tendrilled hands groping, fanged mouth a-drool.

"Go," she said, pointing to the north. It fled along the breeze after Kenir. One by one she called its companions from the wood, and bone-chilling chimerae fled in the track of her enemy. When the last was gone, she sighed. Anyone courageous enough to stand and face those would find them illusion, yet few had ever dared that.

She sighed, wishing that she had the power to bring into being real warriors armed with true steel blades and stout bows. Yet that was futile. She must recruit those who were of flesh and blood.

The chink of her mail accompanied her down the dim path. In

time she paused, listening. Then she called into the gathering darkness, "It is Yarusha. Are my people hiding here?"

For a long time there was no reply, but at last a cautious hail came from the undergrowth. "Is it truly our lady?"

She whistled the signal, and dark forms came from hiding. They were few, but she saw one that was taller than the rest.

"Faron, is that you?"

"Indeed, Lady."

"Kenir has taken his men toward Rostath's keep. I sent after them the shapes of fear that guarded you, hoping to slow them until we can warn our neighbor. Is there someone who is able to run the hidden ways and give warning?"

Faron nodded. "My son will go."

"Then give him this token." She stripped from her finger a ring set with red stones, the symbol of the Kellen, her people. "Now make haste. If a single one turns and faces the shapes behind them, all will know that the host that harries them is only shadow."

She sent the rest to the fortress. In a few minutes she was on her way again, forging deep into the forest in growing darkness. Her feet found the track she sought, almost without thought, as she focused her mind toward the haunts of the League of the Clanless.

A faultless sense of direction was an aspect of her Gift, and she followed it surely toward her goal. Yet she knew that this might be her last night of life, for her Gift did not include invincibility among its attributes. If the Clanless refused her plea, she would die there in the wood.

As dawn touched the treetops, she caught a glimmer of fire among the trees. There was no sound of voices; the wood was still, except for the twitters of birds readying for the flight southward. She moved quietly, her soft-soled boots making no sound on the mulch of the path, and halted at a distance from the fire.

She whistled the call she had used with her own people. Nothing moved. She called, "Will the Clanless hear a warning and a plea?"

Birds went silent in the trees. A hare scuttled into its burrow. The fire burned before her, and she moved forward unhesitatingly. When she came to the blaze, she unhooked her sword and laid it on the ground, reached into the slit of her mail and removed a dagger, which she flipped to bury its point in a tree trunk. She took her strangling cord from its loop and laid it on a stone by the fire.

Her hand shook a bit as she removed the golden chain holding her birthstone from about her neck. That was her birthgift, the sign of her power. Then she waited.

When the sun rose over the treetops, a man stepped from the wood. The fire had burned low, and he kicked the butt-ends of logs back into the coals. When they flared up, he took a kettle from behind a stone and set it in the edge of the blaze, as Yarusha watched, wordless.

Meat and herbs went into the kettle, and when savory smells brought the Clanless to the clearing, Yarusha still waited patiently. All of these newcomers were young. Very young. Several dozen people soon sat about on stones or billets of wood, eating their morning meal. They paid no heed to Yarusha, and she did not speak to them, nor did she sit. From her stance, it was clear that weariness was not a word she had learned.

When the meal was done and the remnants removed, the man who had prepared it approached and stood facing her. "You spoke of a warning. We will hear that. I must warn you in turn that we have little use for pleas and seldom offer aid to anyone."

"I am no messenger," Yarusha said. "But Yarusha Kellen Halonath, Lady of the fortress belonging to Jarob. My husband is now dead, his village in ashes. Kenir of Eastrank moves against his neighbors, seeking to weld all holdings into one, with himself as ruler. Those resisting die.

"You will not find safety here in your forest. Kenir cannot abide those who are free and rule their own lives. He will axe the trees, burn the wood if necessary, to harry you out and put you to death or into chains. That is my warning."

The man laughed. "Why should he come into the forest? No soul has come here for fifteen years at least. The specters at its edge send ordinary folk shrieking away."

"He will come. The specters were set there by one who lives at Jarob's fortress. Fifteen years ago she came. I have control of them now. I have sent them after Kenir's troops, now moving toward Rostath's House. No more terrible shapes guard your western border, Clanless One."

There came an uneasy buzz of talk. The man turned from Yarusha to consult with a cluster of his fellows. She heard worried note in their voices. When he again stood before her, he was less relaxed than he had been.

"We hear. The warning will be heeded. One goes, even now, to see if those who wept in the wood are truly gone. Now...what of the plea?"

"Come with me to stop Kenir. Help me to kill him. We might come upon him before he reaches Rostath, or shortly after, surely. "

The hard young face creased, the smile holding no humor. "We live with death. She is our mistress, our goddess. Why should we court her at your bidding?"

"Where do you find your new Clanless Ones?" she asked. "Do you have only those born in the forest to swell your numbers? Or do you find recruits coming to you from the fort-steads, generation after generation? If Kenir has his way there will be no more youngsters coming to find you."

He flushed. "We have no infants here. We rear no young. Those who want such go out and join the cattle living around the fortresses. Only the free are allowed among our number. But you are right; others come from the steadings. If none came, we would grow older and go out in our turn, and there would be no one to take our places."

She nodded. "You may rely upon it. Kenir would allow nobody to leave his holdings. He crushes his own with an iron fist. He would do no less with those not his own."

A long call quavered through the wood. The youth listened, and then he sighed. "You tell the truth. The watchers are gone."

"Are those I see all the Clanless in the forest?" she asked.

"No. We range the forest, and our calls can send the word from side to side in an hour." He stared at her for a moment. "Wait. We must consult."

She nodded and lay, full-length, on the frosted grass. As she dozed, song-like calls rippled through the wood. Voices, melodies, cries mingled in a great canticle. In an hour, she rose to stand beside the young man in a wood gone silent again.

"You have decided?"

"Not to rape and slay you."

"That is comforting."

"But to join you, for our own protection."

She drew a deep breath. "Have you swift and secret ways to travel toward Rostath's holding? Our ways are to the west. Time would be lost getting there."

"Have songbirds wings?" he asked. She caught a glimpse of the boy he might still be, as he grinned and swung his arm in a summoning gesture. "Others will join us as we go."

They moved then, so quickly and quietly that birds did not take flight or hares scutter from their way. When Yarusha looked behind, she could see gray-clad shapes moving along the track, too many to count. Night did not halt them, and dawn found them at the edge of the forest before Rostath's House. The village was ablaze. Archers on the walls were finding targets among the ruins below.

She stared closely, as she said, "Kenir will be at the rear, directing things. He will move if there is a frontal assault, but he does not risk his life easily."

The boy said, "I give you my name, Lady. Arvin Clinkmail. If we are to die together, that is fitting."

"Thank you. Take a large group and come from the far side of the wood, taking Kenir and his men by surprise. I will take another group and slip toward the place where I believe he is waiting for the time to strike. He killed my man, and I will slay him with my own hands."

"That is fitting," Kevin replied. "Luck be with you, Lady."

"May you live to grow old," she replied. Then he was gone, and she motioned to those nearest to follow her. The hut where Kenir waited seemed to glow in the light of her Gift.

A clamor, after a time, told her that Arvin had made incredible time and fallen upon the troops from the other side. She smiled as a stocky shape emerged from the door of the hut and stood staring toward the uproar. Kenir! She ran, forgetting those who came behind. "Kenir!" she shouted. Her blade was in her hand.

He turned. Yarusha recalled how she now looked. "Goddess, release me from illusion," she prayed. She saw recognition dawn in the bold Lord's eyes.

"Jarob's bitch, is it?" he cried. "Come to join your new Lord, have you?" His chuckle boomed as he thudded to meet her. His blade was snakelike, heavy to suit his brawny arm. His eyes lit with killing fire, but she knew that her own matched them.

She ducked a blow that would have cut her in half and swung at his legs. A satisfying shock ran up her arm, and then she whirled away from another of his efforts. He was stronger by far, but she was light of foot. She dented his helm, cutting away the ribbon bearing a totally undeserved Purple. He blinked as she danced back. Then he came after, limping, blood streaming from the cut on his leg.

Yarusha feinted a swing at his head. As he raised his blade to counter hers, she dipped forward and swung at the leg once more. Something hit her, searing across her back, even through the chain mail, but she had connected. The leg was laid open, the bone showing. Panting, she wriggled away.

Kenir, intoxicated with battle, strode forward to finish her and fell, as the leg refused his weight. Yarusha was ready. She kicked the blade from his hand, which moved speedily to catch her ankle. She caught the hilt of her sword in both hands, swung it high, and hacked off the hand at the wrist.

Kenir's eyes went wide, white rims showing. His breath came in groans, both of effort and pain. "I will not die at the hands of a woman!" he shouted.

She saw then that his attendants were kept busy by those who had followed her, and she stepped back and stared down at him. "A wife. A mother. A warrior. One of the Gifted. All those, besides woman. I would never have troubled you in your own place. Now I will kill you." She cleaved off his head with one adrenalin-charged blow.

Those engaging her followers threw down their weapons. A wail went up, and the clamor beyond the ruins lessened. Yarusha raised her head to shout, "Kenir is dead. Surrender yourselves to the mercy of the League of the Clanless!"

She dropped to sit in the dust beside the headless corpse. She felt no twinge of guilt as she looked into Kenir's dead eyes, but she covered his face with a kerchief. This was someone's son.

Feet appeared before her. Arvin...she rose wearily, her aging bones protesting. The activity of the past days now weighted her with exhaustion.

She looked up at the young man. He returned her gaze, astonished by the change in her. She laughed quietly. "I am now myself," she said. "My oldest child is not much younger than you. I knew your kind value the young, so I made myself look so, not as deception but to gain your ear."

He took her hand. "I thought age was a thing of weakness and lack of will. You have taught me better. This was the one who killed your man?" He touched Kenir with his foot.

"Yes. His kingdom will fall apart now. His troops will flee homeward to forget the war. My children and your people will survive, though it will be a lean winter, for the crops have been burned."

She looked about. The Clanless stood in a circle about her, and there was a longing in their eyes that she suddenly recognized. "What do you need, my children?" she asked.

Arvin fingered the hilt of his bloodied sword. "It has been so long," he mumbled. "A blessing? From a mother?"

She kissed his forehead. "My blessing to all the Clanless. Your western border is secure," she said.

They came past for her kiss and her blessing. Tears formed in her eyes, but she blinked them back. Somewhere, each of them had a mother, and some bit of each of these young spirits still longed for her.

When the last had been blessed, she slung her blade and re-moved her mail.

"What will you do?" asked Arvin.

"I'll go to Rostath and sleep for two days," she told him. "Then home to my children. You'd best be gone, but I might come into the wood to call some evening. Will you hear me?"

Arvin grinned. "Come at your will, Mother of the Clanless Ones," he said.

He ran into the forest, and Yarusha saw Rostath approaching. She waited as he came to her side and took her hand. She shushed his words of thanks.

"Nonsense! Just show me a bed, that's a good boy, and let me rest for days!"

She stared at the forest after another good boy, in his strange way. Safe now as were her own children.

"A good day's work," she agreed, as Rostath led her toward his unbroken home.

Andre Norton got me hooked on fantasies about cats, and this is one of the results.

THE GUARDIANS OF THE SHRINE

The shrine guarded the Navel of the World, its ornate shape covering with its cloverleaf design the place where north met south, east met west. Columned porticoes topped long flights of steps leading down in each direction, but the door on the east was sealed with mortar and stone. Its columns were broken and blasted, and no one looked toward the towering green mountains rising beyond the meadows.

The ginger cat, Tairos, guarded the northern door, sitting in the shell-shaped portico, his green eyes fixed on the chilly waste from which the north wind brought frequent flurries of snow. As far as the eye could see, the hills rolled away, cloaked in ice, studded with boulders frosted like wedding cakes. The broken ground was concealed beneath a smooth white blanket.

The black cat, Ilysis, guarded the west. Her half-closed amber eyes kept close watch on the distant line of desert beyond the golden grasslands. From that direction came, at times, ranks of painfully sun-baked people, their wells dried behind them, their bellies empty and their children hungry. They had been known to attack the shrine, though no food was kept there for any save the cats, and their food was not that of Men.

The white cat, Kyrsos, looked southward into the jungle, from which unseen eyes often stared back. The rubbery leaves of the trees and vines and the brilliant blossoms sometimes moved when there was no wind to stir them, for the savage tenants of the south coveted the imagined contents of the shrine. Kyrsos kept his blue eyes keen, for an attack would come some day.

The gray cat, Grana, had guarded that sealed eastern door, but not one of her surviving companions ever mentioned her name. She was melted into the stone, shattered with the mortar, her blood forming a part of the bonding that shielded the hard-defended portal. It had been a terrible battle, but the shrine still stood, and the pearl at its heart was undisturbed.

The cats guarded the tenant of the shrine, though for many generations of men and of ordinary cats their mistress had not stirred from her frozen sleep. Not since Grana died defending her had she waked, for those who came from the east had set a spell upon her, hoping thereby to take her reins and depose her as guardian. No one had come since, with knowledge enough to break that enchantment, and the cats were not magicians.

The sphere in which she slept was a shimmering globe, its iridescent curves pearled with interior frost, revealing glimpses of the woman who floated in its center. White smoke moved about her, blue light shone upon her, and diamond sparkles sometimes glittered, even upon her skin.

She was pale as milk, her hair a shining swirl of midnight about her shoulders. Into her hands, which were folded on her bosom, went the reins governing each segment of the planetary globe. Ribbons of white light, they pointed the compass, except for that one which should have gone eastward. That line ended in a crisped and blackened stub, as if some force had burnt it almost back to the hand of Tiri-na-oth, Demigoddess who safeguarded the Navel of the World.

Tairos, being the least occupied of the guardians, thought often about the plight of his mistress. There were no attackers there in the north, only the wind and the cold, which he could not stay nor hinder. This left much time for remembering the ages during which he had watched here, growing with his siblings, through those long centuries, far larger than any cats known to humankind.

He slitted his green eyes as wind knifed into the portico, carrying on its edge a freezing slither of rain. The north was growing colder, century by century. The west grew drier, the south steamier and more lush. What was happening in the mountains to the east he could not say, for no one could watch there. But Tairos had an intuition that the world itself was moving in upon the shrine, as if to squeeze it out of existence.

If only Tiri-na-oth would awaken! Her strength, her knowledge, and her fierce will could halt the advance of the winter and the desert and the jungle and whatever came nearer from the east. She had, for millennia uncounted, kept the world in order, its regions holding to their old patterns, and if she could be brought back to consciousness, she could again bring them into alignment.

He slipped backward into the portal and closed the heavy door behind him, slipping its bars, locking its iron hasp with a bronze bolt. He glanced about the shrine, seeing the cold glimmer of the light from the sphere shining on the polished stone and the rubbed wood and the metal sconces that held the weapons for defending the place. It was in order, and the backs of his companions were alert.

He moved to the sphere and stared into its depths, willing the motionless woman to move, to open her eyes, to speak at last. When she fell in sealing that eastern door, Grana's blood spattering her pale skin, she had already been touched by the enchantment sent by her attackers. Once washed and placed inside the protective bubble, she had never again showed signs of recovering, though the guardians had expended much thought and effort toward achieving that goal.

Now Tairos sat upon the mosaic of the floor, placing his haunches on a crimson swirl inside the golden orb. He curled his ginger tail about his toes, grateful for his fur in this cold spot, and gazed into the orb, willing the demigoddess to open her eyes.

He felt as if his strength poured out through his eyes and into her, urging, pulling, pushing at her to come to her senses. There was danger approaching, he knew in his bones, and she was needed in the world as never before.

There was a solid gust of wind that pounded upon the northern door, and a thin wail of icy air moved through the shrine. To the west, Ilysis gave a warning growl and stood, her black tail stiffened like a war-banner. To the south, Kyrsos spat a signal and leaped backward into the shelter of the portico, his paws scrabbling at the wall where his weapon waited for his need.

So. It was all coming together now, the attack of elements joining those of men to override the long rule of Law. Tairos knew that he should join one of his siblings to defend a door. Yet he felt that he might, this once, manage to rouse the demigoddess. And even as he thought that there came the hiss of power against the sealed door to the east, a blast of heat as something tried to melt its way through the stone.

"From the desert! They come!" came the thought of Ilysis.

"And from the jungle," came the answering thought of Kyrsos. "Armed with the best they have, which does not compare with the armaments of the gods. Yet they are many and we are but three."

Tairos strained toward the sleeping woman, his breath forming a mist on the outer curves of the sphere. And one of her fingers twitched. The foreshortened rein leading eastward moved, very slightly, almost imperceptibly.

The black hair swirled more quickly about the smooth shoulders, and she seemed to sigh, there in the timeless haven of her sphere. The ginger cat glanced about, desperate with his need. He had no hands, and paws lacked certain skills.

There was an urn on each compass point of the golden orb formed by ancient artists on the floor around the pearl. They were tall and heavy, and each held incense that had never been needed or used. Tairos leaned against the northern urn and pushed, setting his clawed paws against the smooth floor, using his size and strength to move the thing.

Slowly, hesitantly, it toppled forward, gaining momentum as it moved. The shattering of pearly glass mingled with a gust of chilled and scented air from the sphere, and then both were overwhelmed by the intense odor of the stuff released from the urn.

The black cat was beside him at once, the white one little later. They stared at the ruin in silence, and he knew that they were wondering what he had done. He was wondering himself, for this might well mean the end of all that they had been assigned to do, through all those endless years.

There came a distant shout from beyond the western doorway. Though Ilysis had closed the panel behind him, Tairos could almost see the straggle of frantic men and women running toward the steps. Those who came carried only bows and spears and fire-arrows. The shrine could hold them out.

There came a pounding against the south door, and the rhythmic chanting held primitive power and terrible lust. Those carried similar weapons, and the shrine would not notice their assaults against its impervious walls.

The wind, now shouting at the north door, could not enter here to do harm, though it had tried since the foundation of the world. But now at the eastern wall, against that melted and sealed portal, there came another assault, and at the sound the three cats quailed. This was the force that slew their sister and felled their demigoddess, and it had come again. Already the stones of the wall were growing warm, the steam of the melting frost filling the air with mist. The wall crackled and snapped as the granite and marble heated, and Tairos feared to look and find the stone shattering as it had done before.

This time, he hoped, there had been no enchantment sent ahead of the attack. The demigoddess slept and had done for a thousand years. But now he turned to stare into the face of the woman who now lay amid a tumble of veils at the bottom of the broken sphere. And those eyes opened, the dark irises dim at first with sudden waking and then sharp with comprehension.

"They have returned." It was not a question.

She sat, her movements smooth and untroubled, as if she had not lain motionless for so very long. Then she stood, her veils moving about her as if they were smoke, and she stepped free of the shards of pearl.

Facing the east, she extended her hands. The ginger cat moved to her left, the white to her right. The black cat set her back against that of Tiri-na-oth and her gaze on the two locked but unguarded doors.

The heat grew more intense as the assault from the east maintained its power and focused upon breaking the wall. The demigoddess laughed. From her shoulders trailed the reins of north and west and south. Loosing her hands, she took them, one by one, and moved them through ancient patterns.

The shouting in the south lessened, as if those who tried the door had lost their purpose. The sounds of that horde moved around the shrine, toward the east.

Now those fleeing the desert were pounding at the western door, but a flip of the rein brought instant silence. Tairos knew that those who had gained the steps were looking back to see the longed-for rain falling upon their distant wastes.

"Open the northern door," said Tiri-na-oth. Before her, the stone was cherry-red, the heat dancing over the surface in wriggling patterns as the stone readied itself to snap.

The ginger cat moved to the portal against the slivers of cold wind, opening the lock, taking down the bars, letting the panels blast open against the walls. The heart of winter filled the shrine, frosting the dampness of that melted rime.

The cats' fur fluffed out to shield them from the bitter blasts now chasing themselves about the cloverleaf shape of the place. The eastern wall chilled to gray at once, and the runnels that had begun trickling downward froze into ridges of stone.

The incense powder from the overturned urn blew on the wind, round and round in purple drifts, sweet and intense and somehow filled with power. The voice of the demigoddess rose amid the tumult in a chant of beckoning.

Again Tairos came to stand at her left. Ilysis stood staunchly at her back, and Kyrsos at her right, allowing their mistress to call upon their strengths and their wills, as she summoned the gods whose servants they all were.

A booming cry came from beyond the door they faced. Those

from the mountains were no primitives, armed only with physical weapons, and they demanded entry into the shrine, though their words were in a language Tairos did not understand. But the North had come to Tiri's call, and no merely human power could warm that frozen breath.

Blows from some tremendous power began to batter the damaged stone, and bits of stuff fell from the groin of the roof. Cracks appeared in the sealed place that had been the doorway.

Tiri called more loudly. The cats began to purr, great tearing roars of throbbing power joining her voice as she called to those who ruled this world.

And they came.

Not in body, for they possessed none. Not in spirit, for their spirits roamed the many worlds that existed. Yet in that part of them that cared about this single minor world they came, and the shrine was filled with potency without form.

Tiri-na-oth seemed to grow larger, stronger, more beautiful as she faced the enemy. Tairos felt his body becoming great, his spirit stretching within him, his tail lashing with unleashed power. His siblings, he knew, must feel the same, and he faced the threat now with assurance.

But those beyond the wall knew when the gods came. They had not dreamed that their spell would fail and the demigoddess awaken to call them, and now they drew back and back, leaving their task unfinished.

With sudden understanding, Tairos knew that they would come again, when they felt the time was right. They might, in time, join with those in the west, those in the south, against the defenders of the shrine, but for now they were defeated.

He turned his green eyes up to meet those of his mistress. Tiri-na-oth was smiling, as the potencies filling the chamber set things aright, after so long a time. The urn tilted upright again, the powder reassembling itself and draining into the jar.

The eastern wall smoothed, and the outlines of the door began to appear, first as lines, then as the edges of a wide door to match those others facing outward. Bits of amorphous stuff drifted through the cold air from wall and floor, from mortar and door panel, moving together before the portal.

Tairos felt a surge of excitement begin to build in his faithful heart. A gray shape, furred and graceful, was forming there at its ancient post.

Grana stood again at the portal facing east. Now she was large, strong, filled with the powers that the returned gods had left there for those who did their work in this rebellious world.

Tiri-na-oth loosed the paws to left and right. The three cats, guardians and defenders, moved to greet their sister, now returned from death to her rightful place among her kindred.

A last breeze drifted through the shrine. The remnants of the pearl sphere shivered into nothingness, and the north wind died away. No sound came from south or north, from east or west, as the demigoddess stood among her cats, listening to the silence.

All about the Navel of the World, the orderly patterns resumed their play. Those who would disturb the balances of the powers were left to nurse their long ambitions in frustration. For the demigoddess had waked, and her cats were, all four, on guard about the shrine of Tiri-na-oth.

How lovely it would be to create a world to your own tastes! I have done it many times, on paper, and this is how it feels.

ARPEGGIA'S DEATHSONG

She had never thought about how death would come, though she never dreaded its arrival. Now, with her breath drawn with greater effort, her heart thudding laboriously under her rib cage, she had only one regret. All her painfully acquired knowledge, forged into wisdom by the fires of a long and demanding life, would be lost with her last breath.

Such a pity!

A hand touched her forehead, dripped water between her lips, and she knew that her daughter watched beside her. What could be taught she had conveyed to Astaria, but the distilled essence of thought and study and years could not be passed from hand to hand.

Only a like existence, lived in the same manner, could reinvent the unique creature that Arpeggia had been.

She drew a shuddering breath, knowing it to be the last. Her eyes dimmed, and chill enveloped her body.

* * * * * * *

Chill wind sang about her, its icy blades bringing her back to consciousness.

Although she knew she was surrounded by fields of snow and that what passed for her body sat upon some frozen surface, Arpeggia required some time to orient herself. Once she managed to call vision into being, she was frozen, in her turn, by sheer wonder.

She sat upon a pinnacle of ice rising so high into the air that the world below was only a shimmer of white and silver. Although she knew that about her was the final chill of death, she now had no body to feel it, only a field of thought and memory assembled on this height for some unguessable purpose.

How long she mused upon the problem was irrelevant, for time no longer existed. Her ruminations took as long as they required, and when she came to a conclusion, she leaned over the edge of her exalted seat and stared down at the swirl of pale mist and snowy nothingness lying beneath her, extending to the horizon on all sides.

If she had possessed breath, she would have laughed. "I have been given a new world, untouched and unspoiled. Why, I cannot guess, unless it is to use as a canvas upon which to paint the things I know," she told herself. She felt excitement build inside whatever kind of body was forming to meet her need.

A world—or a universe? The thought roused something like warmth in her non-body and brought all her sentience sharply into focus.

"Do I know enough to shape a universe?" she asked herself. The reply had to be that she did not, if she intended to form one as complex as that she had left behind. But another kind of universe, simpler and kinder, that surely was a possibility.

"First must come the space in which it exists," she mused, and to her amazement her tenuous hand held a wide brush dripping with midnight blue. Without worrying about the effect, she moved it in great swirls across the silver sky above her icy throne.

Everything turned blue, reflecting that sky, even the ice and the mist repeating it faithfully below her height.

When the color was even and satisfying, she turned her gaze upward. "Now the stars," she whispered, and her brush was laden with gold and silver, blue-white and reddish drops, which she flung with abandon across the midnight sky. When there were just enough, yet not too many to attend to properly, she recalled all she had learned about the properties of those distant suns. Some she painted as red giants, some as intensely blue and hot, giving each much thought before committing herself to its nature.

When the suns were blazing, she gave thought to worlds that might revolve about them. Planetary mechanics had been a fascination for much of her life, and she took great pains to make each of those she designed appropriate to the nature of its star, its distance from the sun, and its own makeup.

Sea worlds sparkling with reflections of many moons were provided with vast tides that created interwoven patterns under the pull of the satellites. Some were like Earth, mottled with green forests, rich brown soil, rippled blue oceans. Some were made of metal, gleaming in the light of their suns. A few were dark and mysterious, in the process of finding their own development. The effect was intoxicating.

There was still this place awaiting completion. She shut away her vision for a moment, intuiting what she might need to make the land below a place of surpassing beauty. To see that, she must have a day-blue sky, and in reply to her will it assumed the tender hue of a robin's egg.

Her brush swept rosy mauve across the lowlands, purple-gray shadow, golden-ochre highlights where the sunlight fell. Rocky cliffs rose, touched with brilliant iris blue and streaks of copper and deep rose. She thought of grass, and green meadows studded the lands; forests rose in multi-hued splendor. Opalescent mists rose from below, and she knew her work to be fine and good.

Never in all her intensely creative life had Arpeggia felt such joy. The arts and sciences she had embraced, only to move on to new interests when she had conquered the old ones, could offer nothing to equal this. No earthly palette held colors that could match the ones that appeared on her vast brush.

"It's like being a god," she said to the vast firmament just completed by her will. "I will create only beauty, no cruelty or pain."

As the words came to her, a smudge of darkness appeared at the edge of her brilliant sky, dimming it with a dirty cast. She had considered creating cloud and storm, as those were necessary to a healthy world, but this was a foul, forbidding color, which, as it grew in intensity, began to diminish the loveliness of her creation.

"This has the feel of an evil thing," Arpeggia said to herself. She huddled on her icy peak, considering how to battle it. Her memory, filled to overflowing with many disciplines, produced a wealth of material that might work against embodied ugliness.

"Music," she cried. Though she had no voice with which to sing, she now had the ability to produce what she needed with a thought. From her long years of study and devotion rose the sparkling strains of Mozart, the intricacies of Telemann and Vivaldi, the staccato brilliance of Bach.

Her music rose as a cloud of color, though it was not one the eyes of her kind had ever seen, and it had no name. As it grew in height and breadth its brightness increased, filling the sky, the land, pushing back the threatening darkness at the edge of the world.

This was not the effortless impulse that had formed her universe but a draining labor, and as the music battled the encroaching evil Arpeggia found her energies dwindling.

She curled upon herself, unable to draw warmth where there was no body, but concentrating her will and whatever physical power remained to her into a small shape filled with determination.

Like a rock, she sat on the peak of ice and willed her worlds to live.

As she had not yet created time, there was no measuring how long it took for her efforts to work against that invasion. When at last the pressure of that darkness decreased, retreated, then disappeared, she felt herself to be reduced to the faintest of stains upon her icy spire.

"Wind!" she breathed. "I need a new wind on my world!"

A breeze drifted over the spire, becoming stronger until a gust lifted Arpeggia onto her shadow-feet. She spread herself upon it like a silken veil, feeling something that was almost physical now. Her edges fluttered, her intangible feet lifted from the ice, and she was borne upward, upward, spiraling into the sky she had made and cleansed.

Then she knew she must have her planned cloud, must have storm, though not the devastating sort she had known in life.

"Cloud!" she shouted, and her voice rolled like thunder, her brightness glinted like lightning.

Her being, now drained of all her knowledge, her wisdom, her love, which she had transmuted into a small universe suited to her needs, crystallized into a million glittering flakes. Six-pointed, infinitely varied, each snowflake glinted magically in the swirling wind and the refracted light of her new sun.

Carried by the storm of her creation, Arpeggia fell upon her world as snow, enriching the seeds her thought had planted there. In time, those would sprout into a richness of life that would perhaps support others who searched for wisdom.

I love to speculate about alien worlds and lost civilizations. This was a sort of daydream....

THE PLACE OF THE ANCIENTS

We came to Selene to be farmers and craftsmen, to rear families and build a society that might, eventually, take part in the vast trading empire Earth had created over a thousand years of travel between worlds and systems. Those who sent us prepared well, scouting out the land, making certain that no dangerous disease or native species lurked there to endanger our nascent colony.

Our supplies included short-term necessities, as well as the viral supplies for creating those over the long term. Though nurtured in the teeming cities of Earth, we were trained to survive in situations we had never experienced or dreamed of.

So we came to Selene, the world of the great red Moon, thinking ourselves prepared for any surprise it might offer. For five years we worked together, creating a small but energetic society that promised to become profitable to those who funded our venture. As happens with most societies, we found ourselves, at last, with time to explore the areas beyond our limited boundaries.

And that was when we brought about the terrible fate we now face.

* * * * * * *

The air had cooled with fall, and again I blessed this world that had an axial tilt. Otherwise we would face the punishing heat of midsummer all the year around. Josiah and I had finished our work in the plant sheds, and now we had some free time. I splashed him with the sprayer with which I had been wetting down cuttings, feeling a wicked smile shape my lips.

He looked up at me, grinning, with mischief in his hazel eyes. It was time for play. "Thanks be we're not run on military lines," he said, putting away his trowel and taking off his coverall. "As long as our work is done, we can do what we like, Maris. I pity the colonists who chose to go to the other kind of outfit. Marcus and the other leaders are almost too easy on us, which suits me fine."

Washing perlite and moss from our hands, we caught up our jackets and headed for our unit in the married quarters. "We could go camping," I told my husband. "We haven't seen much of this continent as yet, but there are maps at headquarters. Let's get some lunch and choose a direction."

He nodded. "I've been wanting to go up into those mountains. We'll camp and maybe do some climbing."

We set out toward the east, where the mountains were forested and runnels of water ran down from the snows above. It seemed, from a distance, like one of the miniature re-creations of the primitive Earth that we had seen in museums, as children.

We had no hesitation, for the preliminary scans assured us there was nothing to fear here, or indeed anywhere on this world. Except for small animals and insects, a few birds, and creatures living beneath the soil and the water, we were here alone. It was exciting to know that no other thinking species had ever set foot where we walked, and no words but ours had ever troubled the air of this world.

* * * * * * *

We reached the mountains before evening. Once camped in a grove beside the biggest stream, we rested for the night before tackling the climb. High above, in the sunset light, we had seen shadowed niches that might well be the mouths of caves. Unusual creatures often lived in such dark places.

We woke early, despite a bit of playful love-making in the night, and washed in chilly water. Before the sky was bright we made our way to the foot of the easiest looking slope.

"Go slowly," Jo cautioned me. "I told Tam when I looked at the map that we'd be gone last night, today, and possibly tonight. If you fall and knock me off the wall, they won't begin to worry about us for entirely too long." I smiled down at him and began to make my slow way upward. We took no chances, for though we feared nothing alive, a fall would kill us just as surely as a predator might.

There were thick clumps of bushes thrusting out of crevices in the rock, giving us firm handholds. Occasionally, fair-sized trees leaned out from roots sunk deep into some rock fault, allowing even more secure climbing. Our toes found weathered creases too, and we moved upward more quickly than we had expected.

The dark openings were soon very near. "Caves, and no doubt about it," Jo called up to me.

I'd already reached that conclusion and found the chance to explore unknown caverns extremely intriguing. I went higher and could see, to my surprise, that each opening along the face of the cliff was approached by a stone ledge, much worn by weather but obviously adequate for foot traffic. As I stepped up onto the crumbling pathway, I realized that there were chisel marks cut into the back edge, where some worker had taken out extra stone to flatten the walkway.

As Jo joined me on the ledge, he, too, recognized those telltale marks. We stared at each other, wide-eyed. "Were there tool-using beings here, long ago?" I asked.

Feeling my way cautiously, I edged around the curve of the cliff toward the dark splotch that was the first opening. In front of the cave mouth there lay a much wider apron of stone, in the middle of which a worn depression seemed to indicate the long-ago presence of a fire-pit or perhaps the site of some other primitive activity.

Jo touched my shoulder before he ducked into the low opening. I followed, finding the space inside high enough to stand in and the cave narrow but very long, extending into darkness. Our earliest ancestors, we had been taught, had lived in such places. Did such primitives have a beginning here, only to dwindle into extinction? My mouth was dry with excitement as we moved deeper into the cave. From time to time, Jo reached back to take my hand and squeeze it or to pat my shoulder, and I knew he was as enthralled as I.

As the light thinned, Jo took his Kindler from his knapsack and thumbed the button. Its brilliant beam reflected from a million points of brightness where damp or minerals marked the walls, and the shadows it formed outlined a sunken track worn into the stone floor by the passing of feet or paws.

Jo reduced the Kindler's intensity to a bearable level, and we followed the light into the depths, to a point at which a knee of stone jutted sharply into the way. It narrowed there as well, and we had to move around the obstacle one at a time. Crawling through a cranny filled with dust and grit, I straightened at last to find Jo staring about, stunned, at the place in which we found ourselves.

"This is no natural cave!" he exclaimed.

A vast domed chamber, its seamless interior was the color of polished bone. Here there seemed to be little dust, although the place had to be ancient. As our light gleamed on the curves of walls and dome, another, more subtle light began to glow inside the stone.

In a moment, Jo extinguished our Kindler. Then we stood agape, as opalescence began pulsing around and above us. It was like standing inside a vast seashell under a silver sun.

Opposite the cramped entry-hole, a doorway was framed in a graceful arch carven with symbols. Two half-moon panels closed it, and we crept across that great expanse of floor to touch them, push at them, trying to open that further gateway into marvels.

I fumbled at the door on the right, but my fingers slipped across the frictionless surface without gaining a grip on it. Beside me, Jo was doing the same.

"It's going to take teamwork," he grunted, at last, and we linked elbows and pushed the widths of our bodies against the smooth panels, which moved hesitantly before us until they caught halfway and stuck there.

I went first, and Jo followed me. A band of light from the room behind pierced the darkness beyond the opening, and there, too, light began to bloom. Now we stood in a long corridor, along which circular portholes pierced the walls on either hand. They were some meter in diameter, set about hip-high to me, which told me those for whom they were positioned might be rather small in stature.

I bent to peer into one opening, as we moved past. It was dark inside whatever chamber might lie beyond the transparent portal. Jo flashed the Kindler, and this room, too, began to create its own illumination, very faint but quite enough to allow us to see a round space, like the inside of an egg, which formed the room.

This light was palest violet, and it revealed a row of cylindrical shapes arranged regularly around the curve of the chamber. Sharp pain skewered my temples, and I gasped, feeling pressure inside both skull and mind.

Jo was moaning softly, holding his head between his hands, and the Kindler went out. The violet light dwindled, too, and the pain lessened. Beneath that I felt a sort of pulse, like a weak heartbeat, and a sense of some alien presence as I backed away down the corridor toward the moon-shaped doorway.

"Come on, Maris," Jo muttered and went forward. I forced myself to follow him. What we found here would change the preconceptions of our kind forever, and I wanted to take part in this historical discovery.

We did not speak again for some time. Instead, we now seemed able almost to read each other's thoughts. Moving along that tube-like corridor, we were silent, but I could feel Jo's tension, matching my own.

We took brief glimpses into other round rooms as we passed, but as soon as the violet light began to glow we backed away and shut off the Kindler. One experience of that incredible pain was more than enough to make us cautious.

The corridor was longer than we had believed. As the light advanced with us toward the farther end, we found it seeming to retreat before us. Dozens of portholes slipped past us as we moved, and when we paused to glance back, the door through which we had entered was almost lost in the dimness that moved up behind us.

I caught my breath, but Jo touched my elbow warningly. Words here might, I knew, mean far more than we thought. I moved close beside him and together we continued toward the still invisible end of the corridor.

The complex had evidently been driven deep into the mountain, for we walked the better part of a kilometer before we could see the end of our journey. The bone-colored tube down which we went ended in a decorated wall, on which were painted, in subtle but unfaded colors, the history of a species.

"Look," Jo whispered, pointing to the bottom of the curve. "That is the beginning." I followed his finger with my gaze, and soon it was clear that the story was told in picture-symbols, spiraling counter-clockwise from the center, to cover the circular wall. Breathless with anticipation, I studied the scenes, hoping to find at least one in which the race whose work this was would be depicted. Instead, there was a recurring symbol, obviously intended to represent the dominant species while saving a great deal of detail work. Yet the symbol itself gave some clue to the nature of the beings who invented it. Shaped like a curving Y, it was supplied with an extra pair of marks, obviously arms. Its foot was formed of paired lines, so perhaps those were two-legged, four-armed beings.

They had delved deep into the mountain—that was clearly indicated. Inventions, arts, social gatherings, even families were shown on the wall. There was too much to follow all the way through that intricate history, but when we skipped to the end of the spiral we saw that their own end had come at last. Fewer and fewer of the people were sketched there, and now that long corridor and the round rooms began to dominate. In the center a tight circle held purple cylinders ranged about its perimeter.

Jo caught his breath. "Those look like...."

"The things in the little rooms along the corridor," I finished for him. "Do you suppose...?"

"Eggs?" He sounded dubious.

I thought hard. "Why else would they be stored in those chambers?" I asked. "There's nobody left here, so what other reason could there be? Maybe something happened that led to their extinction, and they left those...eggs or chrysalides or whatever...to survive until it was safe again."

His eyes widened. "Maybe they are deep in this mountain so that only other intelligent beings can wake them with light, which would never get in here otherwise."

It made a certain amount of sense. When we turned back toward the entry, a pale violet glow was touching the whole way. Peeping into the small chambers, I could see that the cylinders themselves emitted that glow, as if they had in some manner come to life.

As we returned to our village, we puzzled over what we had seen, the result of our light on the things in the cavern, and we came to a conclusion. In coming into that place we seemed to have set into motion a process of some kind. When we presented out conclusions, our leaders agreed, though they would allow no further exploration of the cavern and its contents.

"The thing is done," Marcus told the gathered group. "Unwittingly, for good or for ill, something has happened that we cannot change or stop without perhaps destroying the mountain itself. That might set off other and even more disturbing reactions, for a people who could create the things shown in the tapes Josiah and Maris brought back with them could surely place safeguards to protect the site."

We think often about the mountain that looms on the horizon. What will emerge from those eggs? Or will something else, some creation of those four-armed people, come forth instead?

We don't know how long it will take them to mature. Jo and I work hard so our sleep won't be filled with nightmares about the thing we may have caused. There's nothing we can do except worry.

Yet from time to time, we also dream, and we wake with aching heads, as if something squeezes our brains while we sleep. When the aliens come out of their cavern, we are convinced, they will know all about us. But what will they do to or with or because of us?

* * * * * * *

The foregoing account was found in a metal box among the remaining artifacts of the incomers. Because of the mental connection formed between our kinds when the first pair visited the hatchery, we learned their ways of communication, allowing us to understand their writings. This is useful, as their role in completing the Hatching proved to be fatal for their kind.

Now their small encampment lies silent, overgrown by the vigorous plants they nurtured and grazed by the unusual animals they bred. We have not disturbed the desiccated bodies that lie in their houses, some alone, some paired, for that would be disrespectful toward those who were the instruments of our reawakening.

The sight of their shattered skulls makes us sad, but for their kind the life force of our eggs moved into their brains and began to grow. When the time came, our young broke forth, leaving the hosts lifeless.

Three times has our kind sunk into the sleep of death, leaving our eggs waiting in the hatchery. Three times have races arrived from beyond our sun to bring us back to life, and each time they have left behind interesting and valuable gifts from their home worlds.

It is unfortunate that no matter how the violet force reaches into their minds, the result is always the same. To save us they must die. Yet we live and will do so for millennia, for the long swing of our sun around its path through our galaxy will not reach the fatal radiation point again for many lifetimes of our species.

So we add our notations to those of our saviors, hoping that our actions are pleasing to the gods who continue to save the Releeyah from extinction. May this continue to occur, until our sun dies and our world turns to dust.

Something rather similar to this happened in my own area, some time ago, though I cannot know if the old man had such a chance to avenge himself. Yet this is a place where the most unlikely things do manage to come about.

OLD MAN, BAD SCENE

I was never any angel; I have to admit that. I spent my teen years getting into mischief—nothing mean or wicked, but sometimes pretty troublesome to my "victims."

Putting the superintendent's antique jalopy on top of the high school gymnasium was more work than anything I ever did since, but the look on his big red face was worth all the effort. As none of us senior boys could stand the old goat, he had no way to pick which six of us did the deed, so he punished us all. Not one of us got to play in the last few games of the football season.

As far as I knew at the time, nobody resented that, and nobody turned me in, though most knew I had to be the one who got the deed organized and pushed it through.

Turned out, though, that one of them held it against me for the next sixty years. Of course, he and I were never really friends, and through the years we seemed to get on opposite sides of politics and business and quite a few other things. Still, I never thought any sane man would hold that big a grudge against somebody who never actually damaged him at all. If I was in any condition to get back at him, I would, but, being dead now, I can't say that is an option.

I know what you are wondering: if I'm dead, how can I be telling this to you?

Damned if I know. I seem to be stuck here for now. But I was alive and if not well, at least able to survive when somebody knocked on our door, shoved my wife down, and showed me a warrant for my arrest—on a misdemeanor warrant issued ten years ago. I knew my friend Judge Packer had tended to that for me, but there it was, and they grabbed me up from my wheelchair and dragged me out to the deputy's car. They crammed me into the back, hurting my bad back a lot, and drove me the fifteen miles into Templeton.

By the time we got to the jail, I was hurting and mad in about equal parts. I tried to ask what was going on, but nobody would answer a question or even seem to see me as they carried me down the corridor and threw me into a cell. I mean THREW me, and when I hit the floor everybody could hear my hipbone crack. I must have passed out for a while, because when I came to I was in an ambulance. They admitted me to the county hospital and put me in a room. I came and went while a couple of doctors examined me, and they X-rayed me, twisting my leg until I screamed. When they put me back into my room I died. That was no biggie, actually. In fact it was a great relief, because I quit hurting.

Say what they will, I saw no white light or tunnel or anything except my own body—I seemed to be sort of floating above it. After a good long while a nurse came bustling in with the blood pressure thing. She touched me, took my nonexistent pulse, and left. When she came back there were two doctors and another nurse with her, and they seemed to do their best to revive me, but I was gone and intended to stay that way. My mind seemed clearer than it had been in years, and I could see that my death while in custody would make a godawful stink, and surely would bring down hell on whoever had set this in motion. I wondered how they'd cover it up, for knowing Templeton and its loose interpretation of any law there was, I felt certain they would try their damndest to hide what had happened. So even if I had been invited to heaven in that sweet chariot in the song, I would have turned down the ride. I wanted to see what they did with me. And it seemed okay with whoever or whatever was overseeing me in my present situation.

My poor old body lay there for about two hours, and I had to admit that I was even uglier dead than I had been alive. I guess the medics were making some pretty desperate calls to the sheriff's office, and the sheriff was making some even more desperate calls to whoever it was who started this. Also to others, as I learned while following the gurney down the hall and into a van from the local funeral home. So they were going to let my family's own mortician handle me. That surprised me.

I learned better, though. No sooner did they get me to the funeral home than another van showed up, sporting the logo of Finch's from Mount Arum. That was about thirty miles from Templeton. I had a bad feeling that my wife and my uncles and cousins weren't going to know even that I was dead until it was too late to track me down. Sure enough, they got me to Mount Arum and transferred my body to still another hearse, this one from Soledad. Got there and put me in one from Raskin.

And on the way we made a little detour to a crematorium, where I was reduced to a cardboard box full of ashes. This was tossed into a dumpster outside Raskin, and that was that. End of Buddy Norton, businessman, concerned citizen, and one-time prankster, but it didn't set me free to go wherever I was supposed to go.

I was still no angel. I found myself compelled to stay with this until I found out who did it and why. I couldn't recall doing anything so nasty and painful that it would make me such an enemy. And now I realized that I could do things I hadn't been able to do for years—and some of them I never would have dreamed might be done.

So I stuck with the driver of the hearse that had delivered me to the crematorium and later dumped me like a bag of garbage. Not that it bothered me—I was done with that mess, free of its aches and demands and glad of it. But I had a compelling need to find out, and it was the men who were involved who might lead me to the one who started it all.

I had no clue as to what I needed to do next. No guide, no white light, no road map, no nothing. Still, I'd lived almost eighty years in Templeton County, much of that time involved in business or politics or both. I remembered it all, and even more that somehow I had forgotten when I got old. Now it all came back, clear and cold and even beginning to be understandable. In a sort of lightning flash, that long-ago night when we hoisted that ancient Ford to the gym roof appeared before my eyes. I was the only surviving member of the team that did the deed, but there had been eleven more who had been denied the chance to play in the three historic games that won Templeton the state football championship, because of what we had done.

Chance Moore died in Korea. Elton Fitzgerald drowned in the big lake on a fishing trip. Got drunk and fell overboard. Chuck Dennis had a heart attack and died on the golf course. Those I remembered because I had known them well. Of the other eight, only two had been in touch with me through the years. Which one had held a grudge all this time?

I stuck with the driver of the hearse as he drove back to the funeral home in Raskin and went into the office. His trip report book lay on the front seat, and I tried my best to look inside it, but my fingers slipped right through the cover and pages without disturbing them at all. After a while he came out to get the book, and I drifted along like an invisible mist as he went into a big office and set the trip book onto a desk. I was right there at her shoulder when the young woman opened it to post the charges for the trip.

There was a call recorded from the Soledad Funeral Home authorizing the pickup from their van. The expenses and cremation were charged to...the Templeton, Texas, Sheriff's Department. That gave me valuable information, though I had suspected as much all the time. Still, I had no idea how long I would be allowed to hang around, and I was bound and determined to see this through, if possible. I knew I had to get back to Templeton—then I realized that there was no way I could do that unless I had the ability to just...shift myself there.

I thought hard about where I needed to be. It was early morning by now. If I were inside the sheriff's personal office that might be a useful time to overhear people talking about any very secret activities they'd been up to, so I concentrated on being right there in that two-by-four office, waiting for the sheriff to get there. And then I was there, sort of hanging over the biggest filing cabinet. The big clock on the wall showed 6:47. Sheriff Hogue should be coming in soon, for he bragged about being at work by seven every weekday morning. I wished I knew something about haunting people, because I'd have loved to give that son-of-a-bitch a heart attack. Whoever had set this nasty business in motion had worked through the law, and it was the sheriff who'd sent those deputies out to drag me into jail...and my death.

He got there by seven-fifteen, bringing a big cup of hot coffee and a box of doughnuts. I would have given my eye teeth, if I'd had any left in this condition, for a cup of coffee and a doughnut. Then I realized that I wasn't a bit hungry or thirsty or achy or cold or hot. Okay, I could accept that pretty happily. What I could not accept was never finding out who'd set me up to die. So I settled myself in to listen. After yesterday's activities, surely he would call or be called by the one who instigated my murder.

When the phone rang, I came alert. But it was just his wife wanting to tell him she was going to see her mother. Then it was a deputy asking for information about a case. For an hour there was nothing to interest me. But when the clock clicked onto eight-thirty he looked up, checked the time by his watch, and picked up the phone. The private one, not the one connecting him to the dispatcher. I misted down and settled around his neck. He shivered but didn't seem to know why, as he touched the numbers on the dial. Those numbers went into my memory, wherever that was stored, indelibly.

The voice that answered was gruff, as if it came through a throat that had hosted too may drinks and too much tobacco smoke. Not recognizable as one I had heard recently, that was certain. Then I concentrated on the conversation.

"This is Sheriff Hogue. Wanted to tell you we settled that little problem you had. You won't have to be concerned about it ever again."

There came a cackle of laughter from the phone. "You folks do good work, Terry. I'll have to make a donation to your re-election campaign. A big one. That wasn't what you could call a major concern of mine, but I'm gettin' old, and it was somethin' I wanted to put behind me while I still can. You'll be hearin' from me."

I felt myself pulled away from the sheriff. That phony drawl—I knew it. Hadn't heard it for decades, but it was one that had been familiar long ago. Lawrence Thibodeau had faked it, trying to sound like the other redneck boys, but his Cajun accent crept through anyway. The girls had seemed to like him, but the boys thought he was a creep or queer or, worse than anything, FRENCH!

If my girl Lizzie had made eyes at him, I might have felt the same, but we were a real item, as we proved by getting married and staying married until she died twenty years ago. And that comic-strip light bulb came on over my nonexistent head. Larry had made a lot of moves toward Lizzie, now that I came to think about it. Neither of us had thought much about that, because we were so taken up with each other at the time. But he'd cut a swath through the other senior girls, and if shower-room talk that Lizzie passed on to me was anything near true, he'd scored with about half of them. Could he have been so set on getting Lizzie that he'd held it against m all these years?

But then I remembered that night when we all were barred from playing football. He'd been one of the players who had lost his chance to shine. Another memory unfolded. He'd tried to scam the county with a "bargain" deal on asphalt. The group I headed had investigated that, and we discovered that other counties had used the stuff, and it floated away at the first rain. That had probably cost him a lot of money, and it wasn't the only thing we'd found, either. We scotched a half-dozen crooked deals he had been pushing. Though it was nothing personal with me, the idiot must have thought I was out to get him. The one thing I knew for sure about him was that he thought the universe revolved around him.

I knew where he lived, too. Without even knowing how it worked, I found myself hanging in the air above his recliner, looking down at his bald head with its fringe of white hair. He was sipping coffee from a mug, a newspaper open on his lap. He scanned through it rather hastily, and I followed, reading over his shoulder. He had to be looking for any mention of that illegal arrest and sudden death, I knew, but I could see no mention of it, even in the short bits at the back of the paper.

So now I knew. Old Larry, for some twisted reason of his own, had set me up either to serve time or die. I wondered if poor Lizzie, dead now these twenty years, knew what we'd set in motion, back there in our teens. Then I wondered how you'd go about haunting somebody. I'd already proved that I couldn't touch anything. I'd have choked the life out of Larry at that point, if that could be done, but he didn't even seem to feel a chill while I tried. I couldn't even whomp up a good scary moan.

I wanted to hurt that bastard worse than I'd ever wanted anything, and I was totally helpless to do anything at all that he'd notice. Talk about frustration! Being a mind in a mist is not a satisfying state of being. I drifted back up to the ceiling and hung there, trying to figure out some way of punishing the man.

Time passed mighty slowly, I can testify to that. Thibodeau came and went, pestered his wife about silly things, made phone calls to people I knew to be influential and some I thought must be the scum of the earth. If he was setting up some other old acquaintance he thought had done him harm, I couldn't recognize it from what was said.

I seemed to be caught in some kind of limbo, couldn't even go somewhere else, though I tried. There must be some kind of connection between a dead man and the one who had him killed, because I seemed to be tethered there in his study like a colt to a stake. If I'd still had a body I'd probably have gone crazy, but I was sort of frozen in the situation like a fly in amber. It was plenty of Hell for me, though I couldn't really think of anything I'd done in my life that was bad enough to earn me that kind of punishment.

I'd never thought of cheating on the income tax as anything but good clean fun, and I couldn't see God feeling much different about it.

I kept watching the dates on his newspapers and reading over his shoulder, and never a word was printed about my death. I wondered if my uncles and cousins even knew I was gone. We'd sort of lost touch after I got old and sickly, and they were all busy folks, so I didn't hold it against them. I wondered how my second wife was getting along, but I knew she was one tough lady and she'd do fine. No, I was the one in trouble. Where was that bright light and that tunnel folks talked about? How in hell was I supposed to find my way wherever it was I should go, if I was stuck here with this fat, bald bastard.

Then somebody gave him a dog, a yappy little beast named Tab that seemed to see me. First time he came into the study he stopped short, sat down, and stared up at me where I lurked in a corner of the ceiling. He didn't bark, but he lifted his lip and snarled up at me. About that time Larry came in and dropped into his recliner. The dog went over and sniffed his legs, licked his hand, and lay down. From time to time he'd look up at me and snarl, and finally old Larry realized that the critter was actually seeing something he couldn't see.

He got up, grumbling, and looked around the room, followed every step of the way by that dog. That gave me an idea. I started moving around, keeping as much on the opposite side of the study as I could. The dog tried to keep an eye on both of us, but he finally gave up on Larry and kept staring at me. That really puzzled his new master. He kept coming to stand on the spot Tab was staring at, but by that time I'd be somewhere else and Tab would be staring there. I could see that was driving him crazy, and it suited me fine.

Tab and I played that game almost every evening for a week. Then Larry locked up the study and never came inside. After that I could make it to whatever room he occupied, so I followed him around, just like the dog did, and he got more and more frantic. We drove him crazy, old Tab and I, and once his wife had him committed to the funny farm, I found I could turn loose and go just about anywhere.

I checked on my wife and my uncles and what cousins I could locate. Then I began paying attention to things that weren't really obvious, and I found that Lizzie had been trying to get my attention since day one. She really chewed me out, once I realized that the presence I felt was really Lizzie.

I don't really know where we go from here, but she does, and that is good enough for me.

I take wicked delight in devising oddball ways to punish evildoers. Living as I do in an area not unlike that in the story, I know how to do it, too, but I am too old to manage alligators!

THE SWAMP RUNNER

It seems to be getting plumb crowded down here in the river bottom country. I've been running trotlines and traplines and hunting wild hogs and possums and coons since I could walk, and I almost never come across anybody but hunters and once a game warden, but he was dead already. Now it seems as if there's folks behind most every tree and bush. Mostly law folks, now that bank robbers and such have found out what a great hiding place this can be. Too bad they don't know enough about staying alive down here to make it, but if they had good sense they wouldn't be in trouble with the law in the first place.

Course, you could say that I'm in trouble, too, but that's only with the school folks, who think I ought to be cooped up in four walls and made to listen to teachers who can't tell a king snake from a copperhead. I have to admit, though, that they have too much sense to come out here looking for me. The thing that bothers me is that I can read better than most of them and have read stuff they never even heard of. Mama gets books from the library at the college where she works. She is a janitor, but she's good friends with all the librarians and they let her check out what she wants. She has good judgment about what to bring me.

Down here there are always illegal gillnetters and folks hunting deer, either to feed their families, which I never mind, or to sell, which I resent. Mostly I just observe them and let them be, unless they begin cutting trees or messing up the water and the woods. Once in a while a bunch of moonshiners will begin sampling their own stuff and get really troublesome. That's when I drop a hint to my Mama, and she sends a tip to the feds or the state game control people. Usually they clear up the mess pretty quick. I think they've come to rely on those tips, though if they knew it came from a boy under fifteen they probably would ignore them.

Don't make a mistake. Mama sent me to school until I was about ten or eleven, could read anything I wanted and a lot of things the teachers never dreamed I could or would want to, and had enough math to do for the kind of life I intended to lead. Once I knew those things, I had an idea how to find out anything I needed, and the computer Mama bought and set up in our cabin helped me learn more.

Funny thing. She got an on-line degree in history and another in English, but she went right on working as a janitor. She said the kind of in-fighting she saw between the professors and the departments made her sick. "If I wanted to go into politics I'd run for office," she told me. "The idea of spending every day of my life playing politics with a bunch of academics who couldn't find their way out of a bramble thicket is disgusting. I'd rather scrub toilets. Once you do that you have something to show for it, but in the university nobody has anything to show for all their finagling and back-stabbing."

I always thought she might be exaggerating things a little, but she's a smart woman and sees things a lot of people miss. Which is why I chose a life in which politics has only a very remote place. When the time came I guessed I'd register and vote, but the rest of the time I intended to spend with critters I could trust either to try to kill me or let me alone. That can't be said for politicians.

Things went along mighty well for a long time. Mama retired from janitor work, but she missed the university, so she passed the ACE test and enrolled for a Master's Degree in English, which surprised the heck out of her friends there. This meant she could still bring me books from the library, and she figured I could test out for a bachelor's degree in history, probably in literature and English, and maybe even more, but I figured it wasn't worth the trouble. I didn't intend to look for any job in the "real world," that was certain.

So how did I think I'd earn money? You've got to be kidding! The bottomlands are full of valuable plants and critters. I caught snakes for the labs that make antidotes for their poison. I gathered rattan and grapevine and willow and cattail for people who did craft work. There were all kinds of medicinal plants that I harvested for the few old black ladies who still practiced herbal medicine and a growing number of white folks who have caught on to how effective it can be. Mama delivered my gleanings to my customers, though she promised she'd buy me a motor scooter when I got to be sixteen, so I could do my own deliveries. She never got used to those big sacks of mixed moccasins, copperheads, and rattlesnakes. I had to double-bag them and put those into a thick box or she wouldn't handle them at all.

When the Catletts built a fishing shack down close to Peshtigo Creek, I didn't think much about it. People were always doing that sort of thing, coming down from time to time to camp and fish, then getting tired of it and letting the shack fall down. It wasn't as if they owned the land—most of this belonged to the state. Mama and I owned our hundred acres because it had come down from her great-great-great-granddaddy, who got it in a grant from Mexico. The state tried to take it a couple of times, but Mama proved to be a lot smarter than they were. We still had the place and the old cabin, which we'd kept repaired (to the point of almost rebuilding it), and now we had it protected under the historical homestead program.

That was why I never bothered about the Catletts' shack or their weekends spent there—not until the wind shifted one day when I was running my trotlines along the creek, and a whiff of a nasty smell just about knocked me onto my heels. I'd read about meth labs, of course, because I kept up with newspapers and magazines, but that stink matched the descriptions I'd read. I slid up the creek, past the gator hole where a big old bull gator was sunning himself on a mud-bank, and several more were lurking under the water, only their eyeballs betraying their presence.

They paid no attention to me; I was something they were used to. Besides that, I sometimes brought them dead critters I found in the woods or run over on one of the dirt tracks where kids drove their four-wheel drive pickups down to the mud-wallows they used. Once in a while a couple of the young gators would follow me for a while, as the path ran alongside the creek, seeming to hope that I had some treat for them.

As I got closer to the shack, they gave up and slid deeper into the creek, and I went low and silent, for the Catletts were there in their lab, and the stink was terrible. Worse than that, they had been tearing up the woods around it. They'd cut down a big dogwood and two grancy-graybeard trees that I'd watched bloom in the spring since I was about eight. A trail of slimy stuff ran off toward the branch of the creek beside their shanty. Whatever it was, it couldn't possibly be good for either fish or alligators.

I found myself getting angry. People stupid enough to buy their muck were free to do it or not, but the critters and the fish and the gators had no choice. Whatever that gunk running down the slope might be, I knew it was nasty. Make no mistake—I killed game to feed my Mama and me, when things were tight, but every time I did that I thanked the dead animal for helping us survive. Sort of like the Indians used to, I guess. These folks were as nasty as their sewage or whatever that was polluting the creek. I figured I needed to do something to discourage them.

I went home that evening and told Mama what I'd found. She had her nose in a book, as usual, but she came out of it in a hurry when she learned what the Catletts were doing. "We could turn 'em in," she said. "But they're a mean bunch, from what I hear, and they might burn us out...or worse."

I'd seen some things happen in the swamp country that made me sick to think of. There was that game warden who'd arrested a bunch of illegal gillnetters. They went to jail but got bailed out, and before you could get your breath, the warden's house burned down with him and his wife in it. Then there was that girl who turned in the site of a still she stumbled across while on a fishing trip. What they did to her I try never to think about.

I spent a lot of that night thinking instead of sleeping. Just before I finally drifted off I heard a distant bellow from the swamp—a big bull gator sounding off, I knew. And then it came to me, clear and clean and—appropriate. Smiling, I let myself sleep at last.

That was on a Tuesday. I had most of the week to prepare, before the rest of that crew came down for their weekend in the country. I scoured the dirt roads and even went out to the highway and picked up every run-over critter I could find. I got those gators so spoiled they'd follow me along the path, and I baited them closer and closer to that shack. They got as near to being pets as I suppose a gator can come, though I never got too close or turned my back on them. By Friday night I had them ready, if things worked out like I hoped.

Mama didn't like for me to roam the swamp country at night, but in this case she didn't argue when I laid out my plan to her. She knew town-people—no one better—and they were terrified of most of the critters in the woods. Which made me wonder why they risked their precious hides down here in the habitat of so many. Anyway, I was loaded with road-kill when I made my way down to the creek where my gators waited.

And they were hungry! I dropped a squashed possum here and a stiff armadillo there, until I had the entire bunch trailing along the path behind me, the sound of their padding paws creepy amid the chirps and squawks and twitters of the night birds and tree frogs. They were well on their way, and I hoped everyone was asleep in that shanty, for I had to dump the rest of my bait inside its door.

They must've felt mighty secure, so far out in the woods, for they didn't even have anyone watching. I heard only sputters and snores as I eased the door open, after picking its lock (Mama didn't know I had learned how to do that from one of the books she brought me). I felt the gators too close behind me for comfort, so I dumped the bait and jumped aside as far as I could as the reptiles shoved into the building with a grating of horny hides and began chomping into their treat.

Hidden in a huckleberry thicket, I listened, as it was too dark to see anything much. First there were some grunts and groggy questions, then a match scritched and a streak of light came shooting through the cracks in the walls. Then there was a royal shindy. Screams and crackles and crashes were punctuated by the sounds of irritated gators, who evidently didn't appreciate having their midnight snack interrupted.

Then four shapes crashed through different parts of the walls, heading in four different directions. I almost laughed out loud, for I had watched them over the weeks, and none of them could find his way through the woods unless there was a clear-cut path to follow, preferably with hatchet marks on the trees along the way. They'd spend the night lost as graveyard ghosts, with whippoorwills and screech owls making the night tuneful with their weird calls. Before dawn every one of them would think he was in Hell.

I heard a strange noise, sort of a smushing sound, and a flicker near the shack told me that the kerosene lamp must have been upset. Now those flimsy walls were unable to stand with man-sized holes in them, and they were falling in. The whole shebang was going to collapse and burn without my lifting a hand to make it happen.

I went to the path and gave the whistle I used to attract the attention of the gators. But they were not idiots. They were already shuffling back toward the creek, most of them carrying something dead in their teeth but unwilling to stay close to something as alien as fire. When someone came down tomorrow to take part in the family "business" they were going to find something they couldn't explain. When they found their kin, if they did, those who had been there when the disaster happened couldn't explain it either.

The gators had blotted my tracks with their own, I figured, and nobody would ever suspect a mere boy of making this happen. Particularly since I knew very well that my "co-conspirators" would never say a word to anyone.

I went home and told Mama what happened. She laughed herself to sleep. Even if those four Catletts died in the woods, they were no loss to anyone, including their kinfolk, and the world was better without them.

I did some laughing myself, before I dozed off.

Creating myth is terrific fun, and sometimes I have an idea that lends itself to such exercises.

FATE HAS THREE FACES

DEIRDRE, CASTER OF THE STONES:

In the mortal world I am a gardener, providing food for my family and many others. I take joy in my work and would gladly undertake no other. Yet from time to time, at long intervals, I am called to other work, disturbing tasks outside our reality, which can be of dire importance to the World of Men.

For I am she who casts the stones that decide the fate of my kind.

Such a call came to me one gray winter day, when I would far sooner have remained snug in my stone house, planning my plantings for spring. That was not to be, for as the day dwindled the old compulsion rose within me, and I knew that fate was calling me forth to that old and hateful duty.

BELVA, READER OF THE RUNES:

I had hoped never to be summoned again to the Casting. Age and infirmity should have excused me from that painful duty, but on a day hardly to be matched for bitterness the call rose within my ancient bones. I set out for the secret destination, wrapped in thick shawls and heavy leggings and shivering despite them all.

Behind me I left no one who would miss me or care if I froze in the frozen lands, yet I valued my life, painful as it was. The minutiae of living occupied my hands, and the vastness of thought and learning kept my mind active. On this, which must surely be my last calling to duty, I found myself resenting this old obligation. Why, I wondered, and not for the first time, had this been laid upon me who was neither strong nor overly wise?

Yet I am the one who reads the runes carven onto the stones, and the decision cannot be made without me.

MELLORA, INTERPRETER OF FATE:

Serenely weaving a figure into my tapestry before the coal fire, I had no forewarning. The summons came with breathtaking force, sweeping me to my feet with its compulsion. Dropping the tapestry onto its frame, I went to the window and stared out into the forbidding day. I shuddered, not only at the thought of facing the cold, but at the reality of the grim duty before me. Always, the casting of the stones required a reading, and that reading showed me the meaning of the problem and the solution to it.

I turned to prepare my travel pack. After eating a good meal, I donned my fur cloak and boots, took up my bundle, and opened the door. It was a long journey, made longer by the inclement weather. I wondered how old Belva would fare on such a difficult road. Deirdre was strong and able, but Belva had made too many of these difficult and demanding journeys. I wondered who would take her place, when she was gone. Then I reminded myself that over the generations the Caster, the Reader, and the Interpreter had been replaced and performed their tasks without fail. The fate of our world depended upon us.

THOSE WHO WATCHED THE WORLD *sat in their high place, waiting. Once again they had seen the approach of catastrophe. Once again they had called upon those responsible for resolutions to come and decide the fate of a people. Their ways were difficult, beset with perils. If the Watchers had been capable of worry, they would have paid special attention to the oldest of the women, for she faced a terrible journey with too little strength for the task. But it was Deirdre who was in danger.*

DEIRDRE, CASTER OF THE STONES:

I started my trek with my usual trepidation. Five times the call had come, and five times I had answered it. Never had my way been easy, but this time there was an added stress, one I could not quite identify. Something waited among the rocks of the hills, a cold, hard presence that sent a chill to my heart.

Hefting my staff, I strode forward in darkness, feeling my way with the senses that roused only when the call to duty came. A boulder larger than a house loomed before me. Beyond it there was a presence, and I moved toward it, probing with my staff. When the haft went icy in my hand, I knew I had touched the thing that waited. The tingle that always filled me when I cast the stones now quivered in my hand, and I sent that impulse down the shaft into the thing before me.

Then there was pain enough to make one wish to die. Fear lashed at me from that unseen entity, and weakness enveloped my body and sought to overcome my will and my mind. I bit my lip until the blood ran, held onto the staff with a grip that only death could break, and sent my will along the faithful wood to penetrate the creature it pierced.

A hiss like the last breath of a serpent sliced through the air. The presence disappeared from my sensing, just as darkness overwhelmed me. Yet I struggled upward from that sea of blackness at last, pulled myself to my feet and found to my great relief that a gray dawn was breaking.

By day's end I would stand in the secret place.

BELVA, READER OF THE RUNES:

Unfair as it seemed I, the oldest and feeblest of the Called, must face the longest road to the secret place. Though the first span lay across fields and meadows, now they were soggy with wet and slick with ice. Bundled as I was, falling could not damage me much, but it slowed me a great deal, and I made good use of my three-pronged metal stick, which grasped the ice, giving me balance for setting my careful steps. Still, I knew I must arrive last of us three, by a great deal, most like. The appearance of a frost-wolf did not cheer me at all, as the thing leaped from a frozen hedge and made for my throat. Remembering all the times before, I sank to my knees and braced the walking stick, handle downward, just in time to skewer the beast's throat on its prongs. Fortunately, the wolves encountered before did not live to learn from the experience, for which I was most grateful.

By the time I came to the foothills, I was happy that I need not scale the mountain itself. My path ran in loops around its toes, where the effort of moving was enough to leave me exhausted. But on the third day I knew that I would arrive at my destination and I prayed that this would be my last journey to this place.

MELLORA, INTERPRETER OF FATE:

The wind bit viciously at my ears and my fingers, even through their fur wrappings. Before I had gone ten leagues, my feet were numb and my legs were aching, though I paused to eat and to rest as often as needed. Never before had I been called in such weather, and I was unused to battling such cold. Yet I was trained for such duties, and I drove onward, stopping only when I could not move one foot before the other.

Strangely, on this journey I did not meet any of the animal or spirit opponents I had battled before. Only the weather and my own body seemed determined to stop me, and those I could defeat, though with great difficulty. I found myself wondering how old Belva was progressing, if I, a generation younger, was having such problems. Then I was at the foot of the mountain, faced with climbing to the cliff where lay the secret place.

By the time I stood on that apron of smooth rock, I knew that this was going to be a unique Calling. Something dire rode the wind and lurked on the horizon. I found myself dreading the casting and the reading and, most of all, my interpretation. At the end, it was I who must save or doom something—or someone. Never before had this been a thing that I found it painful to do.

No one was there—I was the first to arrive, and that told me that the others had found impediment upon their roads. I found a niche out of the wind, wrapped my furs closely about me, and set myself to wait.

DEIRDRE, CASTER OF THE STONES:

When I came at last to the mountain and the secret place, I found Mellora waiting. She greeted me and moved aside to let me sit with her in her sheltered spot, and I turned to her and said, "I fear for Belva. She is so frail, and hers is the longest road. "

Mellora gazed out over the frozen hills and the flatlands beyond. "Never have the three failed to arrive, when Called. Though I am youngest of you all, that I have learned well. Such a summoning as we have demands an answer. Once a Caster came, cast the stones, and died where she knelt, having battled even death for long enough to complete her task. "

I had heard the tale, I realized, from Mellora's predecessor. "Not only she," I said. "Others have fulfilled their duty and perished, but only after their work was done. This is a thing that gives one faith in Those Who Watch the World, I feel."

She nodded. Then she took from her pack a strip of dried meat and a flask of wine and handed them to me. We sat in silence, eating that ration and waiting for Belva, who must come, whatever her condition.

BELVA, READER OF THE RUNES:

When I pulled myself at last onto the rock floor where the others waited, I was almost done. The last miles had drained me dry, taking what seemed the last of my strength. Still, once I stood erect upon the stone I felt the familiar surge of power that always accompanied this dreadful duty. Deirdre and Mellora rose to stand beside me, and once we touched our hands together, the current linked us and empowered us beyond any ability we possessed as individuals.

Now the wind died away, as if smoothing the way for our work. Deirdre loosed her hands and took from her pack the stones, six smooth blue-gray pebbles marked with symbols. Mellora and I stepped back a pace, and she knelt and shook the stones in her hands. Then she cast them onto the stony floor, and they rolled with a soft rattle to settle into position.

Deirdre stepped back and I took her place, kneeling to study the symbols that meant nothing to anyone except at just such times as this. The marks seemed to writhe before my eyes, and I focused closely upon them, calling out each that lay uppermost as it came into my mind.

"The sigama. The ultine. The makrem. The ellios. The intrimo. The exelem. Those are the symbols I see," I said to Mellora.

I stepped back, and she took my place to stare at the symbols, which had again dissolved into their indecipherable state. Now the reason for this summoning would come, along with the solution to whatever problem it showed us.

MELLORA, INTERPRETER OF FATE:

Never before had I dreaded my task so bitterly. As I knelt on the stone, I felt my heart begin to race, my blood pound in my veins, my limbs quiver. My entire body seemed determined to stop me from interpreting the reading, and I quelled it with utmost effort. Bending forward, I gazed at the swirls of color on the stones.

Into my mind came the names Belva had called out. The sigama. Plague! That came into my mind with stunning impact. Of all the perils we knew, plague was the most merciless.

The ultine. I closed my eyes and into my mind came a picture—a village, swaddled in snow, where men bore forth draped bodies toward a distant graveyard. Did this mean an entire village must die?

The makrem and the intrimo came together, and the meaning was all too clear. A choice must be made. And the exelem—I must choose, on pain of extinction, which of our people must die, an entire clan. It must be that of one of us. I must make the choice, without taking council with my peers.

I sank forward onto my elbows, my face in my hands, moaning with anguish. Deirdre and Belva came to my side and lifted me to my feet. "What do you see, Mellora?" they asked, their voices anxious, but I could not reply. I must make my choice before I spoke again.

Deirdre's clan was valuable, filled with master gardeners, talented sculptors, gifted teachers. Belva's was old and wise, possessing more wisdom than any other I knew. Mine was—young, enthusiastic. Not learned. Not talented, particularly. Not of irreplaceable value to our kind. I must choose to doom my own people, myself included, that the others might live.

The choice was clear. Once it was made, I spoke. "I have pronounced death upon my own clan and myself. Plague will come, and it will take the villages of my people, but yours will be safe, along with all the others in our land.

"Go home, my sisters, and rejoice that your people will survive. I return to my place, my family, my kin and friends and prepare to battle the plague, though I know that will be useless." I felt tears behind my eyes, in my throat, but I went with them from the mountain and camped with them for the night. Rest we must, before undertaking the return journey.

In the morning we embraced for the last time. "I am taking Belva home with me," Deirdre told me. "She must rest and be cared for before going to her lonely house. We will not forget you, Mellora. We will tell all about this Casting. We send our love and grief with you."

When they went away, I turned toward my own place, and if I had come in bitter cold, I returned in worse bitterness. To be forced to destroy my own was a cruel, a terrible doom.

THE ONES WHO WATCHED THE WORLD *turned their gazes to another place, another time, another set of people. There were always disasters to show to those who must deal with them, though few were as sad as this one had been.*

One of my worst nightmares involves having my mind trapped in a totally uncontrollable body. How much worse if that body is not even human!

MINDBEND

The noises in my head are chattering away, rousing me from my long sleep. Chuckles of static and shrieks of interference interrupt my thoughts. I wish I could recall what it is I am supposed to be doing, but I can see just from surveying the landscape that a catastrophe has happened here. I have been injured, I think, probably badly impaired.

I have tried checking over my body, but that is not as easy as I thought it should be. Instead of the anatomy I remember, I seem to be much larger, with layerings of unfamiliar materials. Instead of four limbs and a rounded receptacle for sensory apparatus, I seem to have one large, barrel-shaped area on treads. The "arms" are of metal, with grasping clamps at their ends.

Everything I can access tells me that I should inhabit a human being, and yet all the specifications in my files deny that. At the moment, I am a metallic object with a rational mind, and how I became so I cannot understand or even guess.

The place in which I have come to rest is not a good one, though I have seen nothing that would qualify as "good" since I became conscious. A wide desert of pebbles and sand and arid soil stretches away from horizon to horizon. The light is a strange orange-gray, filtered through dirty mats of reddish cloud; it makes everything look dead.

I have seen no living tree or bush, not even a blade of grass, since I woke in a little cup of eroded soil some kilometers to the south. Insects evidently no longer exist, although it is possible that my altered hearing range might not pick up their shrill squeaks. No bird has crossed that forbidding sky, and no animal or even serpent has moved before my treads as I trundle northward.

There is no purpose served by remaining here. I will go forward, though to what I cannot imagine. There is no sun or moon or star visible to guide me, and only some inbuilt sense of this mechanical body orients me toward my goal. If there is no other sentient being left on this arid little world, what point is there in continuing?

No point, but it is less painful than pausing to wait for whatever doom can befall a creature like me. Or endlessness, which is far worse.

The swells of the desert are growing more abrupt, topped by ragged teeth of rock. Once I almost wept, thinking I saw a city rising on the horizon, but it was only such another formation, mocking the neat buildings I have reviewed in my memory banks.

Heaving up and down the long swells, I find myself growing desperately lonely, and for relief I am going through the computer files available in my system. In an orderly fashion, I am trying to find what and where I am...and why.

* * * * * * *

"He's dead, Ambrose. There's no use in trying to revive him now. Let him go peacefully." Sharon was looking down into my face, and, strangely, I could see both from slightly above and behind her. The crisp cap tilted as she bent to draw the sheet over my cyanosed features.

Ambrose Fenton straightened, his face crumpling with grief. I felt sudden empathy, for I would have wanted to weep if I had stood at his death bed. We had been friends since boyhood, and this was a sudden and painful parting.

What happened to me? Hovering there in the still room, I retraced the events leading to this point, but all I could find was overwhelming pain. The arm, the chest, nausea, a terrible jolt, and then the drifting that had ended here just beneath the ceiling. I died of a heart attack. Being an army doctor, I had seen relatively few such deaths, but the symptoms were there.

* * * * * * *

Shocked, I paused, my treads digging themselves into a spot of soft soil. If I am dead, then what am I doing here? What is this thing in which I ride, using its sensors and, to a large extent, its memory?

I must dig further into the files, learn what has been done to me.

ARDATH MAYHAR * 73

* * * * * * *

It was like being reeled in at the end of a line, an unlikely fish caught out of the peaceful stream of death. I resisted, but I had no substance with which to hold myself in place; the essential "I" went where it was compelled, and once it came into range of the things in the laboratory, I understood what was happening.

A huge metal hulk stood on treads beside a table on which rested a glass container. Inside that, throbbing to the rhythms of an attached pump as it forced nutrients and oxygen through its cells, was a brain. My brain.

I was being dragged back into it, willy nilly, though I wanted to howl and curse. But in I went, whatever it is that forms the entity I am. And I found myself trapped in that blind chunk of brain matter, waiting for what I knew must come next.

I was a part of the team that originated the techniques for implanting brains into mechanisms. All too well I understood what was taking place. To become a destroyer instead of a healer—what a terrible fate for a doctor, even one involved in such inhuman projects as that one.

* * * * * * *

So, I am now a destroyer, armed to the nonexistent teeth with sensors and weaponry. I dig impatiently into the log kept electronically since the implant, and I find that I was assigned to the terraforming of Elektra Six, being given there the task of wiping out the native fauna to make room for specially adapted Terran strains. I shudder—or would, given the ability—at the thought.

Another file. The Kamraon War. I key another in rapidly, for I have no wish to re-examine that catastrophe, but the memories flit around the edges of my memory: Living bodies burst like eggs. Cities crumple beneath the impact of the Sonosystem attacks. Other mechanical weapons not unlike myself heave over the horizon to disappear in a blast of disruptor fire.

And all the while, trapped inside this metal monster, there has been the sensitive human spirit that was mine. Was that why I went dormant, into a sort of mechanical shock, and was out of action while this world was pocked and pitted around me with Impact missiles?

I move forward, skimming or skipping files rapidly. Where am I now? What action had brought my kind to this undesirable little world, where the bloodshot cloud never changes to show that it rotates at all?

At last I find the last entry in the log:

> Assigned: Celeric outpost.
> Purpose: Protect against infiltration by agents of the Rebellion.
> Guard: Protect strategic arms and fuel installations from theft or attack.
> Supply: Provide Franchise ships or detachments with needed supplies.
>
> NO CODE CANCEL
> NO CODE CANCEL
> NO CODE CANCEL
> NO CODE CANCEL

And that is all. *No Code Cancel*—I sped through basic codes to find what that might mean. When I did, I wondered why a guard on an unmanned outpost needed to be programmed so that it was impossible to change its orders. It seems irrational to me.

But evidently the little world had been attacked, for the evidence was all around me. Blast cones were becoming more frequent, showing that a firefight had taken place here between ground forces. Why? I can only hope to learn more as I near the center of the concentration of fire.

Gradually, the memories filter back into my bruised mind. The Rebels had come, but I and the two others set to guard had beaten them off...too easily? Now I wonder. A fleet of Franchise transports arrived soon afterward, and much of the food and equipment left here for them was transferred into their holds.

Before the last shuttle could take off, there was a raid, coming from nowhere, that demolished the Stashes, even those deep below-ground. The shuttle cracked under Impact fire, but many of the men aboard lived to scramble out of range before its fuel tanks went.

Unus and Duo had set their backs toward mine, forming a protective triangle inside which the survivors huddled, firing when there was some target within range of their feeble firearms. I remember hearing Captain Evinrade yell behind me, but I was engaged in firing on a line of Metallics that came over the ridge before me, their weapons busy as they approached.

And there my recollection came to an end. Had I sustained a direct hit?

I stop beneath that unhealthy sky and grip the External Scanner in one set of clamps. The arms are arranged so that I can reach any part of my anatomy, in order to effect repairs. Now it shows me, inch by inch, the pitted metal of my skin. Just behind the shielded spot where my visual and auditory sensors are positioned, there is a mark, old now, but still showing the blackening of fire and the subtle crinkling that denotes a hit by an Impact Bomb.

Below, in the belly of my body, lies the computer with its vital files. Theoretically, that should have been cushioned enough to prevent damage, but I trace the connective cables to the sensors, and I realize that such a "wound" might well have put me out of commission.

Had I gone trundling off across the desert, blinded, deaf, unable to think or to access my orders? What had happened to those I left behind me?

I am going back; I know that now. Some mechanical instinct is taking me in a direct line the way I came...how many years ago? It had been long, for the blown sand has scoured most of the scorch from my metal. But there is no way to count years in a world without season or sun or star.

I wonder how the conflict went for those sent by the Franchise. Were any of the men left alive? Or has it been so long that even the survivors would have died of natural causes?

What of Unus and Duo? And I am...Tray! That opens up another memory, of a long ago communication with my two companions. Unus had been a teacher, a young woman who drowned back on Terra. Duo was...what? I tried to think. Then it came to me.

Duo was a musician, and he managed to make his electronics form notes of exquisite purity as we sat through the endless days on Celeric. He sang many musics to us. Where is he now?

I am hurrying now; my power sources, activated by the sun behind the endless cloud, are able to force a goodly pace. Ahead I can see the shattered remnants of the shielding that covered the Stashes.

Instinctively, I activate my Communicator, sending the signal to any Franchise force left in the Enclave. At this point, I do not care who I find there. The Rebels have political differences, perhaps, but they are not evil people. I will be happy to find anyone, human or mechanical, to ease the terrible solitude.

A star-signal has gone up, brilliant blue-white against the gory sky. Someone is there! I am filled with excitement, though this body has no heart to pump or blood to pulse.

There is movement on the horizon. A Metallic—Rebel, of course, but what of that?

The bulk about me heaves and screeches. Ports open, and a clatter rumbles through my gut. The weapons systems are readying for conflict.

No! No! I try to force my will upon this brute beast of metal, but it is inexorable. The beams focus, the charges build.

I try to blank out my thoughts, to return to the vegetative state in which I spent such a very long time, but I cannot ignore the quiver as the blast roars outward, or the distant sound that is my sole possible companion being scattered to the winds.

I close myself inward, inward, encapsulating everything, folding down. Deep inside, my last wink of thought is glimmering.

I shall shut it down...

Being precocious and intelligent can be extremely uncomfortable. I knew decades before this was recognized that many of the poisons used with such joy by farmers were both dangerous and destructive. If something will kill an insect, if you get enough of it, you can bet it will also kill you!

IN THE LONE GRAY

McGeir plodded along the valley, gray dust puffing about his ankles as he forced his weary feet forward. His entire body must be lined with powdery grit by now, he was sure. His eyes felt sandpapery, his lids rough and inflamed. He blinked hard and lifted his gaze to the mountains ahead.

The peaks rose dark in the west, silhouetted against a dim sunset. If McGeir's calculations were correct, there should be a new moon somewhere in the murk of the west as well, but it was invisible behind seamless gray cloud. It had been a long while since he or any of his people saw a new moon.

He had slowed while examining the horizon, and Loon passed him, leaving him at the end of the line of walkers. He stepped faster, for tail-folk didn't last long. Was he growing weaker?

At first he had led the refugees. He'd been irritated by the slowness of the pregnant women, the small children, the old, and the lame. But he'd been certain he could lead them, at last, to some promised land where the soil was loamy with the castings of earthworms, mountain streams still ran clear, living conifers rose against the sky, and wild animals lurked in the forest, watching them with eyes untainted by sickness. But as they crossed mountain passes, trekked through dead valleys, he had never found such a haven.

He forced himself to pass Loon, then Truda. The grandchild slung against the old woman's back was asleep, his gray-pale face thin, his eyes ringed with blue. McGeir looked away, thinking he could not deal with another dead child.

He wondered if this abnormal weakness had begun when the

last of the pregnant women delivered a dead infant and bled to death in the shelter of that last rock wall. Or had it been when Dolan, who had seemed tough as old hickory roots and who knew all there was to know about survival, had leaned on his staff, closed his eyes, and fallen, straight as a tree, into death?

All the deaths...those were what bled away his own strength, drop by drop, to soak into the gray dust, the gray air, the gray waste that the world had become.

Pushing himself, he passed Garsten, ignoring her inquiring glance as he drew even with her.

Their old intimacy had no place in this new situation. This was a context that she and her peers had brought into being with their earth-shaking discoveries. Their last pesticide, supposed to save the world from insects, had killed most of the earthworms, leaving the soil barren. On the heels of that came pestilence that devastated the world.

The only humor McGeir had found in the situation was the fact that most of the insects had sailed through unscathed. Only when nothing was left at the roots of dead grass or in the decay of cities would they begin to suffer, he was certain. Even then, they would probably survive.

The irony was that his people now ate insects, almost exclusively.

From time to time they found a scummy pool where a few frogs or tadpoles or minnows still survived, and he had used most of his remaining strength to keep his starving crew from eating them. If those could provide a start for another cycle of life, they must live to do it. His kind, having caused the disaster, didn't deserve to destroy them.

Garsten still didn't understand his attitude. Even before the release of the pesticide, he had argued with their employers, trying to make them comprehend the risk. But most of the techs and researchers were city folk who had never seen a patch of land deprived of earthworms, hard-caked soil that dried and blew away on the wind. They insisted that only "bad" creatures would perish. T-36-D wouldn't harm any beneficial element of the ecosystem.

Ha!

McGeir hitched his pants up and settled his holster against his hip. Too many things had been managed to death, literally. Too many stupid decisions had been made. He'd been told, when he was a boy, that anything that would kill a cockroach would kill him, if he got a comparable dose of it. Nobody in charge ever seemed to take that into account.

Now he was coming up behind Seelbach, who turned at the crunch of his steps. With a sinking sensation, McGeir realized he had not looked closely at the scientist in several days.

The blond moustache was straggly, the beard unkempt, the skin bluish. His red-rimmed eyes gave him a nightmarish look, like something from one of the old horror movies.

McGeir grimaced. The old days were not that far in the past. Maybe three months? Or five?

He'd been too busy, in the beginning, to keep track. Then he realized there wasn't much use for it, though he tried his best to count days.

For a while they'd all kept assuring each other that Europe hadn't used the pesticide nearly as long as the U.S. had. Surely someone would come to their rescue. All the while, McGeir felt sure they were fooling themselves.

Look at the sun! he thought. When you only know it's there, because when the pitch blackness turns dingy gray, things are really bad. Never a star had he seen since the beginning of the end, when a huge dust storm devastated the western half of the country and covered the sky with a pall that had to be miles deep.

Seelbach cleared his throat. "It's about time to camp. We're all tired, but tomorrow we ought to make the foothills, don't you think?" Despite his words, his voice didn't sound hopeful.

McGeir nodded, studying the man closely. He was done for— McGeir had seen too many in his condition to be mistaken. Seelbach wouldn't be in the file when the black sky lightened.

Seven of his people had already gone that way, there when it grew dark, and not to be found at all when the light came again.

McGeir pointed ahead, where a low ridge crowned with stiff growth would provide some shelter from the night wind. It was all dead, of course, like the rest of the vegetation he had seen. He spat into the dust.

Seelbach turned toward the ridge, and those behind followed. For the first time in weeks, McGeir stood aside and counted as they passed him. Nine...ten...eleven...Truda and little Pat made thirteen. And Loon—but Loon, who had been tail-man, was no longer there.

McGeir stared back along the valley. Had the man just turned and walked away? Or did some predator still live, stalking them as they moved? What kept happening to the last of the line, time after time? He could see nothing to provide an answer. There was no distant dark spot that might be a body...just nothing.

McGeir hitched his holster again, automatically. Then he followed Truda to the ridge and helped her spread her scanty blanket. Tonight there was not even an insect to eat, but the three remaining children didn't whimper. They sat patiently where they were put, their eyes huge and dark-rimmed in their sallow faces.

They wouldn't last long, McGeir admitted to himself for the first time. First the children would go—no, he'd forgotten. First Seelbach, tall and strong and too highly educated, would be gone tomorrow. Then the children.

Who next? Likely Truda. Determined as she was, she was old; without her grandson to give her the will to live, she would go soon.

He turned to check the others. Garsten had built a fire—there was plenty of dead brush, if nothing else—after digging a hole in the dust to keep the blaze from spreading to the bushes around the camp. The remnant of his group huddled in their blankets around the fire, falling asleep quickly. There was no energy left for talk.

Yet Seelbach, as if knowing what was coming, seemed inclined to conversation. "You were right, McGeir," he said, his voice a dry rasp in his throat. "All the time, you were right, and the Company wouldn't listen to you. We didn't listen, the government didn't listen. Most of us spent our lives on cement, before the Company sent us to the isolated lab in Iowa. We didn't understand how the soil works, not really. Just from books."

Garsten gripped her hands together in her lap. "It should have been enough," she croaked. "The information was there, but it was insufficient. The people who wrote those books didn't really want to know how totally dependent we are on the land and the trees and the creatures that grow there. It all started with water, I think...." Her voice died away as she stared into the fire.

McGeir unbuckled his holster and laid it carefully on the dust. He'd said what he had to say, back when there was still time to save matters. Now he had no energy left for argument or discussion.

Seelbach wouldn't be put off, however. "You knew, McGeir. Others must have, too. Why didn't anyone listen to you?"

McGeir straightened his blanket and stretched out his legs. "Tame scientists told the bosses what they wanted to hear. I think most even believed their own lies. A man can do that, no matter what evidence he has in his hands."

Garsten shook her head. "The scientific method...," she began.

"...Is exercised by human beings, who lie to themselves without even knowing it," McGeir interrupted. "I read once that objectivity is impossible to mankind. True. We proved it, didn't we?" He lay full-length, enjoying the warmth and the rest.

She stared at him, her face gray with dust, her eyes as bloodshot as his own. "You don't think there's anyone much left, do you?" she asked.

He sighed. "Maybe bunches here and there, all as desperate as we are. The plague that came on the heels of the dust storm must've cleaned out the cities right off, or we'd see signs of more people. Unless we can find a place with good water and plants and animals, we're through. Maybe it's better that way, though it's a pity to kill off the world along with our kind. I'd hoped we might eliminate ourselves and leave the rest to regenerate. Ah, hell...." He fell silent.

The fire fell in on itself with a soft rustle. Garsten pulled her blanket over her face and turned her back. Seelbach stared across the glimmer of coals for a long moment. Then he, too, covered himself for sleep.

McGeir lay on his back, ignoring the pebbles beneath him. He couldn't look up at the stars, for there were none visible. There was no place to go from here. No mountain valley, protected from contamination, lay ahead to insure life for this bunch of stragglers.

Maybe, deep in the soil beneath him, there might survive the eggs of earthworms and grasshoppers and other vital creatures. Weed seeds almost surely waited amid the dust, and he knew seeds could sprout, given the right conditions, after hundreds or thousands of years of lying dormant. Food plants had been developed from weeds, back in the beginning.

In the distant future, there might come a day when those things lived again and flourished.

That was too far ahead, too long a time, with too much pain to endure before it came.

McGeir heard Seelbach's furtive movements, his quiet steps dying away into the darkness.

He understood at last what happened to those they had lost.

One could go just so far into the lonely grayness. There were only so many steps in a pair of legs, only so much hope in any human heart. When those things were exhausted, it was time to go.

He fumbled with the cartridge belt in his pack. Twenty rounds left. Enough for all, if they decided to take that route. They'd find the gun when he was done with it.

He slipped the pistol from the holster and moved down the side of the ridge toward a ravine.

The children wouldn't see his body, down there.

One quick move, a jerk of the finger...and he went out into the lone gray.

This was a very early sf story, which I sent to the editor at Galaxy Magazine. *Mr. Gold returned it, saying that I was totally unsuited to writing sf and should find another genre. If he had praised me and told me to go ahead, he might have stopped me. Fortunately, I am one who does not accept discouragement.*

THE DAY OF THE DRUM

Juluah paused on the crest of the ridge. Below her the rift was sinking into black-purple shadow, though the heights along its farther edge were still tipped with red-gold by the setting sun. Her ears were honed to catch any whisper of wrongness amid the sounds of the evening. She lingered for a moment, watching the bright death of the day.

About her the thick leaves of the forest stirred in the twilight breeze. The first boom of the d'hangi came as a shock, shattering the peace. That sonorous reverberation was followed by others, patterned to convey to her trained ear a message as clear as if it were spoken.

Juluah stood quietly, her head cocked to catch every element of the message, but her hand, clenched on the haft of her spear, belied her seeming calm. Her eyes now probed the sheer drop she must descend, not for beauty now but for danger.

A minuke in the tree above her had gone silent at the first note of the drum. Now it stared down at her, and though she did not turn her head, Juluah felt its gaze. Insects and animals alike had gone silent in the jungle cloaking the shoulders of the mountain. Wild creatures had short lives, and she knew none had heard the voice of the d'hangi before now.

Now in middle age, Juluah had heard it in her youth. When the last echo died, she turned her gaze up toward the minuke, which held its small hand before its mouth, shocked by the noise. Its slender body quivered, and Juluah reached up to smooth its golden fur with bronzed fingers. Without her long years of discipline, she too might quiver, she knew, for the voice of the d'hangi was the voice of death.

The sun had now set, but she waited until the trail downward was deep in shadow. Her mission had not been one of grave importance, but all had changed with the words of the drum. She must deliver not only the word she carried from Ellehi, her chieftain, but also terrible tidings to the neighboring people beyond the rift. All were now in danger.

For the three nights of her journey, she had dreamed ill. Now she knew why: the Deep Ones had emerged from underground. Once more they were walking the daytime forest, armed with dark weapons and the hearts of slavers.

Shuddering, she started down the dim trail. Her training as a Messenger enabled her to go down that perilous way; pitfalls of vine and loose shale could not betray her knowing feet. By the time the stars had rolled past the edge of the height, she reached the bottom of the way and made her way beside the river, which had chewed a long and crooked path through the stone of the mountains.

Ellehi called her the swiftest Messenger among the Kora'ah, though she did not allow need for haste to make her careless. She sped along the narrow track worn into the stone by millennia of paws and hooves. There would be no enemy here, she knew, but there were other forces the Deep Ones could call. She could feel danger before her. Shifting her spear to her left hand, she drew her long blade with her right.

The stars gave little light. Juluah's world had no moon. She strained her eyes into the darkness as she moved between the great stone blocks that had fallen from the cliffs over the millennia. Beasts laired among the monoliths, and the way was narrow.

It was hazardous to make a light, for she would become a target for anyone who waited. Yet it would be worse to go, blind, into their hands. Making the holy sign with her spear-point, she reached into her tunic and drew out a smooth stone, cool to the touch. She warmed it between her hands and fitted it into a loop in the thong that had bound her hair. Once the weight settled, she concentrated her will upon it.

A firefly glow began to flicker within the stone. That grew in intensity, radiating outward to light the path ahead, where it pricked out many light-points among the other stones.

Eyes. Waiting.

Juluah slanted her spear forward and gripped her blade as she moved onward. A knobby shape, glossy-black as coal, darted forward to lob a pebble at her head. Deadly in speed and accuracy, it flicked past her ear as she ducked.

She thrust her spear into the dark shape that had flung the stone; it made no sound as she pulled the point free, but it did not move again. Others came at her, dodging and darting, and she hewed and thrust, beset from all sides. The creatures had no caution, but they seemed strangely mindless. The touch of metal seemed to render them helpless as well.

Still those deadly pebbles whizzed past her head to bruise shoulders and arms and jaw. Only her Messenger's agility and warrior's skill brought her out of the rock-maze alive. Behind her she left still black shapes that would, she thought, turn in time back into heaps of rock.

When there were no more, she used her light to examine the path before and behind, but no further enemy could be seen. Removing the stone from the loop, she returned it to her pouch and the thong to her hair.

Dawn found her climbing, for she had crossed the river by way of a chain of boulders formed by some long-ago landslip. Now she moved through even thicker jungle that grew on the other side of the rift. As the light grew stronger, she glimpsed beasts returning from their nightly hunts, and they were not like the animals beyond the river. Even the birds sang unfamiliar songs.

Her way wound in curves and switchbacks. Twice she found great serpents lying across the path, catching the first warmth of the newly risen sun. The first was small, and she leaped over, but the second was huge, its girth greater than her own.

Looped across the cut from tree to tree, it watched with knowing eyes as she approached. The arrow-shaped head, the width of her two hands together, swayed head-high before her. The sheer face, straight up on her right, was indented with gashes of stone from which softer stuff was weathered away, offering a way around.

"Wait here, Old One," she said, laughing. "If one of the Dark Ones comes, you have my leave to greet him." Then she leaped for the wall of the path and clambered up and around.

Before the sun was high, she was at the top of the cliff. From that height she could see a thin column of smoke rising from the compound of the Gelu'ah, and she called a shrill summons into the morning. There was no waiting, for behind her there came the soft sound of an arrow being nocked. She turned slowly, her hands clear of her weapons, to see a boy standing beside a rock that showed traces of a watchfire.

"Who comes to my people?" the boy asked.

She smiled, for he was very young—almost as young as her last son, who had seen twelve summers. She did not smile but answered him as she would have replied to a chieftain.

"Juluah, Messenger of the Kora'ah. I bear two messages for Keloha and your elders from Ellehi and the elders of my tribe."

His bronze face impassive, he regarded her, but she could see a faint quirk at the corner of his lips. "All have heard the d'hangi. Is there war among the Kora'ah?" he asked.

"Among us all, I fear," she said. "I did not come to bring that word, but it overtook me in the voice of the d'hangi. I must speak with your elders."

Those elders waited before the circle of mud-plastered wicker huts, outside the stake fence that kept predators outside the village. Keloha strode forward. "Greeting, Messenger. What word do you bring from my brother Ellehi? Is there war abroad in the land?"

"When I left Ellehi there was peace, and a harvest so abundant that I was sent to bring you and yours to a feast. The drum altered that, for it spoke of the Deep Ones. On this side of the river do you know its language?"

"Only a bit. Yet I have dreamed...." His dark eyes stared into hers, and she knew his dreams must have mirrored her own. "Ill dreams indeed. Come to the Council house, Messenger. We must speak together."

When she had eaten and drunk and rested a bit, the elders came into the house and sank into their usual circle. She began, "Juluah, Messenger of the Kora'ah, to Keloha of the Gelu'ah, greetings from his brother Ellehi. I will not speak his words, for they no longer hold meaning. Instead I will speak the words of the drum.

"Just before sunset, a way believed to be sealed beyond opening was opened from below, and the Deep Ones emerged into our world. Armed with the weapons of rational beings, they carried also tubes of metal that set our village ablaze. Yet some of our boys slipped through a channel too small for their elders. They turned the tubes over and stopped their mouths with clay, slaying with their knives the Deep Ones who operated them.

"Our enemies are left with blades and spears, and even now we battle them. Many have died and will die, yet we know this is not the only place where they may emerge. We are not the only village marked for death or slavery. Aid us, if you will. Safeguard yourselves, if you can."

She fell silent. No one spoke for a time. Then the boy asked, "But who are the Deep Ones?"

The elders nodded, and Juluah said, "Upon our world there were always two peoples: those who live in sunlight and follow the paths of peace, when that is possible; we are a free people and kill nothing needlessly.

"The others live beneath the mountains in caverns and tunnels at their roots, digging out the bones of the heights to melt for metal. They are not demons, though they hide themselves from the light and work in the midnight places. They hate us who walk free, even the animals."

She held up her spear before the boy. "The very weapons we bear were made by them, for we do not work metals. These are the spoils of generations of battles."

The boy's eyes widened. "But there must be things we might trade them for such things. We have little metal, but they surely have too little fruit and cloth. Why do we not barter with them?"

"They do not want the things we make and grow. They want our strong backs and clever hands to work in their mines and smelters. They want slaves, my son, grubbing away our lives in the bowels of the earth to stoke their fires, shut away from the sun forever. Nothing else will they consider, for they will not speak with our kind, considering us cattle.

"Sometimes twice in a generation, sometimes more often, they break forth from the depths and try again to conquer us. Always, they have failed."

Keloha's voice boomed forth like the d'hangi. "Always they shall fail. Rest, Juluah, and tomorrow speed homeward bearing word that the Gelu'ah follow hard upon your heels."

"Ellehi will be grateful, as will all my people. Rest well, elders of the Gelu'ah," she said.

She rose before the sun and was well into the gorge before nightfall, resting in a niche in a boulder for the night. That stone was rooted in the bed-rock, and all through the night she felt growlings and stirrings, as if stone ground against stone. At first light she sped forward toward the distant cliff.

As she passed the moonlight, they shimmered beneath the sun, and about them lay dark heaps that had been her enemies. Bereft of the will that had formed them, they had returned to their natural state. What strange skills, she wondered, could shape moving forms from rock?

She found the path up the cliff at last and climbed it without noticing the lovely light of sunset. With the last of twilight, she reached the crest and rested. A sound reached her, careless feet moving on the narrow ledge running along the shoulder of the ridge. A minuke stirred uneasily, and she shrank into the jungle, melting into the thick growth of trees and vines.

The path was a gray blur, but the dark shape that came stood out sharply. Totally black, surely by use of paint over skin, with broad gray stripes lining its face, it was a Deep One, walking abroad, alone.

His steps thumped arrogantly against the stone, frightening the small creatures. He paused where she had stood to watch the sunset; the minuke gave a squeak, and the Deep One looked up. From his hand, a tube squirted a fine mist into the air, and the minuke dropped, lifeless. His laugh grated like gravel pouring down a hillside.

Leaning her spear against a tree, Juluah grasped her blade and stepped silently into the pathway. "Guard yourself!" she said.

The Deep One whirled, bringing up the tube, but her blade flicked out and sent it whirling into the depths below. His own blade whipped into sight, glinting in the near darkness. "You dare to face me? I am a master of this world. You sun-cattle cannot hope to withstand us!"

"Guard yourself," Juluah said again. She lunged, and his blade barely turned aside her thrust. She parried the counterthrust easily, and her rush moved him toward the edge of the cliff.

He battered her back again, using his greater weight and power, but she held him behind a barrier of steel. That was a strange duel they fought, blinded by night with only gasps and clangs to give Juluah some clue to his position and intentions.

The breeze picked up, and the flutter of his cloak gave her a hint. Taking a chance, she lunged low, hoping to thrust beneath his guard. Metal grated on bone, and he grunted. She heard a swish as his blade swung toward her, but she rolled away and heard his fall.

His blade gleamed in starlight, lying on the path. She kicked it away to clatter amid the stones below. Taking the light-stone from her pouch, she warmed it between her hands and looked down at him.

His eyes glittered with desperation and dismay, but her blade was near his throat, and he was lying along the verge of the cliff. His right bicep was thrust through, disabling him, though it was a clean wound and not fatal.

"Will you listen?" she asked.

He said nothing, and his eyes seemed shuttered against anything she might say. She laid her blade against the skin of his brow, marking it with the sigil of the Kora'ah.

"Now will you listen?" The tip of her sword was at his throat. Those eyes were now aware and afraid.

"We who live in the light do not trouble you in the Deep. Labor there until you wear the mountains away to plains, if it pleases you, but we will not slave there for you. We will not be conquered; we will die before we will be slaves. Corpses cannot delve in your mines or feed your fires. To be master of the dead is nothing.

"I could kill you now, but what would that accomplish? One more carcass for the carrion birds? Take my words back to your people: live as you will. Labor as you choose, but learn that you cannot conquer the people of the light."

He would not meet her gaze, there in the tenuous light. As if he were ashamed to be answering her kind at all, he whispered, "My people would not listen to such words. This time we shall win...you will learn this. This time we cannot be denied."

As if in reply, the d'hangi boomed, rolling across the land and echoing from the mountains. Juluah cocked her head, listening.

"Do you understand the words of the drum?" she asked.

He shook his dark head.

"Then hear them through my lips. The Deep Ones are driven from the valley of the Hasha'ah, and that tribe has come to aid the Kora'ah. The attackers, their numbers much diminished, are trapped in the north angle of our valley. If the Gelu'ah come, we will destroy them. If the Gelu'ah do not come, we will drive them into their tunnels and seal them into the darkness once again."

She looked down at the Deep One, her lightstone bathing his face and making him squint. "And the Gelu'ah will come; they are behind me, less than half a day."

The Deep One groaned and struggled to sit. Now there was fear in his eyes. "You will...free me? Even now?"

"Especially now," she said. "After being driven like vermin into their burrows, surely your people will hear you speak my words. It is easy to forget the mettle of an enemy your parents battled, but one who has just trampled you into the dust must be taken seriously. Go back into the darkness. Emerge, if you can, as reasonable people, ready to bargain instead of to enslave."

He rose, holding his injured arm carefully. She didn't wait for him to choose a direction but brushed past and picked up the tube he had dropped. She carried it into the jungle and buried it deep, with the body of the minuke.

When she returned to the path, the Deep One had gone. She moved forward toward the valley of her people, who would need her skill and her blade.

Once all the Deep Ones were pushed back into the depths, the Gelu'ah would attend a feasting, after all. Perhaps, this time, it would be a feast of hope as well as one of victory.

To a great extent I am this lady, and her solution to her noisy neighbors was one used by one of my sons in similar circumstances.

DEEP WOODS LADY

I've lived in the woods for most of my life. Once in a while someone asks me if I'm not afraid, living out here all by myself, with the nearest neighbor a half-mile away. That's funny! I've never had a bobcat or possum or coyote come breaking in my door to rob me. I can walk down my woodsy road in the evening and no mugger will attack me, though I do carry a snake stick. Water moccasins tend to be mean-natured, and it's just as well to have something to discourage them with.

My road ends at a river that runs into a big man-made lake, and everybody and his Uncle Ned comes scallyhooting down my road, pulling boat trailers at top speed. They go by so fast that they never spot my oddball house, which is hidden behind a thick hedgerow and in the middle of a cluster of big trees, yaupon bushes, and wisteria, Virginia creeper, yellow jasmine, and rattan vines. When I was younger, I used to keep the smaller growth pruned back, but the older I get the more I appreciate my home-grown jungle, so I let it go, unless it impedes something necessary.

I never bother anybody, and I expect nobody to bother me. That worked for decades, though I have to discount those charitable-minded ladies who used to visit me and ask me to chair the Red Cross drive or some such activity, beginning the pitch with, "We know you don't work, so we thought you could do this...."

I write. I paint. I make my living that way, but normal people just can't get their heads around the concept that sitting at a type-writer, easel, or computer and staring at the wall can possibly be called work.

Those finally stopped coming around, and I have spent the past ten years relatively untroubled. And now the acreage north of me has been clear-cut and the Bradlows have built a house there. The clear-cutting was bad enough, destroying a beautiful hardwood and pine forest and leaving much of the wood to rot. Then those philistines came in and built a monstrosity out of tin and plywood and junk, and moved eight adults and any number of totally untaught children into it.

For all my fifty-odd years I have lived down here near the river bottoms, and it has been quiet, except for natural sounds of the woods, and the rattling of pickups along the road to the river. To those familiar and untroubling sounds were added shrieks worthy of banshees, yells that would shame a barbarian horde, and a general hubbub that made anyone within a half mile cringe. Even shut into my study with the air conditioner running, I found myself distracted to the point of being unable to concentrate.

I suspected that civil protest would do no good, but I began with a neighborly gesture. I baked a cake and carried it through the tangle of brush-tops and gouges made by the loggers' trucks to the already ramshackle porch of the house. My knocking finally brought footsteps toward the door, and a frowzy blonde peered out through the screen.

"D'ya want?" she muttered.

"I thought I would..."—I almost choked on the words—"...welcome you to your new home and bring you this sponge cake."

She brushed a strand of hair out of her eyes and stared at me, then at the cake, which I had put in a disposable plastic container with a cover. She slapped absently at a child who came pushing past her jeans-clad legs. Three more came shooting past her (and me), sounding like steam calliopes. "Get outta here, you little bastids!" she shrilled, but she reached for the cake with a small attempt at a smile.

I gave my best imitation smile and said, "I am Lynn Masters, and I live just down the road in the strange metal house. I am sorry you had to build in such an ugly spot, but they cut down the forest a few months ago."

She did her best, I could tell, though polite behavior was obviously not her forte. "I'm Kelly Bradlow," she said, opening the door and gesturing for me to enter the house.

"With all these kids, the house stays a mess, but you kin sit down in the kitchen."

"Are all those children yours?" I asked.

She shook her tousled head. "Just the first one. I got more, but they're too little to let run loose. There's snakes and stuff out in that mess. Most of the ones you'll see belong to Meg and Joan and Lissa.

Our men are loggers. They done the work clearin' out this woods so's we could build. This belonged to Doug's fam'ly. Wasn't till his Daddy died that Duggie and the boys got hold of it legal and could cut off the timber and sell it."

"You're all one family then," I said, feeling a bit sad and helpless. "Is Doug your husband?"

"Guess you could say so. We been together four years and had three young'uns."

I girded my loins and ventured to say, "Well, it's about the children I came over. I'm a writer, and it takes a lot of quiet for me to do my work. The children are rather—loud? If there's any way you could calm them down a bit, I would surely appreciate it."

She stared at me as if I had suddenly grown another head. "You mean you write books and such? And get paid for it?" She sounded both shocked and horrified.

"Yes. Paid rather well, in fact. I paint pictures as well, and sell them through the art gallery in Templeton. "

She backed away as if I might have something contagious. "Duggie says it's sinful for a woman to get paid for workin'. It's all right to work her in the woods or on a farm, but payin' her makes her uppity and self-willed."

I couldn't help breaking into laughter that shook me from head to feet. "What century is he living in?" I asked her. "Didn't he ever hear of women's rights?"

"Women is the spawn of Satan, the root of evil ways. The preacher says we should work hard, keep our mouths shut, and mind our men, no matter what they want us to do." Her voice held the ritual tonalities I had heard from any number of backwoods preachers and fundamentalists. I knew there was no hope for her, poor child. Nevertheless, I persisted.

"Well whatever Duggie thinks, I need quiet to get my work done, and those children make so much noise I can't think. I would appreciate anything you could do to tone them down a bit." I turned and stepped out of the screen door onto the step.

Kelly followed me, rather hesitantly I thought. "Miz Masters, I don't like to be on the outs with neighbors. I'll see if the girls can rein in the kids somehow. I take it you earn your own livin', have no man to do for you?"

"Exactly. I grew up on that land south of you, used to farm it when I was a bit younger, doing my writing in my spare time. Then I grew old and achy and the writing began earning me enough so I didn't need to farm any more. Now, except for what I make selling a cow from time to time, my writing income supports me."

She sighed, and I could see her better instincts warring with her religious teachings. As I walked away, I turned and she gave a tiny wave before going back into the house. What a pity. There was the making of a nice person there, if she hadn't fallen into the hands of a redneck bigot. My impression of the Bradlow brothers was not, I am afraid, a favorable one, if they shared old Duggie's convictions. Still, I pride myself on being open-minded, and I knew I had to give things a chance to work out.

For about three days things were somewhat more quiet. Then there was a knock on my front door that threatened to smash in the screen. I was absorbed in a scene and it took a moment to come back to myself and go to the door. Filling the entire door frame was the biggest man I had ever seen. He was taller than the door—some three inches, in fact—and wider, too.

"You that Masters woman?" he asked, his voice deep enough to vibrate the floor under my feet. "Been fussin' at my woman 'bout the kids?"

Thank God I am tall. If I'd been much shorter I would have had to crack my neck to see his face. I stepped outside and he backed away a bit so I could stand on the porch. That face was no treat. Its expression was worse.

He bent to stare into my eyes. His were washed-out gray, contrasting with the saddle-leather tan of his weather-wrinkled skin. I stared back with all the authority of my fifty-odd years.

"I simply asked Kelly to see if the children could be a bit quieter. Their shrieks break into my concentration, and I earn my living by thinking and writing."

He drew a deep breath. "You got no man to keep you straight. Nobody to make you do right and keep to Christian ways. If you go puttin' sinful notions into Kelly's mind, I'll come over here and make a Christian out of you."

I felt a hot surge of rage rush through me. I stepped closer to him and glared into his eyes. "You come over here with any idea about that sort of thing and I'll blow your damn head off. I've lived down here all my life, and my parents and grandparents before me. We don't have trouble with anybody, because everyone around here knows we have guns and know how to use them. I shot a burglar a few years back, but he was not from anywhere close.

"If you think you can set up a nineteenth-century farm, with bullied women and children, here in the beginning of the twenty-first, you'd better think again. Children go to school. Women have to go to town for groceries and such, and one day they'll wake up and realize that the fact that you men are bigger than they are doesn't mean you have the sense God gave a goat. Now get out of here before I lose my temper."

I backed into the house and lifted the shotgun I keep just inside. I thought his face would burst it got so red. "My family's kids're goin' to make your life miserable," he growled. "I'll see to it."

He started toward the road.

I called after him, "Two can play at that game!" I already had some ideas about that.

Music had been my passion all my life. I had equipment that could equal having a symphony orchestra or an opera company in my own home. I did a bit of shopping on the Internet, and once the CDs came, I simply waited to see what might happen next.

The children had become louder and louder, though from the lack of enthusiasm in their voices I suspected that shouting and screaming to order wasn't nearly as much fun as doing it spontaneously. I let it go on for two days. At just about bedtime on the second, I set up the speakers from my old stereo system, aiming them at the house up the road. Now there were no trees to buffer the sound, and I knew the family would get the full effect.

At midnight I turned on the *Ride of the Valkyries* at full volume. Then I went inside, plugged my ears with the kind of plugs artillerymen use, and went to sleep.

That CD would play all night, with whale calls, train whistles, wolf howls, every wild noise I could think of. Nobody in that house would get any sleep, for I knew what that system could do. It would vibrate the house itself.

It took two weeks. Then they moved out, and I had my lawyer make an offer for that land. They accepted it. I tore down the house, and I am having the former forest replanted with a mix of hardwood and pine. It's quiet again, and in time there will be deep woods there, for my nephew, if not for me...and I didn't have to shoot anybody at all!

This may be my earliest sf story, which I may not have marketed at all—I cannot remember, actually.

WELCOME TO SHIARA

The thing uncoiled slowly, deliberately, the metallic gold of its sinuous body stretching to incredible length. Emerald eyes glistened in the flat head, not the eyes of a mindless predator but those of one aware and alert.

Berthold felt them on him as he froze in place. There was no malignance there that he could detect, but he knew he might be in trouble. He had never intended to disobey orders and venture alone into the intricate ruins of the buried city. Others had disappeared down here, on other expeditions, and he understood that because of the thick layers of metal-impregnated stone above him, he couldn't call for help. If this creature was dangerous (and it looked as if it might decide to be at any moment), he must make an orderly withdrawal from its territory. What he would do if it pursued him he didn't like to consider.

Berthold had lost his sense of direction, and his Locator seemed to have suffered some malfunction—possibly because of the odd metal of the surrounding structures. When the turf underfoot had collapsed, dropping him into the depths, he hadn't been fully aware of the direction in which he'd been going, except that the Locator told him camp was ahead. Tumbling down through layered debris hadn't helped any. When he finished rolling downward, he had found himself in this stone tunnel, which must be far below the levels of the city that had been explored. It was impossible to climb back the way he had come—he had felt stuff crumbling, even as he fell. The weak spot was probably completely unstable.

As he began to back warily away from the shining serpent caught in the beam of his emergency lamp, he drew a deep breath... and wondered how the air in this deep complex could seem so fresh and breathable. Could it be that the serpent-like creature kept air shafts open to the surface? It must breathe, too, he felt certain. The fauna of this world seemed to use oxygen, as those of Earth did.

As he moved, a dim light began to grow around him, and soon he could shut off his lamp. The glow grew stronger, and he found it came from crystalline insets along the upper curve of the tunnel. What sort of power could have lasted this long? The system seemed to be motion-sensitive, for as he moved farther along, the tunnel behind him dimmed to darkness again. Turning to stare back, he saw the liquid shimmer of gold and knew the creature was following him. Even as he watched, the golden shape slithered closer, the head swaying above the rippling curves of the long body.

An opening appeared as a shadow in the now bright corridor, and he ducked into it, causing the light behind him to die away. Frantically, he thumbed the switch of his lamp and found himself in another corridor. Behind him, he could hear the sibilant hiss of scales on stone, and when he turned the beam in that direction it reflected golden sparks.

He turned to run, examining the corridor as he went. At any other time he would have admired the fineness of the stone-work, but now he searched only for some way to escape. That thing behind him knew these tunnels, while he was fleeing like a mouse in a maze, blind and panicky. He glimpsed a cross-passage ahead and switched off the light, hoping to lose his pursuer. He crept forward now, as softly as possible, and at the point where he estimated the other corridor to be he risked one flash of light. Then he nipped into the tunnel and stopped to listen.

Behind there was the leisurely swish of scales. He didn't move, taking time to control his heartbeat and calm himself with the techniques that he had acquired in his long training. Then he clicked on his torch and hurried up the new passage. If this serpent was like those on his world, it might well home in on his body heat. Darkness would be no help to him. Only his quicker mammalian wits might work against what he hoped were slow, reptilian ones.

The passage ended at a cross-tunnel. He'd turned right twice, so far. Now he turned left, for he didn't care to go back to the beginning again. This was a long passage with arched doorways along the sides. Some still were closed with heavy panels, and he hoped there were no more golden serpents behind them. Others had disintegrated, and he dared to peep into one of those rooms. Nothing was there except dust and dimness.

His faster pace had now left the slithering sound far behind. He reached the end of the corridor and turned right again. Doors, doors,

doors, mostly intact and immovable, marked the way. He had to find some way to shut himself away from the thing behind him. Otherwise he might find himself in the position of rats, back in his school lab days, caught in the coils of snakes.

He tried the doors, now, though they had no handles and were made to slide upward into the wall. Hand in slot, shoulder against the wood, he would give a hard push and go on, almost without slowing. When another corridor opened to his left, he took that route. There the doors were made of metal, each solidly shut. He tried a few, but these took more time and soon he heard the distant slither behind. At last he stopped to examine the largest door yet, probing its arch with his bright beam. Indentations marked either side of the arch, a long reach even for him, and he was tall. The coils were closer now, and he stretched to set his thumbs into the notches. He pressed hard and a groan sounded inside the wall as metal screeched and the door moved upward.

Berthold found he had been holding his breath. Now he let it out and stepped back. A room closed so tightly for so long might contain deadly vapors, and he fumbled for the gas-wick the explorers carried for building fires. It lit as he touched the igniter, and he held it toward the opening. To his relief it burned brightly, and he stepped into the doorway. The panel hissed downward behind him, and he searched for some way to secure it. Then he relaxed. The serpent had no hands. It could not conceivably open that door requiring two thumbs and a long reach. He was safe...at least until hunger or thirst forced him out into the corridors again.

The room had begun to glow with the motion-sensor controlled light, now, and he saw that it was huge. Above him in the domed ceiling something began to hum, and a barrier dropped between him and the metal door. A grid of steel...Berthold gripped it before he could stop himself. The mechanism lowering the grid stopped and a soothing voice said, "Welcome to Shiara. Your brain scan shows you to be moderately advanced, and our linguistic program has accessed your vocabulary. An analysis of your biochemistry is being made at this moment, and you may rest assured that your every need will be met, insuring you a long and healthy life in the Shiaran Zoo of Sapient Creatures.

"Even should some disaster overtake our world, you will be cared for without interruption, for our zoo is solar powered, and the cells are made to last forever. Synthesizers will supply your every want or need. You will not be troubled by watchers, for our techniques allow us to observe you without direct vision.

"You may think it cruel to imprison sentient beings, but that is the only way in which to observe them in safety. We hope you were not unnecessarily alarmed by the appearance and actions of our Collectors, which are of a species almost every sapient race finds frightening. They are able to herd specimens into the domicile without being physically coercive.

"If possible, we will find another specimen of your kind with which you may reproduce, and any offspring, we assure you, will be trained in a manner fitting for your kind and released on a planet suited for its survival. You will not be sentencing it to a lifetime of captivity. We find such scruples to be a part of your psychological profile, and we do not want you to be concerned.

"Again, welcome to Shiara. We regret that your introduction to our world must be of this nature, but scientific investigation demands sacrifice. A long life to you, Rale Berthold!" The voice went silent.

Berthold stared blindly at the dome above. He was seeing Elizabeth Gramming, biochemist for the expedition. She had clashed with his views all through their training. When he was chosen leader of their group, she had been furious. She did not control her dislike, as he did. She was the only female in this particular crew. To be trapped with her for a long healthy life in the bowels of this dead world—the thought was unutterably horrible.

Berthold carefully switched off his torch and set it neatly beside his utility belt. He would try to escape, but he had a feeling these beings had built with that in mind.

The walls were changing. A scene of distant mountains, a lake washing against foothills began to form. Plants and flowers grew on the floor, which was now grassy, and the sound of leaves filled his ears. A vivarium...Berthold laughed. After a very long time, he began to cry as well.

If I had possessed good knees I might well have become a ballet dancer. Unfortunately, I had a pair of trick knees, so that was ruled out, though I have always been an avid fan of the dance.

THE LAST *PAS SEUL*

Natya leaned her forehead against the glass, feeling the chill of the night beyond the window. The terrace glinted with frost and moonlight, and sparks of frozen light splashed from a row of chrome and webbing chairs leaned against the wall for the winter. Behind her, the room was clearly reflected: a great cedar tree had been decorated the day before by a group of chattering young women from a local church. There were billowing drifts of discarded Christmas wrappings, among which the unobtrusive attendants moved, assisting patients, straightening their clothing...caretaking. The thought was bitter.

Natya's gifts lay behind her, untouched. One was from Boris, of course, for he always remembered her on holidays. Others were from faithful admirers out of the past. Even the members of the *corps de ballet* sent her gifts for which she had no present use. The gift she needed most was withheld, she thought. She needed to dance! Only that mattered.

Lighted by the backwash of moon glow from the terrace, her triangular face stared back at her from the polished glass. Big dark eyes seemed to search themselves despairingly for some lingering trace of Natasha Grigorievna Petrova. Natasha, the beloved baby, whom the great Diaghilev had lifted to a table-top amid a Christmas feast, many, many years before, and named one of the great dancers to come. She had been fourteen.

Now she examined her reflection critically. She was still straight, still slim (thanks be to God!) for a woman of sixty-eight— she was not bad. Her chin quivered, and she leaned against the window, hiding her face from an inquiring attendant.

She felt useless and sick, thrown away into this chrome-plated junk heap. Christmas Eve had always been a magical time for her, a time of giving. She had reached out and affected those who were not of her own world. She slid out of the present into that warmly remembered past...

Holding a sheaf of roses almost as long as her body, young Natasha made a deep reverence, right, left, center, to her partner, who raised her gallantly and kissed her hand. She smiled up at Boris—the great Boris—through a mist of excitement. His eyes twinkled at her, amused and pleased. The applause wearied at last, they made their last bows, and floated into the wings.

The prima ballerina had been watching, still in her costume and makeup. Taking Boris's hand she smiled at the young dancer. "You danced verry well," she said in her kindest tone. "Will you drrive with us to the rreception?"

Natasha blushed, knowing they would prefer to be alone. "No, I thank you. But I have...plans...for the evening." She hurried up the break-neck iron stair to the dressing room shared with three other principal dancers, hoping they would be almost ready to leave. "I want to dance," she whispered to herself. "I must give something to someone tonight—some of the magic to someone who has none. It is, after all, Christmas Eve."

Natasha paused at the thought, while her two companions passed her with smiles and went giggling down the stair. She smiled as she removed costume and makeup, packed toe-shoes and tutu into a case, and locked the door behind her. She laughed all the way to the stage door.

Late hangers-on surrounded the doorway, hoping to meet some of the dancers, but she knew that to them she seemed a child—perhaps a maid—on her way home. There was no trace left of the fairy-like being who had brought them to their feet so short a time ago. Grinning into the wide collar of her gray coat, she passed them without being noticed.

She looked up and down the street. The lights of a police station gleamed a block away, and she thought that might be the very place to learn what she needed to know. She tapped down the icy walk and up the frosty steps. She looked up at the sergeant behind the tall desk, who was staring down in surprise.

"And what might I be doing for you, young lady?" he asked in a delightful Irish brogue.

"I am Natya, a dancer from the ballet," she said. "I want to dance for someone...for a Chrristmas gift, you know. But I do not know this city or who might like it or would still be up. Could you help me?"

He blinked. Then his ruddy face wrinkled into a smile. "The old folk are abed," he said. "So are the orphans, but the Salvation Army has an all-night open house downtown. It is no place for you to go alone, but the patrol will be going down there in a bit. You might go with them. Then they will come back and see you safely home."

Happiness bubbled up in her. "That will be perrfect!" she exclaimed, hopping from toe to toe. The sergeant's smile dissolved into a ripe chuckle.

Once in that great barn of a building, she had danced to the spirited if erratic music of a drunk at an upright piano. They managed the doll dance from Coppelia, a bit of *Lac de Cygne*, part of the divertissement from *La Belle au Bois Dormant*.

The audience, she thought, had fortified their spirits, before they came, with stronger stuff than the coffee and cocoa this party offered. In a mellow mood, they responded with enthusiasm to this unexpected and unfamiliar entertainment. The Salvation Army officers were delighted, and even the policeman, arriving near the end of her performance, applauded her vigorously before driving her to her hotel.

That night, in a mist of happiness, she had slept as she had not slept since leaving her father's house in Petrograd, two years before. That was the first of her Christmas Gifts to the world. Before or after performances, she had danced for pensioners and prisoners, bums and orphans.

But now there was no longer a need for her. She was treated kindly, but as though she had nothing to offer anyone, ever again. That was a bitter pain in her heart, the treacherous heart that six months before had cut short her teaching years in the only world she loved.

The moon shone as it had done on that long-ago night. Again she was shunning a party. Perhaps, just once more, she might make a small gift of herself, to the starry sky if to nothing else. She slipped from the window, pulling the draperies closed behind her, and left the room. For once, no one stopped her to ask where she was going.

In her cramped room, she caught up the long white shawl from the chair and draped it around her shoulders. Then she sat before her mirror and caught back her hair (white now, instead of raven black) with a practiced hand. Fastening it firmly into place, she set her Spanish comb at the crown, the black contrasting nicely with her white.

Beneath her fingers, the face became, once again, that of Natasha Grigorievna Petrova. The brows winged darkly, the eyes sparkled, the wrinkles disappeared under the makeup. When she was done, she stood and turned on her toe. The pale gray fullness of her skirt swirled satisfactorily, and she nodded at her reflection. "Boris," she whispered, "tonight I will dance for you. Drream of the way we danced, you and I. Dream of me tonight, Boris, in your hospital bed. Perrhaps we will both soon be frree."

The hall outside was empty. She flitted across and out onto the terrace, her dancing slippers soundless on the tiled floor. By the bird bath in the center of the area she paused to look up. There was no wind. The stars were just above the reach of her fingertips, she thought, frozen in the winter sky. She listened for internal music, and when it came she stretched upward, her arms rising, her whole body flowing into motion; as the music moved in her mind, her limbs followed its rhythms.

Her arabesque was still a matter of steely strength and grace. Slowly, turning, she folded into fifth position, made a preparation, and leaped, the *jeté* right, strong, soaring, with the stretch at the top that made her seem to hang in the air.

Still the music moved inside her, and her muscles ached with the old delight, her bones feeling light and young, for all their aching. Turning, whirling, dipping, gliding, she moved upon the tiles of the terrace, a creature of air and moonlight. Startled faces at the windows were inconsequential. Gesticulating attendants were unnoticed, for her joy was almost suffocating. Her throat throbbed with the wild impulse of her blood as slowly, slowly, the music died, leaving only an echo hidden in her heart.

Her shawl became a shawl again, instead of a wisp of moonbeam. The skirt fell gently to stillness, and her hands drifted into repose. She smiled at the dumbfounded nurse, a smile of infinite delight, as she followed her into the house.

Faces smiled back at her, touched with a bit of her wonder and joy. Hands reached out shyly, as if she were somehow magical. The director, obviously prepared to scold her, was unable to find words, and her expression held a touch of awe.

The bitterness Natya had felt seemed to wash from her spirit. In that mood of perfect peace, she knew her final gift had been accepted. Now she could face her future, long or short, with tranquility. She closed her eyes as she sat in her chair, and a sharpness ran down her left arm, across her chest. She smiled more broadly.

"Good night, Boris," she whispered. Perhaps tonight they would both go free.

Cat stories delight me, for I find cats to be almost as independent-minded as I am.

MY FRIEND EDDY

I have to admit it—I worry about Eddy. Not that I'm responsible for him, of course. We're not that kind of friends, both of us being totally independent. He ignores me, and while I pay pretty close attention to him, I try never to let that show. The bozo may be a drunk and a drifter, but he has his pride, just like me.

We both get into fights from time to time too. We have the scars to show for it, and I'm pretty proud of my chewed-off ears and crooked tail, which has been broken more times than I can count. Whenever Eddy truly notices me, which isn't often, he grins. We're pretty much of a match, the two of us, though he lost his right eye and wears a patch over it, while mine is a mess of scar tissue.

Sometimes when he staggers down the street, humming gently between hiccups, I trail along behind him, my tail as straight up as it will go. People stop and stare as if we were some kind of parade, though Eddy often seems not to notice. Even other bums give us little salutes, and poor old Ed thinks they're for him. I know they're for the combination of ragged Eddy, staggering all over the place, and me, marching straight as a string behind him. We have a style of our own.

By now you probably guess that Eddy is a few pickles shy of a pint. He can wander into the craziest situations, and I don't seem to be able to keep from pulling him out of them, sometimes literally. A big tough tomcat can make himself felt, believe me.

We had gotten along so well for a couple of months that I suppose I got a bit slack. When Eddy unexpectedly hopped a slow freight that night I gave a growl, for I hate having to leap aboard those things. Just one second off in my timing, and I'd be ground to hamburger beneath the wheels.

I made it, of course, and found myself in an empty boxcar with only Eddy for company, and this was one of the nights he was thinking I was some kind of delusion. He tucked himself into a corner and covered himself up with the old Army overcoat he'd bought for a buck at Goodwill a couple of winters ago. I went over and nosed him, just to make sure he was all right. Then I curled up with my tail warming my nose and dozed off. The train picked up speed and clacked along for hours before it slowed again in a big rail yard. I yawned and moved to the doorway to look out. It was pitch dark, still.

A heavy boot almost squashed me as someone jumped aboard. Behind him came another big fellow, swearing almost as well as I do. I slid aside silently, baring my fangs at the smell of that boot. Then I scooted through the darkness to the corner where Eddy was hidden by his olive drab overcoat. Many of my scars were given me by men who made my whiskers tingle just the way these two did. I knew bad news when I smelled it.

I pushed up under the coat and nipped Eddy's stubbly chin. He grunted softly—I hoped the sound was covered by the clacking of the wheels. I nipped him again, harder. He fumbled around until he felt me. Then he froze. I had known for years that he usually believed I was a delusion, and that suited me. But now we needed to act together, and he had to know I was real.

Before I had to nip him again in warning one of the men let out a curse. Just what I needed. Eddy ran his fingers over my fur. "Umhmmm," he grunted, almost silently. He might be short of smarts, but nobody without a well-honed sense of self-preservation could ever have survived so long.

Then I heard something that made my fur stand straight up. A small child whimpered, and one of the men said, "Shut that kid up, Moberly. He's worth as much dead as alive, now we've got him. Once they pay off, there'll not be any way they can trace us—or him, if we drop him off in a river someplace."

Eddy heard, and for once he understood what was going on. He went so still he might have been dead, except for the thumping of his heart. Once he'd had a kid of his own—he often talked about him when he reached the maudlin stage in one of his worse drunken spells. I knew there was no way he'd ever let anybody kill a child, no matter how impossible it seemed to rescue him.

I was thinking hard myself. Some tomcats kill kittens, I know, but the thought made my whiskers bristle. I like young things, human or otherwise, and I knew we had to do something to save the child those creeps had in the opposite corner of the boxcar. Still, when Eddy silently slid from under the coat and felt his way up the wall, it almost took me by surprise.

Then I realized what he had seen, his head not being under the coat. One of the men was standing, outlined against the slightly lighter darkness beyond the open doorway. He was holding a big bundle as he moved closer to the opening. I could see it squirming. Just at that moment the engineer blew the air horn for a crossing, covering the sound as we moved. Eddy took the left side and grabbed the kid. I took the right and jumped as high as I could, raking my claws down the man's neck and kicking my hind claws into him. He was completely surprised, and my attack knocked him off balance.

Eddy hurled himself backward, and I could see that he had the child wrapped tightly in his arms. The kidnapper fell forward, toppling out of the door onto the right-of-way. By then his companion had roused himself to action, but, not being a cat, he wasn't able to see what was happening. He headed for the sound of the child, who was crying in Eddy's arms. I wove around his legs and pushed hard, and he fell onto his knees.

"Get out, Eddy!" I yowled, but of course he couldn't understand me. Still, I could hear him scrambling across the floor toward the door. The old boy could get it in gear, when things got tight, I had to admit. The train howled again and began to slow. Eddy jumped out, and I leaped onto the back of the man who tried to grab him as he went. He yelled as my claws sank into his shoulders and my teeth met in the nape of his neck.

He rolled, trying to dislodge me, as the train rattled past the spot where Eddy had gone overboard. When it began to pick up speed again, I jumped free of my struggling captive and sprang out of the door. I had to find Eddy...that other villain might not be so far behind that he couldn't locate him, by smell, if no other way. Eddy tended to be pretty fragrant, most of the time.

I hit running, my paws scrambling among the gravel for an instant before I gained the grass beyond. Now I could see well in the starlight. There was still a half-mile of train left to rumble past me.

I moved into the sunflowers along the embankment and sped back along our track. Eddy would, I hoped, have had the good sense to move away from the railroad as fast as he could. We had to get that child into safe hands before the snatchers found him again. I only hoped he was old enough to know his own name and address.

Once hidden in the shadows among tall grass and sunflowers, I paused and waited for the rest of the train to pass. Then I listened hard, trying to hear, through the shrilling of crickets, the sound of someone running. A mockingbird ran through his repertory, but I could hear nothing that didn't belong among the sounds of the night. A field mouse rustled through the grass and I killed him cleanly and ate, still listening. Then, far down the line, I heard running footsteps. The villain we had pushed out must be following the train, hoping his friend would also get out and join him. Too bad he didn't break a leg in the fall onto the right-of-way.

I gave a low growl of amusement. I suspected the other one would keep going with the train, because neither of the two had the faintest idea who—or what—had attacked them. That kind of human being had no courage, I had found in my rough life, and risking the unknown was probably not in him.

I slipped deeper into the grass as the steps came nearer. Wherever Eddy had gone to ground, I hoped he would stay there and keep the child quiet until this one had passed by. Eddy was no strongman, and though I had muscles I'd never had to put into action, you had to admit that there was a pretty big size difference.

As the steps came nearer, I heard, in the distance, a faint wail. The child was awake. While the villain coming toward me couldn't know that his captive had been taken out of the boxcar, he might investigate a child's cry, out here where there shouldn't be anyone at this time of night. I crouched under a clump of sunflowers, waiting in ambush as he angled toward the sound we both had heard.

When he reached me I hurled my weight against his near knee. He stumbled, tried to balance on his moving foot, then fell full length among the briers and scrub beside the fence dividing the right of way from pastureland. I sprang onto his head and dug in my claws. Then I leaped free.

I shot past him through the fence, heading toward Eddy and our waif. With a pale line showing that dawn was not far off, we had to get the child under cover, if there was such a thing out here in the boonies. I smelled Eddy, then, and headed toward the source of the stink. He was shuffling along cautiously, holding the boy over his shoulder and peering at the dark, uneven ground. I nudged his leg, then got in front of him so he could guide his steps by the white tip of my tail. I hoped he remembered that nip in the boxcar and would keep recognizing that I was real.

There had been cows on that ground—I stepped neatly around a cow-pat that proved it. This didn't mean people lived nearby. I'd traveled a bit in my time, and I knew that, but maybe we'd get lucky.

The dawn was brightening behind us, and now Eddy could see

to walk, so he no longer needed to believe I was real. I had to move aside, because he would step on me, when he was in that mood.

The little boy had gone silent. I hoped he was all right, but I kept an eye on the back trail, too, in case the kidnapper had followed in our steps. Soon I relaxed, as there was no sign that anyone else was moving in our area. Killdeer rose and circled as we passed, shrilling their sad cries, but there was no sound of them back toward the railroad, which was now out of sight.

Eddy was so much taller that he saw the house first. I knew he'd spotted something when he turned off at an angle and stepped up his pace. Frustrated, I climbed his back and looked over his free shoulder, hearing him curse me as a delusion as I stared ahead. The dawn light was stretching long shadows across the grass and bushes ahead of us. Beyond a line of trees a window caught the sun and shone brightly. I jumped down and sped forward, hearing Eddy pounding along behind me. There was a board fence around the house, and I went under the gate and into a neat yard with a vegetable garden on one side and a winter-killed flower garden on the other.

Chickens clucked in a pen as well, and an old lady was scattering grain from a bucket, while they scrambled and quarreled over their food. I dashed to her side and rubbed against her ankle. She looked down, her round face showing surprise. "Well, Tomcat, where did you come from? I haven't had a cat on the place since the coyotes ate poor old Tabby."

Again I wished fervently that people understood Cat, but by that time Eddy was fumbling with the gate and saved me a lot of effort at pantomime. As soon as the old lady saw the little boy he held out to her, she dropped her bucket and took him. They talked all the way into the house, questions smothered by answers, exclamations drowned out by the sobs of the child. By the time we were all settled in the kitchen, Eddy and our hostess with coffee, the boy and me with milk, Eddy had explained as much as he could, considering that he hadn't really understood what was happening until he grabbed the boy and jumped off the train. Even then his wits were so befuddled he had a hard time making her understand.

"A train, we wuz on, y'see. I wuz asleep but somethin' woke me up an' I heard the kid cry. B'fore I could think I jumped at the sound. Next thing I knowed, I wuz fallin' out of the boxcar with the kid in my arms. I dunno where he come from. Dunno where I come from either, comes to that. But one thing I know, this boy didn't belong to the guys what had him. They wuz talkin' about killin' him."

"I'm Mrs. Abbot," the old woman said, filling his cup again. "What's your name? And, by the way, your cat's name?"

Eddy looked even dimmer than usual. "'m Eddy," he mumbled. "Cat? You see 'im? When I see 'im, I call 'im Bozo. Figured he wuz my 'magination."

"I see him quite clearly," she said. "He looks like a scrapper to me. Seems to understand what's going on, too. I wish he could talk; I'll bet he could tell us what happened."

She was right, of course, but she was also a very bright lady. Once she got the boy settled on the couch with an afghan over him, she got on the phone with the sheriff's office. By the time the law arrived, Eddy had revived enough, under her strict supervision, to give a fairly clear account of where he got the child and why he had taken off with him. Then they waked the boy, very gently and carefully. The sleep had carried him through the last of the drug he'd been given, so he could talk with the deputies.

"I'm Robbie," he told them. "My daddy is David Sherman, and we live in Tulsa, Oklahoma. Mama puts the address on the labels in my clothes." And she had, too. Before noon they had taken the boy to town, where his folks met him a bit later in the day. They asked Eddy where he wanted to go, and didn't seem too surprised when he just pointed toward the highway. They could have made problems for him, if not for me, but they were so glad he'd been where he was and saved that boy they hadn't any notion of making a fuss about his hopping the freight train.

They ignored me, which is the best thing about being a tomcat. So now we're moving down the road toward the river and Texas. Eddy has his overcoat collar turned up around his ears, and his new wool scarf, the gift of Mrs. Abbott, leaves nothing but his eyes showing.

I'm plugging along behind him, my tail as straight as I can manage, my fur fluffed up to ward off the cold wind. Now and again I find myself thinking about the stove in that old lady's house and the china bowl she put my milk in. She'd have kept me, if I'd showed her I wanted to stay.

But Eddy and I are independent as hogs on ice. Whether he remembers I'm real or not, I'm the only friend he has.

This tale came as a sort of waking dream, and the fog was very real and chilling.

THE FACE IN THE FOG

The night was miserable. Left to myself, I would have settled down by the gas log in my study, opened one of the new books from the parcel just received from Blythe and Jenkins, and spent a comfortable evening. Before I could unpack my books, however, I was interrupted by a message from my brother Lionel.

When Effie, my housekeeper and friend, tapped on the door at nine-thirty, I could tell she was upset. She had never liked Lionel, with good reason, and her warnings against mixing into his affairs had been frequent over the years. Just her expression told me who had called.

I had never allowed a telephone in my study or my bedroom. My few friends knew never to call after nine o'clock, so when one came I knew it concerned something of importance—or Lionel! When my brother calls, it is always a matter of life and death, of course. Sometimes that has even been true. Usually, however, it has to do with bookies who demand money or blood. More often it means a loan to finance a panicked retreat into hiding, and many a plane ticket I have contributed, along with walking around money.

If Lionel had been disinherited, or otherwise deprived, I might have resented his pleas less, but that was not the case. Our grandmother's estate had been divided meticulously among her grandchildren, and neither Lionel nor I should ever have lacked what we needed or even simply desired. My habits being conservative, I invested mine cautiously and lived extremely well. My twin, being similar to me only in appearance, blew his entire fortune on a couple of hare-brained schemes that a child should have avoided. Once I reached the parlor, I could hear his voice on the phone, all but hysterical. I let him run down a bit, for he was incoherent.

Then I said in my most patient tone, "Go over it all again, Len.

You left me behind completely. Or perhaps it might be easier just to tell me how big a check you need and to whom to make it out."

"No, no, no!" he shrilled. "This time money can't fix things. I haven't time to go over it again...you have to meet me. Far from your house, mind you. Someplace where nobody would dream of looking for us."

"On this kind of night, with fog as thick as it is, nobody should dream of finding us anyplace but at home," I objected.

He coughed, as if the fog tickled his throat. Then he said, "The warehouse. I suppose you still own it and have the key?" I agreed to go, but I was tired after a long day at the office of our family's shipping company. The thought of walking long blocks in the fog was dismal, but driving through the muck would be worse.

"Bring me a suitcase," Lionel said. "Your stuff still fits me. Pack enough to do me for a week or so, would you? And put in Grandfather Morton's sword-cane."

"What sort of nonsense...?" I began, but there was only a click, and he was gone. To say I was angry would be an understatement. The old biblical question about being your brother's keeper had plagued me all my life. I'd reached the point of refusing, some time ago. And yet letting him wait in this bitter cold fog, at the mercy of whatever enemies he had roused against himself, was too painful to consider. Like it or not, I must go this one last time, if only to make it clear that this would never happen again.

I rang for Effie and asked her to pack as directed. She nodded. "Got himself into something he can't handle," she said. But she went upstairs and did as I asked.

In a short while I found myself negotiating the wet blocks to the warehouse that had been built by my great-great-grandfather, when he started his shipping company back in the days of clipper ships. Most of the distance lay along a wide street, well lit even in the fog, but at last I must turn onto the narrow one leading to the warehouse. I could hardly keep clear of the garbage cans lining the way as I turned into the alley onto which our private entrance opened. I could hear a sound there. "Len?" I called softly. "It's Anthony. I've brought what you need, but I want to tell you, face to face...."

The words died in my throat. A face loomed through the fog, coming toward me in the muted glow of my flashlight. Not my brother's face—this one was dirty, seamed with scars, villainous but in some strange way terrified.

"Help me!" The words croaked from leathery lips, but before I could react the man sank forward onto his knees, then went flat.

I fumbled at a shoulder clad in rough wool, finding a neck wound with a muffler. My gloved hand slid down to stop against the shape of a hilt protruding from his back. The thing felt like the haft of a fisherman's knife.

The rough breathing that had shaken the body went out with a groan and did not begin again. I turned my light fully onto the stricken man, though the fog seemed to dim it almost to uselessness. He was dead, I felt certain. But where was my brother? I picked my way around the still body toward the door to our private entrance. My light caught a gleam and I stared. A polished shoe...someone stood against the alley wall, waiting for me to pass. Only the fact that the shoes were buffed to a high gloss betrayed the one lurking there.

I felt suddenly sick and dizzy. All our lives I had teased Lionel about what I called his shoe fetish. He never set foot outside without giving his shoes a brisk polish, and now he stood waiting for me to go past in darkness—or was he waiting for me to go within reach of another knife? I shuddered.

I turned the beam fully onto the face of the waiting man. "Len?" There was no reply, and I stepped closer. "Did you kill that man?" I asked. "I'm afraid I know the answer, but I'd like to have some reason for what you did."

My own face looked back at me through the mist, my face as it would have been if I had subjected it to extremes of physical and moral dissipation for twenty years, as Lionel had done with his. The eyes were black pits, but I could see that his lip was curled in his old sneer. "Still the New England gentleman, Tony? Stiff upper lip, like our English great-great-whatsis? Walk the chalk line, or take your medicine like a good boy? All those Merriam customs got crammed down your tailor-made gullet, not mine. I got myself into this jam, I admit, but I'm getting myself out of it, and that's your tough luck.

"Big Wally had orders to drop me in the drink. Nothing to do with money, this time...I ran afoul of his boss. Now Wally is dead, and I'm going to be, for all anyone knows. You're going back to your nice cozy house and your tidy income and your hellcat of a housekeeper, and nobody is going to know which one of us was found here, stabbed by a known enforcer, who was found dead nearby, killed by Grandfather's sword cane. You think I can't fool old Effie?"

The light was fully in his eyes, and I knew he couldn't really see me, but I nodded. In his own warped terms, it made sense. Who would think to check fingerprints against those on our school and military records? Here would be poor Lionel, dead at the hands of

Big Wally, who couldn't testify to anything. It was neat, with no loose ends. I never thought Len was stupid. Neither am I. I had put down the suitcase when I stooped over the stabbed man. When I rose, I retained the sword-cane in my left hand. Now I twisted the shank to free the blade. There was the slightest whisper of sound, and Len jerked his hand up, holding the twin to the knife in Big Wally's back.

As he lunged for my heart, I skewered him through his own. He fell at my feet, and I could find no sign of life in him, though his limbs twitched reflexively for a moment. Tears fell onto his coat and shone there in the beam of my flash, as I wiped the cane, closed it, and filled the wound in his chest with the knife taken from his lax hand.

"You forgot the most important of the Merriam traditions, Len," I whispered. "A pity you didn't pay more attention. You'd have remembered the most important—when our family produces a real, dangerous wrong-un, we attend to him ourselves."

I had no blood on my clothing or my shoes—fastidiousness runs in our family. I dropped my gloves into a drain beside the main street, going beyond my home to do it. There was nobody at all on the streets, and I was grateful for that.

When I returned to the house, Effie met me at the door and noted the suitcase I still carried. "Didn't show up, eh?" she asked.

I shook my head. "He told me to meet him in the park, the third bench from the rose garden. But he never came. I have a sad feeling that this time he called for my help a bit too late."

She sighed sadly. "It had to come," she agreed. "I've heard things I never told you, knowing how it distresses you. He's a bad one, Master Tony. And just in case he has been particularly bad tonight, we'll just say you never left the house. Is that all right with you?"

I looked intently into her wise old eyes. She knew me very well, did Effie.

My smile was a poor effort, but I replied, "Just as well, perhaps. I shall be in the study very late, if anyone should call."

She plodded away to unpack the suitcase, leaving me to clean the sword cane carefully and put it into its unobtrusive place in Grandfather's collection of unusual weapons. It took me a long time to wash my hands, and even then they didn't feel quite clean. Probably never would again, I thought.

Now I am sitting before the gas log, a glass of port in hand, a pristine book in my lap. I cannot read, however. I am waiting for

Effie's tap at the door.
    I expect another call before the night is over.

Although never faced with the problem this character had, I was the dairyman who did all the work described here. I loved walking that trailer tongue, as it seemed wonderfully dangerous, with a pair of trick knees.

NORTHER

The norther slammed in like a great gray fist, flattening the grass and wrenching at the trees. Gustav Berg shuddered as the tractor topped the hill and caught the full strength of the icy wind. Huddling down into the slight protection of his denim jacket, he headed for the belt of wood-lot on the south slope. Followed by a solemn procession of cows, he set the tractor in its lowest gear, walked the tongue of the trailer back to the loosened bales of hay, and began to fork big blocks of fodder onto the gravelly hillside.

Berg worked alone, lived alone, ate, slept, and, infrequently, laughed alone. Now, his hands busy, he felt, behind his wind-burned face, the ache of loss. But the tractor neared a row of trees, and he turned, with almost a dancer's grace, to run back up the wagon tongue, lean forward, and turn the wheel of the tractor to avoid the obstacles.

Now he swung into the metal seat and guided the machine into a narrow track leading into the woods. Here the wind was only a roar overhead, a gentle ruffling in the dry leaves on the ground. He stopped the tractor and began carrying forkfuls of hay in as large a circle as he could manage. The ghost of a whistle murmured from his lips as he trudged back and forth among the hungry animals.

Finished, he drove back up the hill toward home. He realized he must start a fire before he changed to his heavy coat, so the house would begin to warm up. He would be chilled when he was through with the second haying and the milking. Coming into a toasty-warm house was always a comfort.

"Maybe tonight I'll finish carving the puppet for the boy," he chuckled, heading toward home.

The morning had begun fair and warm, but it had turned into a raw and overcast noon. The wind no longer came in gusts, but swept steadily from the northwest, bitingly cold. Berg was now feeling the chill painfully, sitting still on the tractor, his hands going numb and rheumatism striking into his wrists. He shifted into fourth gear and bumped down the hill toward the house. Pulling into the tractor shed, he sat for a moment, easing his hands and waiting to regain breath in his chilled lungs. He stripped off his work gloves and moved out of the shed, entering the house through the back door.

It was cold already, even in the short time the norther had been blowing. Berg frowned. "An empty house seems emptier in cold weather," he muttered. His fingers felt thick and dead, tokening more rheumatic problems. He fumbled with kindling and paper, wasted several matches, but at last a blaze flickered amid the kindling in the fireplace. Settling back on his heels before the spark of warmth, he watched the flames grow larger, eating into fat pine splinters, and burst into vigorous life. How Martha had loved that wood fire, he remembered. She had not minded feeding the ravenous fireplace.

He felt nearer to her when he watched a fire burning. It was so much more like her nature than the stiff, unflattering pictures she'd had taken over the years. Steady warmth, occasional sparks, and cracklings—those mirrored her personality. He sighed and glanced around the room she had created for him and their son. Even after her death, it still spoke of her. Her clock ticked on the work table, where his carving tools waited, her strange little paintings lit the rich pine walls with vivid color, and her hand-loomed fabrics hung at the windows and cushioned the ladder-back chairs.

Putting the fire screen in place, he went into the kitchen and sliced cured ham, fried eggs, baked a can of biscuits (far inferior to those Martha flung together with reckless speed). His blunt hands laid the table, placing colorful pottery and plain silver on a yellow cloth, the food onto serving dishes. That was how Martha served meals, and he did it the way she had taught him.

Once finished with the meal, he cleaned the kitchen, put away the dishes, and shrugged on his heavy parka. It was colder outside, the wind icier, and the soil underfoot was chilling rapidly. In the morning, he knew, it would be freezing and fair. The pond and the creek would steam like kettles of soup, their waters, still warm from today, interacting with the freezing air.

He thrust his hands deep into his pockets and moved to the big hay barn. Haying and milking, haying and milking took up all day, every day, in winter on a dairy farm. He climbed into the loft and pitched down alfalfa hay for the milk cows. Darkness would come early, beneath the low gray mat of clouds. That done, he battled the wind to the dairy barn. Lighting the water heater, he sterilized his equipment, put feed into the troughs, and moved to the sliding doors. "Hooooeeee!" he cried.

The call was whipped away, but soon a cow appeared at the top of the hill, and the entire herd met him at the gate, lowing gruffly and jockeying for position behind the shelter of the barn. He milked with easy competence, using intelligence to make up for the lack of a second pair of hands. But even after two years of doing this alone, he still missed Martha's quickness, her jokes, her teasing. He wished the boy were here with him. Life would be easier with someone to work for, to share with, and to plan for. But Martha's mother had insisted that he was too young to live without his mother's care...and maybe she was right. Ten is very young. He stopped suddenly. Tomorrow was Sunday. Teddy would be with him all day. The thought spurred him to renewed effort.

It seemed a long time since last Sunday. "A man needs someone around to keep him pinned down, or he rattles around in empty todays and tomorrows and can't keep them straight," he grunted, shutting down the milker. The silence was startling, even with wind rushing over outside. He cleaned the barn until it shone white and sterile, scrubbed his vessels and sterilized them. With his hand on the light-switch, he paused to stare about him at white, empty walls. "Like me," he thought.

He flipped the switch and trudged through the darkness toward the house, avoiding with accustomed feet the uneven spots, the ruts, the ripples in the ground. The house was toasty warm. Snapping on a light, he had one moment of unreasonable expectation. Surely Martha would step into the kitchen with his house slippers in her hand and an admonition on her lips. "Hurry! Supper's just ready, and Teddy and I are hungry, if you're not!" with a twinkle in her eyes that belied her tone.

She didn't come, of course, but he took comfort in the indefinable feel of herself that she had left in their home. Some women, perhaps, would have gone away altogether when they died. Not Martha. She put so much of herself, her energy, her forethought into her home that he almost felt her living presence. He kept the house as she had, constructively as a continuing project, and it was still vitally alive.

Changing his shoes, he busied himself with supper, whistling softly as he worked. The bang of a car door interrupted his preparations, and a crease appeared between his eyebrows. "Maybe a neighbor needs to use the phone," he murmured as he went to the front door across the warm, pine-scented living room. He peered toward the gate, after switching on the outside light. It clicked open and shut, very firmly. A small shape, burdened with a big case, marched up the flagstone walk and looked up at him.

"Hi, Daddy," said Teddy. "I told Gramma I just had to come home. After we talked for a while, she said she supposed I really did, but to be sure not to miss school or get sick. Uncle brought me home, but he had to go right back for a meeting." The boy's brown eyes looked a bit worried.

Berg stared down into the small replica of his own homely face. A rusty smile began to grow at the corner of his mouth. "Been needing a hand in the dairy," he said. He reached for the suitcase in the boy's hand, opened the door again, and let out the smell of frying chicken and hot biscuits. They entered, side by side, and it seemed the entire house settled around them, relieved to have the two of them together again.

In the kitchen they worked together easily, laying the table, pouring milk into tall yellow glasses, placing food in the serving dishes. Neither said much, but their eyes smiled when they met. Teddy's appetite would have astonished his grandmother, Berg knew, as would his willingness to help wash the dishes.

"Daddy," the boy said suddenly, "I won't have to go back to live with Gramma, will I?" Berg hung the dish towel neatly on the rack to dry. "No, son, I guess we both belong here together, just the way Mum left us." He reached down to take his son's hand and glanced out of the window, which was now beginning to fog over.

The norther had spent much of its strength, and the wind was dying away to a murmur, a whisper, stillness. Frost was glinting now beneath the cold, starry sky.

Tomorrow would be fair and cold...but only outside. Inside it would be summer.

Visiting the strange countries in my mind is a marvelous adventure. This was a most interesting one. I also like goats—used to milk one, in fact. Nonetheless, I never was quite satisfied with this tale.

PER CASTANEA

The Mountain rose in ascending slopes, its entire face marked with streams.

Their courses knitted into lacy patterns against the grass, twining around the bases of towering beech trees, and watering the fields below. Ela the goat-girl thought it the most beautiful thing in her life. The crown of great beeches circling the crest surrounded a giant of their kind. In a clearing just below it three rough-hewn stones stood in a huddle, the space within that triangle bare. Nothing grew there; no living creature ventured into that barren spot.

In summer goats grazed the Mountain, tended by Ela. Since she was six she had followed them as they worked their way gradually up the Mountain in the wake of the sprouting grasses of spring. By midsummer her flock always reached the beech tree, and she made a habit of resting in its shade while the animals browsed. She often wondered if her goats would have entered the angle between the stones if anything had ever grown there.

When she was younger, she had entered that space, thinking it good for playing or thinking. All had seemed well. Then her skin crinkled, her hair crawled on her neck, as if wicked eyes glared at her from the stones. Shivering, she had retreated and never ventured near the stones again. The goats stayed clear even of their shadows, and there was a rim of uneaten wild roses outlining their shadows.

Sitting beneath the biggest beech, Ela looked about, checking on the goats. Then she took out her cheese and bread. So often had she done this that birds of all kinds came for the scattered crumbs. She had come to realize that they did not fly over the standing stones but circled about the spot. Although she was not exactly afraid of this place, she was always very cautious as she went about her duties. Anything that could keep a goat from eating rose vines was something to consider carefully.

Thinking was what defined Ela. Other children had little time for thinking, but Ela's long days on the Mountain allowed her to examine the world around and inside her, which gave her a unique ability to deal with the unusual and the unexpected. As there was little in life to challenge her innate curiosity, she came, in time, to consider the stones, using both logic and imagination.

When winter came, and she was almost fifteen, Ela took her handwork with her to the firesides of the oldest villagers, where she made baskets and asked questions with equal persistence. Learning all the tales about those three stones should be of help, she thought, and the elders were willing to tell their old tales to a fresh pair of ears.

Mam Pauli was the best storyteller in the village, but Ela did not go to her. She had noticed that Pauli's tales seemed embroidered with details that nobody could possibly know. Instead the girl went to Grandmam Seela, whose tiny hut did not attract many visitors in winter. When Ela tapped on the door and spoke her name, the old dame welcomed her into the dim room, lit only by the flicker of a very small fire.

"A cold evening," she said as she stooped into the room. "I will mend your fire, if you do not object, so I can see to weave my baskets while we talk, for there is a tale I would hear."

Seela was more than pleased, for she had to carry the peat for her blaze from the village stack, and it wore hard on her old bones. So the goat-girl took a big basket from the hearthside and brought it back full to the brim, enough fuel to keep the grandmam's blaze burning for two days. Then she sat and began to twist and weave the willow withes together, as she asked the old woman her questions.

"I do not know all you ask," Seela said at last. "It has been many summers since I last set foot upon the Mountain or saw that spot you ask about. Yet when I was young, perhaps your age, I, too, wondered about those strange stones and that spot where nothing grows. My own great-great-grandmam was alive then, and she told me the tale she had heard when she was young. Weave your basket, and I will try to recall her words."

Seela paused and drew a deep breath. Then she began to speak: "In the oldest of days this land stretched from the hills in the east to the river in the west, for no Mountain yet loomed over our village. There was then no ruler in the south to require heavy taxes, and we lived well, with no hunger in winter as there is now. This meant that in spring, after crops were planted, the young folk could venture into the grasslands to play in the sunlight. Now it would seem mad to waste a moment in such things, but then there was no need to use every moment of life for survival.

"One of these was a scholar, old enough to be wise but young enough still to be vigorous. He fancied himself a wizard of sorts, for then there was no penalty for pursuing the occult arts, and he hunted the rocky slopes at the edge of the valley for minerals and the pasture-lands for herbs.

"He had huge and ancient books in his house, which he studied by firelight after finishing his day's work, teaching the children. Not a single person was allowed into his home, for he defended his privacy fiercely. Our people were innocent and hard-working folk, then, and no one was overly curious about his activities.

"Yet there came a summer when those researches brought about a terrible curse upon the valley and its people. Nobody knew exactly what blasphemy he committed, for only some children playing in tall grass saw him go into a hole in a hillock, and what he did there he did not return to tell.

"They only knew that in the midst of peace and sunlight there came a thunderous sound, and the ground shook. Those who were standing fell, and those lying in the grass amid the flowers clung to the soil as if fearing to be flung into the sky. When the shaking ended, the Mountain had risen from the hillocks.

"The people were stunned and astonished, and they stumbled back to their shaken homes as if in a daze. By nightfall they had begun to ask each other what had occurred. Then a bright blaze appeared on the top of their new mountain. So bright was this that it outshone the full moon, but no single soul ventured to climb the new slopes to investigate. When, weeks later, three hunters climbed the height they found the stones standing as they do today, though then they still held soil in the crevices and the broken edges were not weathered to dullness. The space between them had been burnt to black dust. So said my great-great-grandmam, and she was a truthful woman, though her tale had been handed down for generations," Seela concluded.

The goat-girl secured the last strand of willow. Then she rose and said, "I thank you, Grandmam Seela. An interesting tale, indeed."

* * * * * * *

Over the winter Ela found more bits of the tale among the elders, but not one of those hinted at a reason why the stones should hold such an aura of fear. She went at last to the schoolmaster, who had a store of ancient books left by generations of his predecessors. He allowed her to explore those volumes at will.

Almost every evening, by the dim light of an oil lamp, she examined the books. They were stored in securely sealed containers the attic of the teacherage, and amid the scutter of mice and the soft rustle of snow sliding down the roof, she tried to decode the crabbed texts, the earliest in a language she could hardly understand.. Yet line by line and word by word, she began to make sense of them, finding that the earliest must be the writing of that ancient who had caused the Mountain to rise.

The first relevant information she found began thus:

> I have founde amidde the Hillocks to the east an Opening that seemes to runne deep into the Rootes of the Worlde. There be strange Attraction there that biddeth me Enter and Explore, but there also be a Sensation of Danger that warneth me away. I must Medidate uponne this before Takeing any Actionne, yet I am Torne between my Desires—there seemes greate Wisdome to be gained by the Studye of this Place. Maye the Gods grante me Guidance!

So. The ancient seeker after the unknown had been warned by some inner sense that this fascination might be perilous. Little had he suspected how terrible that danger might be, Ela mused. Still, she felt a surge of the excitement that old seeker must have experienced. She, too, would have decided at last to explore that hole and its secrets. In her own situation, she considered the space amid the menhirs to be her own goal.

Since first she had led the goats to the mountaintop, those stones had drawn her, and that space between them had equally repelled her. Now she was of an age to marry, if she chose, and fully competent to determine her own activities. Being a sensible person, she continued her researches during the winter, and before snowmelt she found another page on which the writer mentioned his visits to that intriguing hole.

> Each Foraye into that Forbidden Opening leads me more Strongly towarde fulfillinge my Desire. The Spirit Guardinge the Place is beautifull to See, and his Warninges are now less Forbiddinge. When the

Fieldes are Planted, I shall goe there again, and this
Time I shalle enter into the Deeper Mysteries and
finde my Goale.

And after that Ela found no more writings in that precise hand.
Surely, she thought, the ancient curse would have worn away with
time, even if that hole he had entered still existed. By now exploration of that triangle should be a safe project to attempt, if it were
connected at all to that ancient disaster.

She found a contemporary account of the sudden upthrust of the
Mountain that was reasonably similar to the tale Seela had told her.
Putting together the generations, the size of the giant beech tree, and
common sense, she decided this must have happened something like
a thousand years in the past, not an unreasonable span given the long
history of her people's presence in this valley.

As winter waned, Ela began to consider what she might do
when she entered the blighted area. The healing woman of her clan
seemed a possible source of help, and she went to her to ask about
potions or herbs to ward off evil influences. This was a rather difficult thing to do, for Atelle, the healer, was as curious as a cat. That
was why Ela began her request with a white lie.

"I have been tending the goats on the Mountaintop for most of
my life, Atelle," she began. "But I have never grown used to those
stones near the big beech tree. There is something about them that
feels evil, and even now that I am grown, I cannot feel comfortable
there. Have you some herb that wards off that sort of threat?"

Atelle paused in her work of pounding roots in her mortar and
stared at the girl. "You have never feared anything, Child, even
those matters that should terrify you. Why do you now fear so familiar a thing?"

Ela shrugged. "Perhaps I have only just become old enough to
realize how fearful those stones can be and how strange that spot is."

Atelle wiped her hands upon her work apron and turned to in-
spect a collection of pottery pots on the shelf behind her. She drew
out a squat jar whose lid was wired down to its stubby handles. "I
know of no cure for fear," she muttered, "but this may help you find
the answer to your problem." She unwired the top, took a tiny horn
spoon and dipped out a dose onto a scrap of parchment, which she
handed to Ela. "Add this to your herb tea before you sleep," she
said. "You may be…surprised…at what happens next."

"What?" Ela demanded, but the healer would not answer.

Not really content with the result of her visit, the girl returned to her home, where supper waited on the table, and her mother scolded her for staying out so late. She no longer protested that she had been earning her own way for half her life and should no longer be treated like an infant. She understood that to her mother she would never be a grown-up, even if she should live to have children of her own. She only smiled and sat to eat, discreetly adding Atelle's contribution to the mug of herb tea beside her plate.

After the evening meal the family went to their sleeping room, and soon the house was quiet. Because Ela did not know what might follow her herbal dose, she chose to sleep before the hearth, in case she might need the light of the coals in the hours of darkness. Wondering what the night might bring, she closed her eyes and waited for sleep.

Without any interval, she found herself drifting, seemingly bodiless, far above the world. The sensation was strange and should have been frightening, but, disembodied as she was, there was no fear. There was delight when she found herself floating above the starlit clouds, as she rose higher. She looked down upon the mountain, across the river, over the hills, while the world grew smaller below her.

Fascinated, she moved at great speed until she seemed to hang among great suns, cool planets, gazing at them as if she, too, were a star, equal to those about her. As if carried along in some antique dance, she was moved among her companions, often swirling entirely around them before going forward to her next partner. Delight filled her, a sense of sureness she had not felt since she was a tiny child.

As she joined in the celestial ballet, she began to sense words, not quite hearing them, for she had no ears, but knowing their meaning. "You are a part of all this," they assured her. "Never be afraid. So long as you are of good intent, there is no need for fear. Follow your truth, trust your instincts, and neither fear nor guilt may tarnish you."

Then she was released from the dance, moving away from the clustered worlds and suns. She could see the shape of the universe spread all around her, an intricate filigree of brilliance. If she had possessed breath, it would have stopped in her throat. If she had still had a heart it might have halted its beating. Having neither, she simply observed, absorbed, as she spun like wool back onto the spindle of her world. When she opened her eyes again she lay before the hearth, and the coals had not yet lost their glow.

Ela drew her knees up against her chest, preserving the warmth that had blossomed inside her on her journey. The dream, if such it had been, offered no explanation of those stones and suggested no solution for her exploration of the question they posed. Yet she felt strangely satisfied with Atelle's contribution. That spin among the stars had given her something real, though intangible.

* * * * * * *

The winter was almost over, and Ela waited impatiently for spring to begin. The goats became anxious to browse on the young leaves. When that happened, she put on her rough smock and her shoulder-bag of bread and cheese, took up her staff, bade her parents and brother goodbye, and went to the goat pens. One by one she opened the gates, letting the flock of each family free to follow her.

Day by day spring advanced, with only a few late snow showers Ela grew even more impatient to climb farther up the slopes. Yet no one can hurry spring any more than she can hurry goats. She greeted the new growth each day, as the goats climbed the slopes, moving closer and closer to her goal at the top.

By June they had reached the huge beech, but Ela felt it was too soon to begin her investigations. First she must rethink her winter plans; here she must either discard them or put them into action. So she spent the first day lying under the beech, going over all the things she had thought while winter wore away. On the second day she warned her parents that she might spend the night on the Mountain. The goats would be safe there at this time of year, so they bade her goodbye cheerfully. They had, of course, no idea what she planned to do.

All the way up the height, she considered her plan. The tiny bit of herb she had saved, twisted into the parchment, might serve her well, when the time came to confront whatever she might find. Deciding when to venture into the angle between the stones was important, and to find that ideal moment she must use the last of the herb.

When the sun grew hot in the afternoon, the goats always gathered in the shade and napped, and when that happened, Ela did the same, though this time she chewed the last of the herb before closing her eyes. Strangely, once she began to drift into sleep she found herself rising to her feet. Then a glimmer began against the stone ahead of her. Guided by something outside herself, she moved toward the huddle of shapes, taking her place inside their angle to sit on the bare ground. Not until she was settled in her new location did she realize that her skin was crinkling with chill, though it had been too hot outside.

There was no sound. Even the whisper of breeze among the beech leaves had died to silence. Insects had lost their voices, and no hawk or falcon shrieked overhead. Such silence she had never known before, and she drew her knees up, waiting for what might come next. The light had dimmed, though the noon sun still burned the grasslands below. Yet inside that narrow space the night was coming. A last she sat in blackness, into which even the daylight did not intrude.

Then a glimmer began to glow against the stone. As she stared, the space seemed to grow larger, the light stronger. She could see that she was now enclosed in a sort of cave whose walls glowed with phosphorescence. There was a strong earthy smell that told her she was below-ground—had she fallen into that hole the ancient scholar had found? Even as she wondered, she began to see a shape formed by the glimmer, a very old man who sat cross-legged and stared back at her with interest.

Ela felt colder than she had before. How many hundreds of winters had passed since this man had gone into the hole and somehow triggered the birth of the Mountain?

"And how did a child like you find her way into the Secret Way?" he asked. "I have been here for several years now, and no one has ever appeared before." His accent was strange, but the tongue was that of her own people.

She pulled her skirt about her goose-pimpled arms. "It has been far longer than that, if you are the one who explored a hole you found among the hillocks. The place where I waited for something to happen was formed after you went, when the Mountain was created."

He sat straighter. "Mountain? There is no mountain here!"

"You have been gone for many lives of men," Ela told him. "The Mountain holds trees that have been growing forever. I was told great-grandmothers' tales, and I read the ancient books stored in the teacherage. Even your name is forgotten, though myths tell of the rising of the Mountain beneath which, if I am right, this cavern lies.

"Three great stones stand together on the mountaintop, forming an angle in which nothing grows. Even my goats will not go into that space. But I risked drinking a tea made from a rare herb; then I came to the standing stones. Again I tasted the herb, and some force brought me here."

He leaned forward, his eyes burning with green fires. "Why?" he demanded. "Why should a child do such a thing?"

Ela calmed her quaking bones, and considered deeply. Why indeed? Then she said, "I am one who cannot abide unanswered questions. Once I knew about that hole and what followed your entry into it, I had to understand. Nothing else will satisfy me."

The shadowy figure began to shake with laughter, which echoed through the dark cavern. When he calmed a bit, he said, "One after my own heart, who cannot abide the unexplained. When I lived in the village, I was the only one who asked questions. And now there is another."

Then he sobered. "How long has it been? What is the year?"

She shook her head. "This is the sixth month of the Year of Corn. I think your years may have had other names. Yet if you could see the size of the great beech tree on the Mountain, I think you might have a better idea of the time that has passed."

"It seems so short. I think I slept for much of it, though it seems that I learned much, even in sleep." He shook his head, and as he clutched his hair in both hands he seemed to notice for the first time that it was white. He felt his face, running his fingers through his extensive beard, as if surprised to find one at all. His waxen pallor faded to gray. "I have been...gone...for longer than I imagined. "

Then he stared at her, his eyes growing keen and bright. "What name have you?" he asked.

"Ela Castanea," she said. "Daughter of Per Castanea and Ellana Betula."

He gave a deep sigh and stood, as if suddenly energized. "I had a son," he told her. "My line runs true, for my name also is Per Castanea. You are my descendant, I have no doubt."

Staring into his faded eyes, seeing the familiar set of his jaw and angle of his cheekbones, she could not deny it. Her grandfather had looked much the same, when he was very old, and her father himself shared the shape of his face. "My most honored ancestor," she said, "I am amazed to meet you, but I do not understand the purpose of this meeting. Is there some task I might perform for you? Do you need anything from the earth, here in your ancient cave? "

Those dim eyes widened, as if he had not considered such a matter. He leaned toward the wall and fumbled out a bundle, whose wrappings fell apart .His wrinkled fingers stroked three copper rods thus revealed. Each was topped by a sphere of quartz, one pale blue, one the green of moss, and the third the brilliant yellow of daisies. He held those carefully, one in his left hand, two in his right, separated by his fingers.

He gazed at them as if dreaming for a long moment. Then he looked up into Ela's eyes. "I think this is no accidental meeting, granddaughter. When I ventured into the hole, I was seeking for wisdom that would help me protect our valley, for there was a terrible drought. I found these wands. I tried everything I could think of to make them work, but at last I fell asleep with them in my hands. I dreamed a terrible noise, but I could not wake for a very long while. When I waked at last I was sealed in this cavern and could find no passage out. I have been here ever since, sleeping."

She thought hard. Then she said, "The noise you heard was the mountain forming. That must have changed things so the drought was not a devastating one, for there is no tale of such a misfortune in the records."

The old man laid the rods into her hands. "Is there anything threatening the valley now? Any enemy who might raid for grain or goats?"

Ela shook her head. "If there is, we have had no forewarning of it. If there is a reason why I am here, it has not yet appeared to us. What do you think? Yet you cannot know what happens above, I know. This is so confusing."

They sat for a long moment, in the glow of the walls, while the silence surrounded them like a blanket. Then the copper warmed in Ela's hands; her fingers tingled with some strange energy pulsing from them. The crystals began to glimmer.

Per Castanea shivered suddenly. "They did that just before that terrible noise. It almost waked me. These rods...they must appear to the one who needs them. That is a guess, but I think it may be a good one. You must go back above, Ela Castanea, and learn what is happening, for there may be great need of you."

She glanced around, wildly trying to see some opening that could lead her out of the cavern. "How? I don't know how I came. If you have not found a way out, how can I?"

The ancient closed his eyes. His head drooped to his chest, and Ela thought for a terrified instant that he had gone to sleep—or died. Then his head came up, his eyes glimmering in the dim glow of the walls. "Use the rods," he said, his voice suddenly sharp and clear. "Hold them in your fingers, roll them between your palms. I believe they will take you up again. And now I may go to my rest. I am glad to have met you, granddaughter. Thank you for taking my burden." Then he was gone, his body sinking into a heap of dust.

Ela fingered the rods, rolled them, and breathed upon them. The tingle began again, stronger than before. Filled with hope and despair, the goat girl visualized the space between the stones and willed herself there.

Darkness filled her, and she was disoriented. When she came to herself again she was sitting on the mountaintop; the sun was setting, gilding the stones with reddish light. Yet the angle was wrong—the sun should have hung in its spring position, but now it indicated late fall. How much time had passed while she sat talking with her ancestor? And where were the goats?

She rose to her knees, her legs stiff, as if she had sat here for months. Pulling herself up by one of the stones, she stood, looking around her. The foliage was wearing its fall colors, and the grass was eaten to the roots. The goats would already be retreating down the mountain. She knew she had to go down and see to them, but she found it difficult to walk. With a pang, she realized that her parents must have given her up for lost, even now, mourning her, in their quiet way. She must hurry to comfort them.

The village lay silent below her as she descended the last slope. Too silent. With the sun only just set, there should be some activity, if only Seela seeing to some sick person. But no one stirred, few windows glowed with lamplight. Filled with foreboding, Ela stumbled to her mother's house and pushed open the door.

The smell of illness met her. The lamp was not lit in the front chamber, but a dim gleam shone through the door to the kitchen. A clink of a spoon told her someone was there, and she forced herself forward. When she entered the room her mother turned a haggard face toward her and almost fell at the shock of seeing her.

Ela ran to her and eased her onto a stool. "Mother, what has happened? Who is ill? How long have I been gone?"

Ellana shook her head. "Stop!" she commanded. "Now tell me, slowly and carefully, where you have been and how you manage to come at this time when almost all are very sick—or dead—with this strange ailment."

Ela drew a deep breath and sat, facing her mother. Then she told her, in the simplest terms she could find, what had happened. When she was done, Ellana thought for a long time, holding onto Ela's hands. Then she sighed and said, "You actually spoke to the ancestor of our family—that is a great thing. And it was he who raised the Mountain all those aeons ago. Time must work very differently where he was. But now it is time to see if those things you brought back can work to save our people from this plague. Even Atelle has never seen its like. The books in the teacherage do not mention anything resembling it. Four have died, two of them old, two of them very young. Your father is very sick as well. Let us try first with him."

Ela felt her heart grow cold. Could she learn so quickly to use those alien rods? Beginning with her own father was a terrible test, but she took the things from her satchel and followed her mother. Her father, big and burly when she had left, now seemed shrunken and pale, his skin hanging loosely upon his bones. She knew the look of death, for many illnesses plagued her people, and she knew that if she could not control those strange rods her father would die within a day.

She touched his forehead, and he opened his eyes. "I am here, Father," she said, "with something that may help you. I am not sure, but this is better than nothing."

He could not speak, but he blinked and waited for her to do what she must. The rods warmed in her hands, and she began to tingle all over. She concentrated her mind and her will upon her suffering father. His color improved, and he seemed to be in less pain,. She sat in the chair and rested, while her mother examined him.

"He is better, but he is wasted and weakened. It may be that he will never be the man he was," Ellana said. "But your brother is also sick, there on his cot. Try with him, for he has less resistance than your father had."

Ela knelt beside small Urban's side and touched his forehead. Instead of the heat of fever, she seemed to feel the chill of death. She took the rods in hand again and worked with them to heal. Now the tingle seemed to flow into that of Urban, and he drew a deep breath, his stiff body relaxing. She laid the rods on either side and on his chest, and his breathing eased. Now he looked much better.

The door opened quietly and Atelle looked into the room. Once she learned what had happened, she said, "You must come with me, Ela. Many more are very low tonight, and some may die without your help. You are weary, I know, but they are dying."

Ela straightened and stood, putting the rods into her satchel again. "I must eat something," she said. "Mother, do you have food prepared?"

Ellana nodded. "I will bring it after you. Go with Atelle now. I will be there soon."

The night was very long, despite the hot soup and fresh bread her mother brought. Of the fifteen most serious cases, the rods improved the condition of twelve. Two were marginally better. The oldest of the Elders died, much to her grief. When dawn broke, Ela returned home and dropped into sleep. She dreamed of the old Per Castanea, who spoke to her with great seriousness, though she could not recall exactly what he said.

When she woke, Seela stood beside her, staring down with a strange expression on her wrinkled face. The girl stood up with a murmured apology and went to wash her face in the stone basin beneath the pipe from the cistern on the roof. "Now I am more respectable," she said, turning to look at the old woman.

Seela did not smile. "I have brought you the command of the Elders," she said, her voice more stern than Ela had ever heard it. "You must marry Atelle's son Jerob today, and he will take from you those rods and give them to me, for it is forbidden for me to take them myself."

Weary as she had been, Ela found herself angry—angrier than ever before. This was what the ancestor had warned her about in her dream. She drew herself up, squared her shoulders, and spoke directly to the Elder.

"I will not marry Jerob or anyone else. I will not relinquish those rods to anyone, for they were put into my keeping for the protection of our people. Possession of them would corrupt your spirit, Seela, however old or wise you consider yourself."

"We will force you...," but the old woman's words were interrupted by a humming sound, as the rods rose from Ela's satchel and zipped through the open door. Ela laughed. "You could not use them, even if I obeyed your orders. They are a Mystery from the ancient times. I had them from the hands of my distant ancestor, and he came to me in dream to instruct me. Go back to the Elders, Seela, and tell them the rods are gone. I will follow them. Never, save in winter, will I live in this village again."

"You would leave us unprotected? We need you!" Seela cried.

"I will be near at need," Ela said. "Blow the ram's horn. I will hear, for I will build a hut on the Mountain beside the standing stones. If you try to force me to stay here, there will be no help from me, for attempting that will deny this valley grace forever."

Seela snarled, "This is Power! You are a mere child, unworthy to wield it. We who have borne the responsibility here will find them and take them. We will control all the places beyond the mountain chain." Her face was distorted.

Ela took her by her withered elbow and forced her out of the door. "The rods do not obey; they perceive need and fulfill it. They will appear when I need them and hide themselves when I do not. You have proven to me that age does not necessarily being wisdom. Even the oldest can be corrupted by the promise of power."

To her parents' dismay, Ela moved from the village into a sturdy hut built near the standing stones. She snared small game and gathered herbs for food, though winters brought her down to her parents' house. Always she returned to the height in spring. Three times, in dire need, she used the power of the rods, but always they returned to their secret place when she was done.

In time, Ela became the Eldest. When she died the village grieved, but when they prepared to bury her body, it was missing, for it had gone back to that deep cavern where her ancestor's spirit waited.

Having been a dairy farmer during most of my young years, I found it interesting when the livestock mutilations began being discovered in the West.

THE BLUE-FIRED COW-KILLING CRAZIES

Some folks think I'm a bit timid nowadays, but I don't really worry myself about it. Being a country doctor suits me fine, and there's no need to be a hero for that. I don't have to hunt stray critters, and I don't have to sleep on the ground. Since I quit my job as a cowhand, I never, ever, camp out any more. I never told anybody why, but maybe the time has come.

* * * * * * *

When the blue glare hit, I was hunting a lost cow and calf down a scrubby dry wash, cussing old Ginger every time he bashed my knees against dead junipers or rocky outcrops in the wall. I could hear the calf bellowing somewhere up ahead, but in that clutter there was NO WAY I could hurry, even though it was getting darker by the minute, and I should have been on my way to the bunkhouse long ago.

Ginger had just walked head-on into a half-dead juniper and stopped, making me get down to untangle his ears and bridle from the stickery mess, when the whole world lit up like an explosion in a gunpowder factory. Except...there wasn't any noise, and the explosion was bright blue.

I had hit the dirt (mostly sharp rocks) when it started, but I rolled over and looked up into the sky in just about the same motion. There, ghosting away northward, was a round doodad with little green lights around its middle. A mighty strange thing it was, flying through the night easier than a train along a track, quiet as midnight. I could still hear that calf, so I left Ginger standing and stumbled down the wash. It was now too narrow for a horse anyway, and the calf sounded close.

Sure enough, in the half-light I could see the little fellow standing in a round clear spot that had been hollowed out of the wash by some long-ago eddy of runoff water. There was a humped mass beside him. I went over to take a look.

Old PieFace hadn't been much of a cow. A pest she was, and a loner, with enough personality to have been given a name, alone out of the thousands of head on the Star7 Ranch.

I hadn't liked her, but I wouldn't have wished on her the kind of end she'd come to. Somebody (way back in my mind I substituted "something" for somebody) had cut her open from forelegs to udder. They hadn't killed her first; I could tell from the hashed up ground and the way she was lying. They'd taken part of her insides, and I knew they had cut off and taken her udder.

Not a scrap of meat was taken; not the tongue, not a steak's worth of flesh. The work looked as if it was incredibly precise, and I wondered at that. Being a former medical student, I could recognize good scalpel technique when I saw it.

I went back to Ginger and got my little old lantern out of the pack I always carried with me when I was looking for lost animals. The sulfur matches were in their waxed box, and I lit the lantern and returned to the spot where PieFace lay. By the feeble light of the lantern, I could see the cuts fairly well. There was no hacking or sawing, just clean surgical cuts. Something very sharp, wielded by someone who knew what he was doing, had made those incisions, some of which were very unusual and thought-provoking.

As I said, I was in a position to recognize the skill. I was in my third year of medical school when I got a gut full of Willingham Institute of the Sciences (founded by my grandfather, cuss him, which meant that I wasn't allowed to go to a really good school). I cut tracks one Sunday evening and left no forwarding address. Which led to my being there in the middle of the night, with a dead cow and a lot of unanswered questions.

I stood looking at the ground. The only visible footprints were mine, but there were some round, poddly marks all around the cow. In the middle of the clear spot was a dark ring that looked scorched. There were no ashes, just darkened sand and stones.

I cornered the calf and picked him up. It was so easy to catch him that I realized why the mad surgeon had cornered the pair in that pocket of rock. Range cows and calves are not all that easy to catch.

It took me half the night to get back to the ranch. I put the calf in the stock pen and turned in without seeing a soul, but the next morning I saw too much of too many wide-awake wits to suit me at all.

I told them what had happened. First, the straw boss laughed himself sick. Then the owner, who happened to be spending a week in the big house with guests for the partridge hunting, didn't know whether to laugh or send me to the nearest insane asylum. By then I knew nobody was going to believe me, so I just started saying we'd lost old PieFace. And that was that.

I spent the next week building fence. They wanted to keep me under observation for a while, I think. I whistled and sweated and did my job without fuss. The week after, they'd forgotten the whole thing and turned me back to my main job, which was finding strays in the washes and gulches gashing the foothills. That suited me fine.

I took to staying out at night, claiming I was too far out to make it worthwhile to come in. I watched the sky closer than I had since my first year in the high country. I waited. I had a hunch that whoever it was that had killed old PieFace would make another move. I intended to know it if they did.

I didn't really intend to be as close as I turned out to get.

It was a moonless night. The stars were hanging like Chinese lanterns. You'd have sworn that you could see which were nearer and which were farther off, their shapes were so three-dimensional. I'd been lying in my blankets, looking off to northward, when some instinct made me turn my head. Right behind me, maybe thirty feet away, sat that round thingamajig, its green lights twinkling.

I jerked upright, my blanket falling every which way. I found my rifle in my hand—it always lay alongside as I slept, and I blessed the fact. Too soon, as it turned out. As I raised the rifle, a thin pencil of light shot out of the hemispherical shape and paralyzed me where I stood. Not a muscle could I move. Even my eyelids were hard to blink; I could still breathe, very slowly, and that was all.

There was finally a sound from the thing, a sort of purring, and a round section unscrewed and fell back against the side with a dull clunk. A set of steps, like a sort of ladder, slid down to hit the dirt. From the inside of the thing came hard blue light like a continuous lightning bolt, and in its glare I could see two funny shapes thump down the ladder.

They reached the ground and stood there, making gestures and gabbling at each other. I could see their fat round hands and fat round feet, but their bodies were rather skinny. Their heads were roundish, I could see, but what their faces might be like I couldn't see—their backs were to the light.

Now, don't assume I was just standing there cool and collected, observing those creatures scientifically. I was so scared I'd have wet my pants, but those muscles weren't working, either. When you can't move, can't yell, can't *anything*, you don't have too much choice. So I looked.

They weren't any race ever born on earth, I was sure. Besides, that thing they traveled in was no balloon. No country that called itself civilized had anything remotely like it. If anyone had told me, "Will Brendan, in this year of Our Lord 1903, you will see men from another world," I'd have laughed as loud as the straw boss did.

Every brain cell I owned was working overtime. I'd given them a good long rest for three or four years now. They seemed ready and eager to go to work again. The first thing they came up with was the fact that if those critters intended to do to me what they did to Pie-Face, I was in trouble. I had nothing to fight with—I was so rock-hard stiff I couldn't wiggle a finger joint.

I whipped those brain cells into a gallop. How could I get across to those things that I was a thinking, intelligent being? Not a dumb brute like that cow? I came up with one answer. The only thing I had that worked was my mind. I had to think at them!

So I did. It stood to reason that they wouldn't understand English. I had my doubts about Latin or German, too, so I thought in pictures. I gave them pictures of Boston, the only city I knew much about. I showed them railroads and hot air balloons and Gatling guns and every sort of mechanical device I could think of. I showed them a drop of water through a microscope, and the microscope itself. I relived one of old Anderson's lectures on anatomy, and I found I could recall the garishly colored charts in exact detail.

Then I looked toward the ship. The aliens were about three feet away and seemed to be studying me with much interest. One of them pointed to my chest and began a long dissertation. The other stood there with stubborn disagreement oozing from every pore (if any).

When Number One had finished his lecture, Number Two leaned forward and tapped me on the top of the head. *"Glyrht hraht!"* he said. There was no room for argument in his tone.

The other seemed a bit wilted, but after a moment he scuttled back into the ship and brought out a long case, which looked woefully like one that could hold knives and saws and all sorts of uncomfortable surgical instruments.

I hadn't really enjoyed wielding them in my youth, and I liked even less the idea of being on the receiving end. Desperately, I racked my imagination. What would impress them? They had gadgets that made the best my world offered look like toys. What could seem sophisticated to them?

Then I had it. Never in my life had I been accused of being imaginative, but from some hidden place in my mind I drew forth a really wild notion. Those brain cells were in full flight now, with sheer terror nipping at their heels. They came up with the one thing that just maybe might impress those gadget-rich critters.

What if my race was so powerful it didn't NEED gadgets? What if I could just THINK things done, and they were done? That just might shake them up.

I pictured myself standing on a platform, looking up into the night sky. I pointed to the moon, nodded with satisfaction, and, as light shone blindingly, my shape gave a quiver and blinked out. I hoped I had conveyed the notion that I was now on the moon, without the aid of a round ship that shot out blue fire.

To drive the point home, I shifted the picture to the spot where I had found PieFace. Again I envisioned the light, the nod, the pointing, this time horizontally. I blinked out. Then I pictured the spot where I now stood, with myself appearing suddenly from thin air. As an afterthought, I had my pictured self look around, shrug, and snap a campfire and a bedroll into being.

I was drenched with sweat now. Holding onto those visions, making them real while I held them, was harder than building a fence. I thanked my luck that Ginger had elected to graze at a distance tonight, for his presence might have aroused inconvenient questions in the minds of my visitors.

By the time I finished my efforts, I knew they'd been seeing the things I conjured up. When Number Two reached out to unsnap the case, Number One spoke to him so sharply that he shook all over and scurried back into the ship with his burden.

Number One was left alone, facing me. For a long time he studied my face, my body, my hands, the rifle, and the blankets. He walked around me and studied me from the back. He came back around and looked into my face again. I could feel, as clearly as language, the sheer frustration and puzzlement that I posed for him.

After a long time, he turned toward the ship and began walking toward it. He stopped. I could see his shoulders slump. He seemed to draw a deep breath, and then, I'd swear on my own grave, he shrugged. A truly Gallic shrug that said as plainly as could be, "Here he is. I don't know whether to believe him or not. There's nobody to ask who would know. The hell with him!"

As soon as the round ship was well aloft, I found myself able to move. I built up the fire and huddled over it until Ginger came nibbling near in the dawn light. Then I made a trail for the ranch, a train, and Boston.

Medical school looked better than it ever had in my life, and I finished it at a gallop. Seems as if I had motivation that I'd never known before, as well as the memory of that dissected cow and their unheard-of surgical techniques. In some way, I learned a lot in my short confrontation with those critters who cut up PieFace.

I'm not the greatest doctor in the world, but this little southern town seems to like me well enough, even if I am a bit timid. The men hooraw me when hunting season comes around and they take to the woods with guns and dogs. I really like to hunt, you know, and I miss it.

But there it is. I don't camp out any more. Ever.

This began with a scene, the knife stabbing my heart, the instant re-action—writing action is much more fun than LIVING it, you better believe.

PURSUIT

The knife blade caught the light, a feather-shaped sliver of steel aimed at my heart. I didn't focus on it, for there were more important things to do with my last breaths. I must try to kill Regnard, or at the very least prevent him from killing me.

Intent upon the deadly blade, I found the great hall about me dimmed to nothingness. The torch on the wall beside the tower stair gave faint illumination: enough to see my attacker...enough, I prayed, to allow me to survive. Even as my arm rose, slowly as if in a dream, I dreaded the bite of steel in my flesh. Better in the arm than the heart! I thought, as I drove my left arm against the knife and hurled my body against Regnard's larger and heavier frame.

He grunted with surprise. The blade was embedded in my flesh, its scrolled haft caught in the fabric of my sleeve, but I twisted and pulled it from his grasp. At the same moment I tucked my heel behind his and pushed again, this time tripping him so that he fell backward onto the flagstones.

I drew the blade from my arm; before I could use it I was forced to leap aside, avoiding his vicious kick at my legs. My own dagger was a gift from my brother Frederick, a toy, for he would never give me a true weapon. I did not consider drawing it from its sheath.

Regnard was clambering to his feet again, this time regarding me with more caution. He had thought a youth who had no weapons training would be an easy target. My brother had told him so, I was certain, and probably had offered a suitably small payment for my removal.

I almost grinned. Not even Frederick knew of the skills I learned from my elderly tutor, who had traveled far and learned strange arts. The old monk could disarm a warrior with his bare hands, at need, and had taught me to do the same.

I sprang backward and sped up the steep flight of stairs toward my chamber in the Franciscus Tower. Its door was stout oak, barred with iron, and Regnard could not afford the noise required to break it open.

The murder of a secondary heir to the throne is not uncommon, even in more sophisticated places than this, but it is also not supposed to be so blatant as to cast suspicion upon the ascendant heir who would benefit by it. The attendants and the Guard, here in the Rulers' House, would not see what it might be dangerous for them to see or hear what it was unwise for them to know. Yet even they could not ignore an attack upon the younger prince by a flunky of his older brother.

Safe for the moment, I barred the heavy door and thanked God for the sheer height of tower walls beneath my arched windows. No one could climb that way, and there was no eminence nearby from which anyone could descend by ropes to their level.

Nevertheless, I knew I could not remain here forever; now that Frederick's purpose was clear, I must flee or die. Regnard, I knew, was lurking outside my door. To go down the tower stair was to die at its foot of a broken neck.

Behind the arras on the west wall there was a small chamber where my clothing was kept and a basin and ewer awaited my use. Dripping blood, that was the first place I visited, stripping away the blood-drenched sleeve and laying my forearm in the basin.

The water in the ewer was cool and eased the pain somewhat as I washed the wound. That was deep but not wide, and I managed to pack it with cotton wool and bind it tightly with strips of old linen. When I had the bleeding stopped, I washed myself from head to heel and donned clean clothing. Not the fine stuffs I was required to wear about the Rulers' House, but the practical garb used when training with Father Janvier.

Unknown to Frederick, I had crept, nine years old and grieving, into our father's chambers after he died, to bid a last goodbye. There I took for myself the little blade that had been his since he was a child, kept in a chest at the foot of his bed. He had shown it only to me, because Frederick cared nothing for Father's things or, if truth be known, for Father.

Small though it was, the blade was fine steel, the hilt decorated with engraving. I had laid it at the bottom of my clothing chest, and now I dug it out and concealed it in the garments I rolled into a blanket.

Though it was spring and warm enough by day, I took my winter cloak and boots suitable for running as well as for riding. Who knew what pursuit Frederick would send after me?

I was thirsty with blood loss, and I drank what remained in the ewer. Though my arm throbbed with every beat of my heart, I made a final check about my quarters.

I must go now, I thought, feeling my body beginning to shiver. The window would be watched. But who ever knew a small boy who did not have a secret bolt-hole through which he could find his freedom, from time to time? I was still small and slender enough, despite my sixteen years, to manage the passage.

I returned to the cubicle and pulled the arras over the doorway. The floor was very old, very worn. At one side I had long ago managed to loosen the ancient planks and make a hole into the empty storage room below my chamber. From there one could slip behind the supporting wall of the stone stair, a route known only to rats and small boys. The planks slid easily back into position.

I could still negotiate the old way, but when I was safely beneath the stair, I found I was trembling and dizzy. I sat on cold stone, hearing rodents chittering about me, and listened to heavy steps ascending the stair.

Not Regnard; he was silent, as a good assassin must be. No, these steps held the arrogance of authority. The Regent, I thought, had come to see that Frederick's requirements were met.

Feeling almost gleeful, I listened intently. Above there came a pounding on the door; "Goliard! Goliard! Open this door, I command you!"

I giggled softly, and the rats seemed to giggle with me. Regent Lefevre intended to remain powerful after Frederick was crowned. He would kill me himself, if necessary.

Now I heard a crash, as they attacked my door with axes. That took it down quickly; then there was quiet for a long while. They were searching for me, though there was no place to hide. They would be looking out of the windows, sending others to check the roof, but they would not find me. I had drawn the planking securely behind me, and most men do not consider escaping through the floor.

I slept then for what seemed a long time. When I woke, the house was quiet. At last I crept from the understair into the narrow hallway leading to the sculleries. I followed old routes to my childhood exit, a scuttle hole through which refuse was dropped onto the midden below.

Regents and rulers did not think of such openings into a great

House, I knew. If I should ever return with armed men at my back, I might well use them.

The night was cool. Even reeking of the midden as I did, I felt grateful to be free of that house. The stables were on the other side of the kitchen garden, and I crept through the rows carefully, not to disturb the young plants.

Old Josip, the keeper of horses, rested above the stable, but he was deaf and slept like the dead. I managed to accouter Pelly, my gelding, in darkness, tying my pack behind the saddle pad. Leading him around to the back, I found the spot where the wall had fallen before I was born.

I managed to get the horse over the stones, and then we were in the edge of the forest. There I mounted and rode slowly toward its farther edge, where a shallow river flowed into the vale below. Moving into the edge of the water to conceal any track, I left the home of my boyhood.

Before dawn I was trotting over the pasturelands into the hills beyond the vale. When the sun rose higher, I dismounted and led Pelly into the cover of a thicket, where spring grass abounded. A trickle of water ran from beneath a stone, and we quenched our thirst. Then I slept while the gelding munched.

Distant sounds of shouts and pounding hooves along the road came to my ears, but again the habits of adulthood protected me. No knight or noble would think of leaving the traveled way, unless to engage in battle. No track or pile of horse dung would draw any after me. I had chosen my route with care and checked behind us to remove traces of our passing.

Now I was entirely alone. There had always been people about me, some attending, some actively spying on me.

I slept for hours, there in the shade, with the murmur of water in my ears. When I woke the sun was going down beyond the hills, and the sound of birds was all I could hear. Time to move on, I thought.

But where? My people were isolated, and I had never known anyone who lived beyond the hills. To the north were fens and the sea, chance travelers had said. Westward lay long stretches of moor country, sparsely inhabited and dry.

To the south, beyond dangerous forests and rivers, was Kendria, the principal city of our realm, where the King ruled over nobles governing small fiefdoms. My father was one of the High Dukes, kings in their own countries, who were allied to the great King. My brother now held that place. I would not go southward.

No one traveled east from Garenda. I knew nothing of what might lie there. I would go east.

I unrolled my pack and laid out my belongings. There were hose and tunic and smallclothes, in case I got wet, the boots, the sword that had been Father's. I had saved the small bag of gold since I was small, every birthday gold piece as well as gifts from kin, as if I had known I would need money to escape. I knew I could purchase what I needed, exchanging the gold for copper or silver when possible. Gold attracted robbers as honey drew flies, Father Janvier told me.

I rolled everything together again. Father Janvier's sister was heir to an outlying farm. He told me her husband left her well provided for. Maybe she might change some of my gold, if I could find her remote steading.

I gazed through a screen of shrubbery, looking out over the vale. No one moved on the road, so late in the evening. The distant village was only a blur, but I could see no activity there. Father Janvier had said his sister's farm was not far from the South Road to Kendria, served by a wagon track. There would be a moon in time. I would see if I could find Dame Lallia.

Leading Pelly, I set out through the twilight.

Had it not been for the Dame's donkey, I might never have found her house, which was the color of fungus, almost invisible. But the donkey, hearing Pelly snuffle, brayed loudly, giving me a direction to follow. Feeling our way carefully through the trees, I came at last to the wall around her garden; beyond it I could see the sky, filled with stars and moonlight.

The scent of growing things filled my nostrils, hints of sage and rosemary. She was a healer, I recalled. I raised my voice cautiously. "Dame Lallia! It is Goliard, your brother's pupil. Will you open your door to me?"

A faint line of light appeared beyond the shutters. Then the door opened, spilling lamplight down the flagged path. "If you are not Goliard," said a quiet voice that was filled with iron, "then you will regret pretending to be."

I moved up the path, leaving Pelly to graze outside the wall. Staring up at the figure silhouetted against the doorway, I let her examine my features at length. When she sighed, I knew she recognized her brother's description.

"Come inside, Prince Goliard," she said. "Let us close the door."

The room into which I stepped was not large. Dame Lallia set me at her table and put before me cold vegetables and rabbit, together with a cup of goat's milk. I was ravenous; until the food was gone I said nothing.

Then I sighed. "Lady, I am grateful. Your brother's training saved me from death this morning, and your food has done it again tonight. Today Frederick sent his assassin to end me. I escaped, and I hope no one noted my passing. I hoped you might change my gold for copper or silver."

She nodded. "That I will do. Janvier told me the time would come when you must go or die. He left a gift for you, as well as some advice. 'No one travels to the east,' he said. 'For that reason, no one will search there.' I think he is correct."

How strange! I thought. I looked into her dark eyes and tried to smile. "I had come to that conclusion for myself. But I know nothing of what lies there. Is there any tale you have heard that might help me understand what I might find?"

She leaned forward, her nightcap frills framing her narrow face. "We came across the eastern land, when we were little more than children," she told me. "Our homeland suffered a plague, and all who could escape fled. My family came west, but all died except for me and my brother, and we were almost grown by the time we reached Garenda.

"Janvier left me here, newly married, and continued to roam. When he returned, he had become very wise. I remember the eastern country, though I was very young when we crossed it."

She stared into my eyes as if determining the depth of my courage. Then she nodded, as if satisfied. "You will need to carry supplies, for it is an unforgiving place. The land rises into mountains that are cut with ravines and tangled with forest never touched by the axe. Not until you pass into the plain beyond will you find human habitation. There was a manor house set back from the track we followed. An old woman welcomed and fed us and let us rest with her until we were ready to go on. She will be long dead, of course, but perhaps some kin of hers still dwell there. The house has a roof of red tiles. But remember, there are dire influences to the east, dangerous to all."

Somehow I had felt that to be true. A chill gripped my heart, but I nodded. Wherever I went, I would be pursued. Better by a new enemy than those sent by my brother!

She spread me a pallet before the fireplace; I slept deeply all the night through and well into the next day. To venture out before dark would be foolish, we agreed, so I rested, while she led Pelly into her own stable, fed him grain and hay, and groomed him with her strong old hands.

When I objected to her doing that, she said, "Garenda offered me a home and a life, a husband who was kind and true, and a heritage that will see me through my life. It has given my brother useful work and an interest that keeps him young. I owe much to your house, Prince Goliard. Allow me to pay my debt."

So she tended both my horse and me, and when I set out before moonrise she led out her donkey, laden with supplies she insisted I must have to survive. Filled with gratitude, I kissed her lined cheek and mounted Pelly. As quietly as possible, I rode away into the forest, keeping before me, when I could see the sky, the bright constellation we call the Sickle.

For a long while we moved through familiar forest land, but before the sun rose we reached a deep canyon. At its bottom a thread of water moved among boulders, but its banks were steep and treacherous. I searched the edge for a possible path. At last I found a spot where a landslip had tumbled rock and soil to the bottom, making a rough but passable route. I led Pelly down to the water, where he bent his neck to drink. Rolling his eyes after the first draught, he snorted, choked. I tied him to an outcrop of rock and dipped a finger into the stream. It tasted terrible, like sulfur and metal, and I knew Lallia had been correct. Finding good water here would be difficult.

* * * * * * *

We found the mountains just as she had described them, difficult to traverse, frustrating in the thick growth of trees and bushes. When at last we came down the other side, the plain lying before us looked no more cheerful. Gray and tan, it rolled toward the horizon, with never a field or a house or even a wild beast to break the monotony.

We had found a few fresh springs as we came through the mountains, refilling Lallia's water skin each time. Now I realized we might not have enough, even with that, to cross this waste. We camped, the last night, beside the last of the good springs on the mountainside, drinking our fill. When night fell, I searched the plain for some hint of light, but not a glimmer could be seen.

We traveled for three days, following the only track. It wound among small thickets of thorny scrub, over hummocks that reminded me of great tombs, worn away by wind and weather. We camped on the third night under the shelter of a ruined wall, the first trace of the work of human hands.

Pelly seemed nervous, grazing very close to my small fire of brushwood, and more than once I felt as if eyes watched my back. I covered the coals with dirt and prepared to unroll my blanket, but I looked once more along the way ahead. And there, very distant but quite clear, there was a reddish glow. The house Lallia had mentioned? I could only go forward and find out.

I slept fitfully, waked by every breeze rustling the new leaves of the bushes. When dawn touched the sky, Pelly nosed me, as if to say that he, too, wanted to leave. I was only too glad to go, without rekindling my fire or eating a bit of the bread Lallia had packed for me.

We had been weeks on our journey, and spring had progressed to early summer. The track, which showed prints of strange animals and birds, was dusty, and from time to time tiny whirlwinds would twist the dust into spirals and dash it into our faces. So it was that when we came to the house we had sought, I was blinded at first by the last attack of a dust devil.

When my eyes cleared, I saw a red tiled roof. Pelly hurried his steps, and I leaned forward, trying to see any sign of the one who dwelled there. The drive, overgrown with shrubbery, was closed by a rusted gate, whose grillwork was marked with an A, surrounded by leaves and vines. When I pushed at the latch, the entire gate fell to fragments at my feet.

Pelly backed his ears when I tried to lead him forward. I loosed his reins so he could graze and left him behind, feeling very much alone as I trudged between hedges of flowering vigelia and cantropus. Rounding a curve, I found myself at the front entrance, which had been imposing before most of the granite columns fell. Now there was only a narrow slot through which I could approach the front door.

That was ajar, and I called, "Is anyone here? A traveler, weary and in need of water, would like to speak with you."

An echo repeated my words, distorted beyond understanding, down the long hallway I entered. No answer came, but a door at the end of the corridor creaked open. Taking that as an invitation, I strode forward, my steps setting up an army of echoes as I went. The open door revealed a long room with a fire on an open hearth at the farther end. Broad windows let in light, greened by leafy vines that almost covered them.

For a moment I thought the room was empty. Then a voice croaked, "Come in. Come in, Prince Goliard. I have been waiting for you."

Taken aback, I moved forward and stared about. A sofa, empty. A deep armchair, also empty. A wing chair, in which I could see a tenuous shape, gray clad, gray of skin and hair, almost invisible against gray velvet. Could this be that woman, old when Lallia was young, whom she and her brother had met here, all those years ago?

Reading my thought, she chuckled softly. "Indeed, young Goliard, things are not all the same in all places. Here time goes very slowly, and things change little. Here came young Janvier, when he had his sister settled, to study with me. We learned much together, and now we are engaged in an interesting task." She waved a wispy hand, and I perched uneasily on a dusty chair, facing her.

"You have work to do," she said. "The land you left behind in unworthy hands must be reclaimed, else your people will suffer even more than they have done under the rule of your Regent. Frederick, Janvier tells me, is cruel and capricious. When he ordered you killed, that was the signal to set our plans in motion."

I stared, confused. "But I have been weeks on the road," I said. "No one has passed me to bring word to you."

"No need, no need," she muttered. "We have our ways, Janvier and I. You will learn. We are going to arm you for a strange kind of battle, and send you back to reclaim your country from despotism. Frederick was always unfit to rule, and Janvier so informed his father and the Regent, though neither wanted to believe. Now all who live beneath his control are learning, to their cost, the truth of his words."

She shook herself, and dust rose about her. Then she reached a skinny hand, and I took it and helped her rise. How long has she sat there without moving? I wondered, feeling the flutter of her fingers in mine, the lightness of her frail body.

"There is much to do, to learn," she said. "Come!"

She led me into the corridor and through another door. There I found a sort of study, filled with equipment I could not name. There was no dust to be seen, as if it were used every day.

She noted my bewilderment and laughed. "I no longer have to handle these tools with my body, though you must begin so. Sit in that chair. Face the mirror. Then focus your mind upon Janvier."

I obeyed. The mirror was framed in iron and polished until it seemed more real than the room it reflected. My own face stared back at me, pale eyes wide with wonder, pale skin now browned with travel. And as I stared, I found my features dissolving, to be replaced by those of my tutor.

"Father Janvier!" I gasped. "Are you truly here?"

His deep laugh boomed. "No, Goliard, I am in my own chamber in Garenda. But my mind and my spirit are there, as they are here, for your guidance. Listen closely, for this communication is draining on the old, and both Arlese and I are very old. I can come only once more, and that only if there is great need." He waited for my reply, and I nodded.

"This is what you must do...."

He had trained me well, forcing me to memorize intricate mathematical formulae and long and demanding verses. As he spoke, I allowed his words to soak into my mind, and when he was done I knew there were stranger matters in my world than I had ever dreamed.

He stopped, and I said, "I understand, Father Janvier, what I must do. It will take time. Will my people suffer much while I prepare myself to return?"

His sigh was clear, even at so great a distance. "They will, my son. But suffering that has an end is far better than that which might go on for Frederick's lifetime. Work hard, work quickly. Call me only at need. Arlese knows the way of it. Now I must sleep." His face was pale, his dark eyes circled; I knew this had drained him badly. Then he was gone, and my own face looked back at me.

* * * * * * *

For a year I lived with the lady Arlese, who seldom moved from her chair, but who instructed me at every step. I learned rituals whose meanings were lost in the depths of the past. I manipulated substances whose effects astonished me to my soul.

When we were done with my education, we had achieved a cartload of long, thin staffs, beautifully decorated, which seemed totally harmless. Yet by using them correctly, I knew I could establish just rule for my people.

In the stable of the ancient house we found a cart, shabby and dusty, yet stout enough. Pelly, understandably, refused to draw it, but the donkey, being of a less arrogant breed, seemed willing enough. A year from the day when I had fled my home, I set out again, westward along that dim track, leading the donkey, which in turn pulled my cart.

Pelly remained with Arlese, for a poor peddler must not possess a steed obviously of proud breeding. I heard his sad whinny as we plodded out of sight, knowing I might never see him again.

I found travel on foot and with a donkey of determined mind far different from riding. By the time we struggled over the mountains and found the chasm, I was a far stronger and larger man than I had been before. When we reached the canyon, I disassembled the cart and carried it and its contents across and up the farther cliff. The donkey scrambled along easily enough, and when all was put together again we conveyed the very image I wanted.

I bore south, to approach Garenda from the direction of the Capital. When we came over the line of hills and saw the vale spreading below us and the hill that held my House, I felt tears fill my eyes. Whatever its faults, that was my home and those were my people, the charge of my family for endless generations.

To my surprise, I was challenged at the bottom of the last hill by a mounted man bearing sword and shield. "Who comes to Garenda?" he called. "King Frederick allows no beggars or poor men to enter his kingdom."

I had learned, among many other things, humility in my long absence. I doffed my wide hat and stood looking up at the guard. "I am but a peddler, not wealthy, but neither am I a beggar. I bring walking staffs from the woodlands to the south, and you can see that they are nicely shaped, suited for the use of those who need support for feeble limbs."

He sneered, looking with contempt upon the handsome carvings decorating my stock. "Few who are feeble are allowed to stir from their homes these days," he said. "And no one has the time to walk the forests or climb the hills. Our King forces all to work who can, and some who cannot."

I did not frown, though I wanted to smite that arrogant jackanapes. I nodded. "Then perhaps those who serve the King would like to see my stock. These make fine ornaments, when hung upon the wall."

He thought, then gestured for me to go forward. Slowly, weary from my long journey, I plodded toward the walls of the keep and the House of my fathers. No guard at the gate recognized me, browned and grown as I was, and I led my patient beast into the stable yard and left him to the care of Josip, who looked at me strangely but said nothing.

When I appeared at the rear door of the House, the housekeeper, Malina, met me. She had known me from swaddling clothes, but now she did not recognize me.

"I have fine staffs to show the nobles. Where may I set them out, my lady?" I asked her.

"Spread them in the stable yard," she told me. "I need no clutter in the House."

"Then tell those who are interested of my presence," I said. "And thank you."

Before I had my staffs leaned against the wall and the cart, or arranged in rows on the ground, Frederick's courtiers began to arrive. New goods, it seemed, were no longer common in Garenda, a natural result of Frederick's new policies, I suspected.

They wandered about, knocking over some but handling the staffs with increasing enthusiasm. At last Frederick himself arrived to see what so occupied his nobles. I had made one just for him; and knowing his character as I did, I created a piece he could not resist.

When he reached for the staff with the great crest of our House carved into its upper segment, I began the silent internal chant. The other nobles now had staffs in their own hands, and it took a while for them to realize that the staffs now held them.

"My hands!" roared Frederick. "Unstick me from this staff, peddler, or suffer the consequences!"

Though I had removed my hat upon arriving, I now pushed back the scarf I wore about my head. Staring into my brother's eyes, I began to speak the words aloud. His mouth sealed tightly, his hands clenched, and he stiffened, holding the staff before him, its tip on the ground. As if drilled together, the nobles did the same.

Josip peered into my face. Then he knelt. "Prince Goliard," he said. "The gods be praised! Our prince has returned to free us from this tyrant."

Malina came from the doorway to stare, as well. "Is it true? Is this the infant I dandled on my knee? It is!" She took my hand and kissed my cheek, and I was much pleased.

Frederick, trapped and raging, could say nothing, do nothing. Held by the ensorcelled staff, he must do as I bade him, and when I turned and went out onto the road, he must follow. Behind him came the nobles, none of them worthy men, some as corrupt as Regnard.

We walked all the way to the home of Dame Lallia. She came to meet me, closing the gate of her garden behind her. "Welcome, Prince Goliard. You bring these men to be educated in humility and kindness? Come with me to my orchard."

I followed her, leading my column of marchers, until we came to the long arc of cleared land bordering Lallia's fruit trees. She gestured, and the staffs pulled their prisoners forward, stopping them at regular intervals until they stood like a planting of strange trees.

"Now, Goliard," she told me. "Complete the ritual."

I looked to the sky, to the forest, to the orchard, and I sang the last of the chants. "Take root," I sang. "Be nourished by rain and earth. Learn from the trees and the birds and the animals. When you are ready, you will be freed to resume your places among humankind. Lallia will keep watch and will know when your time comes." Before me, the ranks of men and staffs shimmered, becoming ranks of young trees, larger than saplings but not full grown.

I turned to Dame Lallia. "You have served your adopted country well, Dame. Would you like to come to Garenda and live with your brother?"

She shook her gray head. "I will remain here, where I was happiest. I will watch your crop, and I will bring these men to you when they have ripened and dropped their bad habits."

* * * * * * *

That was one year ago. Since returning, I have ruled Garenda, but I have not been crowned. The rain has fallen, and snow. Wind has whipped the trees, sap has risen and sunk again. Fruit has ripened and dropped and set again in Lallia's orchard.

And now I see, moving up the road, a line of men, who walk as if they have newly discovered their own legs. Behind them comes Lallia, riding the donkey. If she has freed my brother and his courtiers, then they are now fit to rule.

I now set my seal upon this parchment, for I will go to meet them, welcome them home. Then I will return eastward, with Father Janvier, to our ancient friend Arlese, and our work together that may, in time, free other lands than this from tyranny.

My old friend Bill was visiting me one Christmas, and he got me wound up in the writing mode—and this resulted.

LALIQUE

Ariane Lalique stood before her mirror, adjusting her pale silken gown, her pale silken hair, her pale silken face. Should I wear the diamonds? she wondered. But she shook her head. Étienne did not care for diamonds; in particular, he hated those Maxim had given her during her marriage.

She turned with a sigh to her jewel box and chose a white-gold necklace set with moonstones. "Why do I trouble to try pleasing them?" she asked herself. "I care nothing for the men who provide for me; if I am honest, I do not care for myself."

Her gaze turned inward, toward her childhood, before Papa was killed and Maman went mad. Then she had cared for a few people, but that had proven too painful to continue. She had survived the years in the convent school, the misery of her arranged marriage, Maxim's rejection of her, but she had slowly discarded her emotions.

Staring into her mirrored silver eyes, she wondered why the men who supported her lavish lifestyle found her so irresistible. There were many women more beautiful, more accessible, less expensive, who reacted with at least simulated emotion to their advances. She did not and never had, even with her husband.

"I do not care," she whispered. "I have never cared, not for Maxim, not for Jean, not for Armand or any of the others. Only for my father, who died and left me. Why do they beggar themselves trying to buy my affection?"

She shook her head and backed away from the mirror, examining the effect of her silver-gray dress, her silver-gilt hair, the subdued jewels about her slender neck. "I look like a figure made of glass—or ice," she said. She laughed aloud, though without mirth. How many have had their self-esteem shattered because of me, have ended their own lives because they failed to arouse any response in me?

There was a tap at her door, and she turned amid a swirl of silk to meet Étienne, who followed her maid into the sitting room. He carried, as usual, a singularly tasteless bouquet, which she took with an icy smile and handed to Fleurette.

"Good evening, Étienne," Lalique said. She turned to allow him to wrap her fur about her shoulders. His fingers against her neck made her wince with distaste, and he withdrew them quickly with a muttered apology.

She led the way to the gilded cage of the elevator. "Where tonight?" she asked him.

"The artists' haunt, Lapin Dormant," he replied. "The carriage is waiting, and I have arranged for a most unusual surprise." He smiled, and Lalique wondered what he thought might amuse her, who never reacted to anything.

She wondered suddenly if Étienne would be one of those who died of desire for her. What absurdity! Why pay court to one who gave access to her body but could never offer even a morsel of her heart? Men were fools!

As the carriage clattered over the pavements, Ariane rode in silence, while Étienne tried to engage her in conversation. At last she gave a sigh and asked, "What is this surprise, Étienne?"

He looked surprised, for seldom did he succeed in arousing even the pretense of curiosity in her. "I have asked Henri Carondel to join us. I saw you admiring his work at the Academy, and I thought you might enjoy meeting him and talking about his paintings. He is a charming fellow, quiet and unassuming, yet extraordinarily talented. I think you may like him."

To her own surprise, Lalique found he was correct. Carondel was very young to have had such acclaim from the critics. He was shy as well, which roused a dim sense of compassion in her unaccustomed heart. Yet he could talk with great enthusiasm about his own work and that of others, Monet and Renoir and their associates, who were his idols.

He was a charming youth, his dark hair curling over a low forehead, his eyes sparkling with life. He even had wit, and she found herself, to her own surprise, laughing at his observations about others in the restaurant.

At first delighted with the success of his surprise, Étienne soon became silent, his eyes narrowed. He knows he is about to lose me, Lalique thought, amused for once inside her secret self. And he is blaming himself for his own stupidity. Perhaps this time...but she turned from the thought and began to flirt shamelessly, though without emotion, with her new conquest. This one could not afford her, but she could, she knew, afford him—for a while.

* * * * * * *

Olivier Levec of the Sûreté sat, as usual, in a shadowy corner of the restaurant. His "good friend," Monsieur Mouton, the maître d'hôtel, placed him in the perfect inconspicuous location from which to observe his quarry.

She sat at ease at the most prominent table, her present paramour opposite her and the artist Carondel at her side. Now why would Étienne Lavoix invite a potential rival to his *tête-à-tête*? The question troubled Levec as he sipped wine and considered this new piece of the puzzle that was Ariane Lalique.

Too many who had loved her had died by their own hands. His superiors suspected she might blackmail her victims, driving them to self-destruction, but the inspector had his doubts. A commoner sort of demimonde might do that, but Lalique was a courtesan of the old school, too well bred, indeed too noble to indulge in such vulgar behavior.

He had investigated her past in depth. Her lineage rivaled the best in Europe. She had been educated by nuns, respectably married, and then most unrespectably discarded by Maxim Delacroix, who had fallen into the hands of a voluptuous widow with the shrewdness to manage a fool. His wife, young, wounded, naive, had no weapons with which to fight her. Or perhaps—Levec had come to this conclusion after long investigation and longer thought—she did not actually care what became of her husband or of herself.

Now, watching from the shadows, Levec admitted to himself that he was fascinated by the woman. She was like sculpted ice, all silver and glimmer, and as cold. Her face revealed nothing that he could discern, and he had watched her under many different conditions. What a waste!

He thought of his wife Polyphème, his companion of a decade, mother of his son. She had never stirred him as this woman did, though he felt deep affection for her. Why did her emotional eruptions leave him unmoved, while Lalique's lack of reaction to anyone troubled him to his depths?

Almost, he felt, he was glimpsing the answer to his questions, but it slipped away when Lalique rose to leave with her two escorts. Between the two dark-clad men, she looked like a lost moonbeam, wavering away into the dim foyer.

Levec sighed heavily. One day that one would discard a lover who would not accept her decision, and he would cut her exquisite throat. That would be a tragedy. His own opinion was that she should be supported at public expense, a rare work of art to be observed from a distance by those who appreciated such matters but needed to be shielded from frostbite.

He finished his coffee and rose, knowing that the evening would now be devoted to the theater and dancing. It would end, he knew, at Lalique's apartment, and he thought he understood which of her admirers would be chosen to remain for the night. Lavoix would not be happy, but Levec doubted the man would be driven to suicide or murder. He was too cool, too controlled for that.

* * * * * * *

Madame Polyphème Levec, sitting with her brother at an obscure table even deeper in shadow than her husband's, watched Olivier move quietly after the trio who had just left. She understood that his superiors had assigned him to this work, that he was observing a suspected criminal, that this was altogether innocent and impersonal.

Yet she knew, with the instinct some women possess, of her husband's obsession with this woman who seemed made of something less substantial than flesh. What about her made Olivier look at her with such sadness and longing?

Never had he looked at his wife so, she recalled with bitterness, in all the ten years of their marriage. They had laughed together, quarreled hotly, and made up passionately, and cooperated well in rearing their son. She had no bad memories of their time together, but she wondered if Olivier did.

She nodded to Raoul and they rose. "He never looks at me so, *mon frère*. Why does he gaze at her with his heart as well as his eyes?"

Raoul was solid and middle-aged, as unromantic a figure as she could imagine, yet he turned to her and said, "She is of the stuff of dreams, little sister. I look at her so myself. And yet she is not one who could become a reality, a companion, a wife or mother. Do not trouble yourself about Olivier. For him she is a fantasy." She could see in his eyes that he truly believed his own words.

Without protest she allowed Raoul to take her home, but even as she went she knew that something must be done.

* * * * * * *

Ariane knew that artists seldom had money, but this was, in reality, not her first consideration. In the years since her father died she had been seeking desperately for something she could not define. Some stir of emotion, perhaps, some small melting of the ice that filled her spirit. Sometimes she found herself thinking with longing of the peace of death.

As they talked, Carondel had waked a glimmer of something inside her. That was more than she had felt in years, which was payment enough for her attention. She managed to shed Étienne at her door in the most subtle and tactful manner, but her subsequent activities with Carondel were no more moving or interesting than any others of the kind. Yet the boy seemed dazed with pleasure, impatient for another meeting. Lalique could not understand the addictive effect she seemed to have on men. For her, the act of love was less than nothing. When she bade Carondel goodbye, she knew she would not see him again. Perhaps she would not see Étienne again, either.

Laying aside her negligée, she sat before her mirror and stared into her own eyes. Nothing looked back at her.

"I am nothing," she whispered. "Oh, Papa, where are you? Only for you was I a real person, and when you died, I died with you. Only my shell is left here." She moistened a towel and began removing the subtle *maquillage* that enhanced her features.

She was moving toward her bed when there was a peremptory rap on her door. Fleurette looked at her questioningly, but Lalique nodded. "Monsieur Carondel may have left something behind. Attend to him, will you Fleurette?"

As her maid tapped toward the door, Lalique stretched on her bed, weary and dimly sad. The sound of voices made her open her eyes, and she sat and swung her feet to the floor.

"Who is it?" she asked.

"I do not know the lady," the maid said, appearing at the bedroom door.

Someone behind her pushed her into the room and entered, looming like some dark specter in the pale boudoir. Lalique stood, shocked and somewhat frightened by the red-faced woman in her chamber.

"Who are you? What do you want of me?" she asked, pulling her negligée about her shoulders.

The woman stood still, gazing at her—through her, she almost felt. Her eyes were the dark brown of the south, her black hair curled beneath the brim of her bonnet, and her skin was warmly tinted as if from the sun. Although she was stocky and inelegant, there was something about her that shook Lalique. She had the look of one who had loved.

"What...?" she began again, but the woman caught her shoulders and shook her roughly.

"I can see what you are now. But you cannot see yourself. You have caught the eye of my husband, and he is fascinated by you. But you do not exist, do you? Have you ever wept in the arms of a lover? Have you ever nursed a child? Have you ever considered working among the poor?" She paused for a reply, but Lalique had no answer for a moment.

Then she said, "You know, I am sure, that I have not. But I do not know your husband."

"Levec of the Sûreté," said Polyphème. "He follows you, as he is ordered, and each night he returns more deeply involved, until he is unable to see me any longer. Even his son cannot gain his attention."

Lalique sank onto the edge of the bed, sick with shock. "The Sûreté—they have me under surveillance?" Never had she dreamed of such a thing, although the deaths of three of her former lovers had shaken even her.

"They believe you blackmail them and they kill themselves rather than pay you or risk having their secrets revealed," said Polyphème, knowing she was betraying Olivier's confidences. "I think, seeing you, that they are wrong. You care nothing for them, do you? Or for yourself. You are not alive. Why do I dread a dead woman?" She turned and left the room, leaving the other two stunned and silent behind her.

Lalique gazed blindly at Fleurette, who was wringing her hands. Could she bear being arrested, tried, even sentenced? She could hardly tolerate the sounds on the street or steps on the stair. Noise and dirt would kill her.

Filled with more purpose than ever before, she rose and said, "You may go to bed, Fleurette. This distressing incident is over." But she knew she had learned the truth that had determined her life, and she could not live with it. She had not been alive for years.

When the woman had gone, she turned to her armoire and opened a drawer at the bottom. A leather box lay there, and she took from it a vial of clear liquid, which she tilted into her mouth. One gulp of the fiery stuff made her cough, then gag.

With a sigh she sank to her knees. Then she slipped onto her side and lay like a puddle of moonlight on the carpet, at peace for the first time since she was a child.

Several decades ago, at a science fiction convention, I met a man who lived this story and told the tale to me. I have great respect for him and his abilities, though I have altered the structure of the tale to suit my needs.

THIS IS THE NIGHT!

He lay staring up into the dimness of the thatch, listening to the boots of his captors, as they paced the compound. The agony in his abused hands had died away to a throb that timed itself with his heartbeat, and the pain in his kidneys was something he pushed out of his consciousness.

The night was raucous with shrieks of birds and beasts. He listened to those, too, for their intensity told him nobody was moving through the jungle tonight. No patrol was coming in or leaving, and that was good.

Nobody in his condition could possibly escape. If he did happen to get into the jungle outside the compound, any escapee would die. That was the wisdom of Captain Quang, and it had been proven valid for three years, in different areas of the Viet combat.

Sergeant William Redknife grimaced. Quang had not held an Apache before this. He thought all Americans were like the ones he had mishandled here over the years. It was obvious that the Cong officer knew nothing whatever about any kind of American Indian, and he would not have believed it if Redknife had told him. Pre-judgments were always hazardous, when you let them dictate your policies.

The sergeant flexed his right knee, then his left. He clenched his fists, though the nail-less fingers were torture, and the damaged tendons did not tighten as they had before. The hands were usable, though minimally by his standards. Redknife was certain he could stand and walk on his battered feet, when the time came.

Tonight had to be the night. If he waited longer, even his tough body would be incapable of doing what must be done. When the officer came to check the prisoners, it would be Muong. It had to be Muong—he had watched closely for the weeks he had been in the camp, and the rotation was rigid. Muong was the only officer tall enough.

He tensed, hearing the decisive clip of boot heels on the veranda of the officers' hut across the compound. The one who made the last inspection of the evening no longer took guards with him. The men here had become too weak to be dangerous, after the weeks of starvation and torture. That was an error he couldn't blame them for making, for he had pretended to be as helpless as the rest. He'd made the most of his bloodstains, his "useless" hands, his warped and "broken" feet.

Now Muong was in the third cell down his side of the compound. The heels thudded on the damp soil, clacked on the boards: next cell, now. And then the officer was bending to enter the low doorway. Redknife lay still, not breathing.

Alarmed, the Cong officer bent over his still body. The hands shot up with blinding speed, and the sergeant broke the thin neck instantly. Muong died without so much as a gasp, and only the stink of feces betrayed his death.

Rolling away from the body, William let it fall onto the bamboo shelf. With all the quickness he could muster, he stripped the body, laid his own filthy rags over it, and donned the uniform, which was now less than immaculate. Muong's stench almost sickened him, though he knew that he himself smelled as if he'd been dead for days.

The entire action had taken perhaps a minute. He straightened, drew a deep breath, though that agonized the cracked ribs, and stepped briskly out into the night. Without a break in the usual routine, ignoring the firelight and the pacing guards, he inspected the motionless men in the rest of the cells. Then he strode back to Muong's quarters and went in.

There was a bowl and beside it a pitcher of water, both sitting on the floor. In the corner beside the cot was a hook, from which hung another uniform. Thank God! He'd have hated to tackle the jungle, stinking to high heaven of Muong's shit.

He stripped quietly, pausing to listen from time to time. The rhythm of bird squawks and howls and chirps and squeaks from the jungle did not change, and the pacing of the guards continued. In about another hour—he gauged the passing of time by his own heartbeats—the guard would change. He would go near the end of this watch, before fresh men came on duty.

The clean uniform (that was, he found, only a comparative

term) was a bit too short, but he had lost so much weight that the looseness at chest and waist allowed it to hang, concealing that pretty well. He used Muong's spare shirt to make bandages for his hands, for the raw ends of the stripped fingers had to be protected.

The boots were hopeless; Muong's feet were much narrower than his own. But there were sandals with bamboo soles and a thong between the toes that would protect his feet. His years in the White Man's Army, with obligatory boot-wearing, had made his soles less tough than they had been when he was a boy on the reservation.

Almost time. He moved to the back of the hut and pushed a strip of the bamboo wall outward. It moved with a rustle, but there was not enough noise to travel far. He slid sideways through the gap and pushed the wickerwork back into place. The light from the fire centering the compound penetrated the darkness behind the huts only in random flickers, making it harder, rather than easier, to see clearly.

The palisade had been in place for months, and the bamboo had softened and split. Again, he managed to part segments in order to slide through. He noted with satisfaction that his old skills had asserted themselves; his passing was silent. The uproar from the jungle covered only familiar sounds—strange ones would have stood out from the cacophony and caught the alert ears of the guards.

The hem of the forest had thickened along the clearing edging the compound. He moved along in the shelter of the wall, searching for a way to pass through without disturbing the birds or changing any note of the jungle's voice.

The main path into the place was on the west side of the compound, and he was now on the southeast of it. Any path he found should be a game trail or one used by locals as they came to the compound with food or traveled to other areas.

He had moved around to the southwest before he found a spot thin enough to accommodate his passing. His adrenals were now at full flow, and the pain of moving, of using his hands, of walking on his battered feet was forgotten as he made his way, inch by inch, into the thick growth. He was hidden, at last, from the staring stars and the watchers who should be in the flimsy tower overlooking the camp.

This was country entirely alien to his kind. The lush, damp growth contrasted strangely, even after so many months, with the starkness of his native high desert and mountains. But he could sense the presence of many lives, large and small, amid the trees and vines and huge ferns surrounding him. If he had been one of his comrades in arms, urban in experience, frightened of wild things, those creatures would have known it at once. Fear roused predators to fury, which was probably why every escapee from Compound Forty-Three had been found dead not five miles from the palisade, in all the time Quang commanded there.

That was something William had been told, of course, by the few survivors who had heard it from their predecessors. Deep in the night, when pain kept them awake and the guards watched the area outside the camp, the imprisoned men whispered through the flimsy walls or tapped in code, conveying messages from end to end of each side of the quadrangle of cells.

They had not only kept the history of the compound alive, handing it down from generation to generation of captives, they also told stories and exchanged scraps of memorized poetry. The long nights held madness for anyone left totally alone, unconnected to the human race, during the black hours of misery.

In the interminable weeks Redknife had spent there, he had known of the deaths of fifteen men, out of the capacity of thirty that the camp could hold. Those had been the ones who had been there the longest. When he left, the men interned just before his capture had begun to die. Even a couple caught after him had already breathed their last, after long sessions in Hell, which was what the prisoners called the torture cell connected with Quang's quarters.

Being who and what he was, he knew that he would not have been lucky enough to die quickly. His tenacity would have held him inside his body long after he longed for death.

Even as it was, he had been hard put to keep his stoicism, as he underwent the attentions of Quang.

He found himself standing still, listening again for any sound from behind him. But the camp was quiet, and the creatures around him, finding this moving body giving off no aura of panic, were ignoring him. Their noise went on, keeping time, it seemed, with the throbbing of his injuries.

Now it was time to move. He must cover ground, between this moment and the beginning of the search. That should start with the dawn prisoner-check, and he must get entirely out of range of those who would surely follow.

He moved along the dim track, avoiding the clumps of fern or the outspread bastion roots of towering trees. The path came and went, but beneath the canopy the ground was not as cluttered with growth as he had thought jungle should be, when first he came to this hellish peninsula.

His nerves settled again, and the constant pain returned to remind him at every motion that he should be in a hospital, not speeding through the jungle. He ignored that, of course, as he had been trained to do all through his boyhood.

He did not stagger, and he did not stumble. His feet moved along, the sandaled toes feeling out the ground before putting his weight down, his hands sliding past overarching growth. He realized, after a time, that he was moving on automatic, allowing his reflexes to carry him along while his mind rested. He knew that one less sure of his directions would be running in circles by now, but something inside him was certain which way was southwest, where he must go.

When he could see the sky as a paleness beyond the distant tangle of treetops and vines, he knew it was time to stop. Even his determination could not hold out forever without rest.

He moved up a slight rise to a tremendous tree, whose bole was fluted enough to allow easy climbing. He wanted to get off the forest floor, and he had to sleep. He doubted that the search would come so far; if it did, he felt certain the searchers would not believe him capable of climbing.

When it came down to it, he found that he almost wasn't. The painful progress up that tree trunk was among the most terrible things he had ever done. His hands almost failed him, time after time, and his bare, raw feet, the sandals lost long since, shrank from contact with the roughness of the bark. But he persisted, and at last he reached the first layer of branches.

He went up still, though now it was easier, as he could stand on the lower ones to reach the higher. He passed a long dark serpent, lying flat along a tree-sized branch, but he did not pay attention to it, nor it to him. At that point, he would have welcomed a relatively quick death from snakebite.

At last he found a wide branch, satisfactorily far from the ground, where he would be completely invisible from below. He used the last of his energy to survey it for anything poisonous; finding nothing worse than a huge chameleon, he settled down, leaning against the trunk with his legs stretched along the limb.

He slept for hours. When his eyes opened, he was totally awake. Voices spoke softly below his perch, and he eased to the edge and risked one eye over the concealing branch. He couldn't see the ground at all, for a thick layer of leafy branches intervened.

He listened intently, and at last he sighed. These were peasants, not soldiers. He had learned, in his months of captivity, the ways in which the Cong communicated, and this lazy and careless conversation was not any of those. He leaned back again, as the group moved away down the slope and their voices died away in the distance.

When he woke again, the sun was far down. His hands and feet, arms and legs, ribs and back had stiffened, and it took him some time to bring himself back to mobility. Then he climbed again, going as far up the tree as he could manage. From that vantage point, he could see a great distance, for this ridge loomed, on the south, over a wide sweep of lowland.

He could see no activity there, though the cloaking jungle would hide it, of course. But there, to the southwest, lay the firebase. He must get back with the last words of Colonel Justiss complete in his memory. Some hundred and fifty miles of jungle lay between, but he knew that he would make it, and he dismissed the difficulty from his mind.

The thing troubling him, as he descended from the tree, was the memory that he had suppressed all the while he had been in the hands of Quang. It was, of course, the thing Quang had been determined to wring from him, but he had never admitted that he had found Justiss and his crashed chopper. That would have brought Quang's full attention down on him, which might have been fatal to others besides himself.

Now he had information to carry back to his superiors. But along with that, he also carried another memory, both bitter and strangely sweet.

As he held the pistol to the Colonel's head, freeing that shattered body from its pain, the man had smiled. In all the time he had spent in this god-forsaken country, that was the only comforting thing that had ever happened to William Redknife.

He sighed, stretched despite the pain, and moved down the small knoll. It was time to cover those terrible miles. It was time to deliver the information the Colonel had entrusted to him. He was, after all, Apache. He would succeed.

Being a born loner, I spent much of my childhood roaming the woods of my East Texas home. There I found spots that held...something. Some were simply alien, but a few held fear as well. I never knew what those meant, but in time I came to suspect there was more to those odd feelings than I knew at the time.

STONE CIRCLES

I was a solitary child, forever playing alone in Arizona's high desert country, where my Apache mother had grown up. From her I gained my love and understanding of the countryside, and from my father I got my hard head and grim determination. She told me, when I was old enough to roam on my own, of the stone circle, rough-hewn and seemingly natural, that stood some hour's walk from our isolated home. In many ways, that circle changed my destiny.

The day I was six years old, Mama called me to her and pointed off toward the northwest. "Now you are old enough to visit the Stones," she told me. "I grew up here, inventing my own games and amusements, and I know that you will soon become bored and restless. If you go there, I think it will give you...other things to think about."

Her gaze was rather wistful as she stared at the distant shapes against the sky. But she said little more except, "Miranda, watch out for rattlesnakes."

She packed sandwiches, told me to be home before sundown, and loosed me into a world of mystery and fascination and infinite potential. I followed her directions, though my short legs tired and I began to wonder what I might find at the end of this first lone journey. Then I began to see the goal she had set me.

A spire of rock rose ahead. It was a blazing hot day, with a vulture circling almost out of sight, as I crossed a low ridge and stood in a cup of rock. In the middle of the circle of stones stood the perfect playhouse, its doorway one of those wind-carved stone arches so often found in that part of the country. That led into a pebbly floor surrounded at intervals by sculpted teeth of red rock, spaced so regularly that the place almost seemed to be man-made.

I felt Mama's presence, even so long ago, and I settled in at once. Little girls can make household furnishings from anything they find, from pebbles to bird feathers, and I soon had my house in order, the rag doll that rode in my backpack enthroned on a divan made of flat stone slabs.

The morning went quickly, and I ate my lunch in the shadow cast by the stone arch. Then, weary with my efforts, I dozed off with my head on my pack. I dreamed of music, the notes of a bone flute. Then I realized that faces gazed down at me from—no through—the curving stone shape above me, as if it were a window into some other sort of world.

In my dream (or did I wake?—I have never been clear about that) I stared up at those faces, which shone silver-gray, like light on water. Long and narrow, with shadowy features, they seemed as interested in me as I was in them. I rose and moved toward the brightest face in the arch, standing in that opening while some kind of energy or impulse moved from me to it.

Then another kind of energy came to me from that beaming face. As it filled me, I felt light enough to walk on the air, and all the colors of the day turned so vivid that they hurt my eyes. Music welled up in my heart, and I was again drowned in sleep.

The first cool of evening woke me, and I gathered up my doll and the pack, leaving the playhouse ready for another day. Then I hurried homeward, for though my mother gave me freedom that city dwellers would never consider for their children, her one iron-clad rule was that I must be at home by dark. With that enchanted playhouse waiting for me, I wanted to take no chance of being confined to the house and yard.

Looking back now from middle age, I realize that my home was that stone circle. Not that Mama and Papa didn't give me love and security—from them I learned independence of mind and ethical behavior—but I learned things in my playhouse that are not taught in schools.

In the center of that complex of energies, I learned to project my mind to become a spider or a lizard or a hawk, and to see the world through their alien senses. I learned to subdue my physical self until my spirit seemed to stand alone in the winds of other dimensions. I suspect that my mother knew these things—she sometimes offered a hint of such things—but I have never known another person who did. Who, after all, could teach them those skills, if they had no stone circle to offer a door through which spectral instructors might come?

By the time I was fourteen, I had finished the school that Forked Creek afforded, but we ordered books through the mail and I continued to learn everything that interested me, from history to astronomy. I still went to the playhouse, but now for other things.

There I considered my own changing body and emotions, my mother's growing silence, my father's worried glances as she became thinner and paler. The conclusions I drew were my own, for the faces counseled only patience and kindness. Those are hard attributes to sustain at fourteen.

There was no one in my school who was the sort of friend who could share the mysteries of growing up, far less those of becoming aware of my mother's mortality. There were no girls of my age, and the Gadworthy boys, who came nearest to it, were repulsive to me.

George, the oldest, must have been twenty, Sam about fifteen, and Tim, the youngest, thirteen. They were all big and sandy-haired and cruel to anything or anyone smaller than they were. It never occurred to me that they might be interested in me, for I always kept a low profile at school.

They must have watched me for a long time to learn where I went. My trips to the stone circle were now infrequent, for I was busy caring for my increasingly sick mother.

However it was, they laid an ambush, just beyond the ridge above the circle.

No one ever came to the red rocks on our ranch, except for me. Never had I met anyone in my rambles, but I was not alarmed when I found them there. Men and boys went hunting at odd times of the year, when the notion struck them, I knew. I nodded and passed on the path.

They gave me no time to think—George tackled me, and we went rolling down the slope, almost under the arch itself. Whooping and grinning, his brothers came running down and grabbed me by the arms and legs. Being no fool, however young, I knew their game.

Though I was terrified, I was also angrier that ever before in my life. That made me struggle so fiercely that I kept knocking one or another loose from their grip on me. But there were three, all bigger than I was. I knew I had to lose.

Long strips of my shirt ripped away, as I looked up past George's shoulder and his flushed face. I cried out to those faces that had come to me so long ago. "Help me! Show me the way! Give me a weapon, please!"

George's knees were holding mine down, his rough hands pushing against my bare shoulders. But now I seemed to see inside him: lungs heaved, the webbing of veins throbbed with the passing of his blood. I sighed with relief, knowing my cry for help was answered.

I reached out with that sense I had learned to use so long ago. It meshed with his heart and squeezed it hard, stilling it in his chest. He sank on top of me, limp and heavy.

Sam was standing over us, and I stared into his pale eyes. "You might as well haul him off me, Sam. He's dead. If you want to try what he did, you'll end up the same way."

The surviving Gadworthies knelt beside their brother and lifted him off me, turning him on his back. Sam felt for his heart, then turned pale. "God, Tim, he's gone! Grab hold of him and stretch him out. Maybe we can pump some air back into him."

Filled with unnatural strength, I rose and stood over them. "I didn't touch his lungs, just squeezed his heart. You won't bring him back that way." I set my back against the stone arch, and the energy that sometimes charged that spot flooded into me. I looked down at the three without pity.

"You will take your brother and go home. You will never tell anyone what happened here, for nobody would believe you anyway, and you had no good reason for being here. Never will you come back here for any reason. Your brother had a bad heart—and that is God's truth—that nobody suspected. You will never remember anything else...nothing else at all."

Their eyes turned strange, as I rammed the message into their minds, using the energies that came to me from the stone itself. Then they lifted George and carried him away over the ridge. I never saw any of them again.

Still I stood in the stone circle, my heart sore, my body bruised and skinned. For the first time communication came into my mind clearly in words, and offered a measure of comfort.

"It is time to go out, Miranda. Your mother is dying and will soon be gone. Your father will need to go himself to soothe his grief. See the world with him. Learn what you can of human beings and their ways. When time turns round again, you will return to this place, as all things return at last to their origins.

"Forget your anger and your pain. Feel no guilt. Forgive those who have hurt you, for they are trapped in blind flesh. Go home now, for your mother needs you. She was ours, long ago, and she will soon return to us."

I went away from the stone circle, my clothing in shreds, but my heart was mending already. I knew that my mother would not be gone entirely, just in a different place. As it was, I told her I had fallen over a cliff, and she smiled and understood.

We had never spoken about her illness, but now I felt bold enough to speak out. "I know something is wrong," I told her. "It has been for months now. Tell me. Not knowing is worse than anything could be."

My father, who had been out on the porch, came in and took my hands. His eyes filled with tears. "Your mother is dying, Miranda."

Mama nodded, but she didn't look sad or afraid. "I have known ·for months now, but I didn't want to worry you, Miranda. Now, somehow, I feel it is time to tell you about it." She settled back on the couch and patted the cushion beside her.

I sat and put an arm around her shoulders, which felt thin and fragile. Papa sat on the other side of her, and we each took one of her hands.

Mama went on, "I want you to take my insurance money and travel, the both of you. The hands can take care of the ranch for a few months, and you both need to get away.

"Miranda needs to learn more about the world, and who could be better than her father to show it to her?" Papa and I glanced at each other over her head and nodded gravely. I knew her wish would be granted.

* * * * * * *

We lived for six weeks together, and we were all kind and even happy, in a strange way. When Papa and I stood together in the cemetery, while they lowered Mama into her dusty grave, I knew with certainty that she was not there. She had returned, after all those years, to the circle of stones and the waiting faces. She had gone home, as I would, one day when I had completed my life. We returned to the weathered stone house and made plans to take a tour of Europe and the Far East.

While my father went to cathedrals and Great Houses, I visited the old stone circles of Britain, which seemed to vibrate with untapped power beneath my fingers. At such times I seemed to see dim replicas of those other faces in the lichens covering the stone, and I knew we would return home soon. A sort of chronology had been set in motion by Mama's death, and I would follow faithfully wherever it led.

When we returned to our own country, Papa put me into a good school, where I completed high school. Then he sent me to a small college, where I acquired enough credentials to teach at the Forked Creek School. By the time I was twenty I was teaching, and I have recognized among my students some children who are of my kind, good material for encountering the faces in the arch.

I always send them to play in the circle of stones. I do not need to accompany them, for I have been there and know what will come to those with the necessary abilities.

Who knows what the final result will be? Perhaps, in generations to come, there will be enough enlightened people to turn our kind from its present course and to preserve what is good in our species. I suspect that the faces in the circle of stones will find a way to eliminate the worst traits in us, if we do not self-destruct first.

Over the years, I have received many rejection slips that complained that the tales lacked conflict. I consider this an indication of immaturity and sheer ignorance. Having been a farmer for much of my life, I know all sorts of conflict that does not include fisticuffs.

CONFLICT

MEMO

From the Desk of William Thister
Editor
Adventure Stories Magazine
New York, NY

To John Cranville
Bonterre, Louisiana

Dear Mr. Cranville:

   Although we found the enclosed story extremely well written and very interesting, as we would expect from a writer with your reputation, my colleagues and I agree that it lacks conflict. As our publication specializes in tales emphasizing that quality, we feel that the lack of interpersonal friction and even violence makes your story unsuitable for our needs. We urge you to try putting two men together in this context and having them slug it out! That is what generates conflict.

Sincerely,

William Thister,
Editor

I crumpled the rejection note and flung it at the wastebasket. Conflict! If that idiot had been in my office right then he'd have had conflict to spare. How could anyone expect fist fights in a story involving a lone survivor of a plane crash, who was battling terrain, weather, and dangerous animals to reach help?

He had to be a city-bred man, without the faintest glimmer of understanding of what it means to face natural dangers, whereas I lived in swamp and river bottom country, among the predators I wrote about. Face that sucker with a water moccasin or a panther or bobcat or a hurricane ripping in off the Gulf of Mexico, and he'd get to understand conflict very quickly.

A metaphorical light bulb went on over my head, exactly the way it does in the comic strips. What use was all the money I'd saved from my very profitable travel-adventure books if I couldn't use some of it for...educational purposes?

I picked up the phone and called my sister-in-law at the Bonterre travel agency. Before nightfall I was on the way to New York, and before noon the next day I'd enlisted my literary agent, Lon Pfisten, in my cause.

I didn't have to twist his arm at all. He agreed that Thister was a first-class twit who badly needed a dose of reality. He had no trouble making up a dilly of a tale, which, while putting Thister into my clutches, kept his own tail out of any crack.

At four-thirty the two of them were sitting in a bar, busily talking about a promising writer who was going to be pure gold for both of them. At four forty-five they went into the restroom, where I waited with a very convincing fake automatic pistol.

Leaving Lon convincingly knocked out and insecurely tied up in a stall, I hustled Thister, his hands bound and his face muffled in his own jacket collar, down the dark hallway to the rear exit. There the used car I bought that morning waited for us.

I fastened him securely into the passenger seat and headed out of town. Every time he offered to signal for help, I nudged him with the "gun." He had no taste whatsoever for conflict at the personal level, I found.

It's a long drive from New York City to Bonterre, Louisiana, but I'd driven it before and knew how to stop for catnaps along the way. As Thister didn't dare sleep while I drove, and was too tired to stay awake when I slept, it worked out just right.

We made it in two and a half days, keeping to the old U.S. Highway system instead of Interstates. Before we reached Bonterre—all three blocks of it—I blindfolded my prisoner and pushed him down onto the floor-boards.

You may wonder why the trip seems to have been made in complete silence. Actually, he asked desperate questions for a while, but once he finally understood that I was not going to answer them, he clammed up.

I timed things just right. It was after nine o'clock in the evening, which meant that the sidewalks had been rolled up and put away. By the time I pulled into the dead-end track leading to Alfonse Dupré's fishing camp on the river, I was tired but elated.

Alfonse was away for the summer, guiding fishermen down on the Atchafalaya. I had made my preparations before starting for New York, leaving the necessary equipment neatly packed in my old pirogue, covered with plastic.

The car went into a dilapidated shed behind Alfonse's shanty, and I hauled my terrified victim through the bushes to the ramshackle dock. Around us the river bottoms and the adjacent swamp were alive with noise; a screech owl quavered its eerie call in the distance. A whip-poor-will's fluttering cry was answered by a shriek from some small creature falling prey to a bobcat or a mink. The croaking of frogs mingled with the chirring of crickets and the lapping of water against the sides of our craft.

The night sounds were punctuated by the chattering of Thister's teeth. He stared wildly about, once I lit the kerosene lantern. Hundreds of bright sparks among the willows and reeds and lily pads marked the presence of frogs and other small creatures.

As the pirogue slid silently downstream, the eyes of a half-submerged alligator glowed, and my passenger ducked as low as he could and began to moan.

"No conflict, eh, Thister?" I asked. "You're about to learn the meaning of conflict when I maroon you on the ridge in the swamp. The time will come when you'd welcome a good solid fist fight, I suspect."

"Maroon? Swamp?" he quavered. "Cranville, have you gone insane?"

"No more than usual," I replied. "You have to be pretty crazy to do the work I do, going places and doing things that put my neck in danger every day of my life and writing about them. Then I write a fiction piece, using real life as the basis, and you tell me I have no conflict. I finally snapped, I think. You are about...to...learn."

A gator bellowed somewhere ahead, and I think Thister fainted. He was still out when I grounded the pirogue on the ridge. I unloaded the canned goods, making sure there was an opener. I put them onto the sleeping bag, laid it all on the tarp, and towed them through the bushes to the huge magnolia grandiflora that would offer shelter when it rained. Its hollow had held off the weather on many of my own camping trips.

By the time I had set up a reasonably good camp for him, he had come to, and I led him to the magnolia. When we reached it, the sky was lightening and he could see the gigantic column of the trunk, the great buttress roots, the triangular opening into the hollow, and the pile of equipment I had arranged beside the fire I'd lit to keep off the mosquitoes.

His eyes were wide, his face pale as milk. "What are you going to do? Leave me here to die?"

I laughed. "Nonsense. I have everything you need for survival. Plenty of canned goods and an opener. In case you never used a manual opener, this is the way to do it." I demonstrated with a can of peaches. A good thing—I could see by his expression that he'd never used anything except an electric, and probably not that very often.

"I also have fresh water in this five-gallon can. This is for drinking only. You can wash in the river, but never, ever drink that river water. You'll wind up sick as a mule if you do."

I went over my mental checklist and continued, "Avoid all snakes. There are a few kinds down here that aren't poisonous, but don't count on being lucky. If you ever meet a gator on solid ground, stand still. You can't outrun him. It's better to stand fast and hope. And don't go swimming. The river has treacherous currents, and contrary to folklore, a moccasin can bite under water."

He sat suddenly, flat on the damp ground. "You mean you aren't going to stay here and show me? You're going to leave me here alone?"

"Keep the fire going. The bugs will eat you alive if you don't. There's plenty of dry wood, if you hunt around, but don't ever put your hand where you can't see what you're putting it on. If it rains, get inside the tree and wrap up in the tarp. You'll be chilled and get sick, if you let yourself get wet. Down this close to the Gulf, it rains often."

It was already very warm, the humidity feeling as if it collected on your skin, but the editor was shaking all over. Nerves, no doubt.

"I'll be back in a couple of days. You should have no trouble lasting until then, though you are going to learn entirely new definitions of conflict before I return. Just remember what I've told you, and don't eat any wild plants or berries, because you won't know what is good and what's fatal." I looked up through the treetops at the sun-streaked clouds.

"Now I'm off. Have fun, William Thister, and learn a lot about the real world." Then I trudged off along the river bank and got into the pirogue. As I poled back upstream I could hear his frantic yells behind me. Before I was out of earshot, they had degenerated into sobs. I almost felt sorry for him.

* * * * * * *

I busied myself with proofreading galleys that day and most of the next. Resolutely, I kept myself from thinking about what might be happening to my captive editor. I truly didn't intend to kill the man, just to show him that his limited world of pavements and sky-scrapers was not reality but the most artificial sort of fantasy.

I had a phone call from my agent, who had been questioned closely about the "abduction" of Thister. Lon had not been suspected, but he was beginning to have second thoughts.

"He'll be back in New York the day after tomorrow, none the worse except for a lot of mosquito bites," I told him. "I'll pick him up tomorrow evening, take him to New Orleans, and put him on a plane. I'll call and let you know when he's on his way."

I drove back down to the river camp just before dark and set out in the pirogue. I must admit that I was curious about the state in which I would find my victim. Would he be fit to travel?

I could see the glare of his fire through the twilight, long before I reached the ridge. He must've collected every bit of deadfall he could find to keep it going so briskly.

When I pulled the pirogue up on the muddy bank, I could see his dark shape between me and the fire.

I had to stop and quit laughing before going on. He looked like something between a scarecrow and a clown. His hair, worn longish, stood straight up, filled with pine straw and twigs. His natty suit had evidently been laid aside, for he was clad in shorts and undershirt, both smeared with equal parts of soot and mud.

He didn't hear me coming, so I cleared my throat so as to keep from startling him. Wasted effort! He all but jumped out of his muddy shorts.

"How did it go?" I asked as I hunkered down beside the fire to keep the mosquitoes off. "Learn anything?"

His eyes were so wide the whites showed all the way around the irises. His face had obviously been washed in the river, but he forgot to check for algae in the pool he found, for he had a sort of green moustache across his upper lip.

"You will go to prison for this, Cranville!" he grunted. "I will personally see to it. Now get me out of here."

"Well, if that's going to be your attitude, I'll just go right back home and leave you here. Nobody knows where you are, and nobody but Alphonse and I ever come here. He's way down the Atchafalaya for the summer and won't come back until the tourists are all gone. Think you can survive for six weeks or so?" I rose as if to go back to the pirogue.

He grabbed my arm and began to shiver. "No! No, you take me back and I'll...I'll never mention conflict again to anybody, for any reason."

I believed him. I still do, though he spent a while in a convalescent home when he got back to New York, recuperating from his ordeal and the malaria he picked up, probably from drinking river water. I warned him, but he was one of those who thought he knew everything.

He bought the next story I sent him, which also had "no conflict." I suspect he couldn't bring himself to learn if I had any more mean tricks up my sleeve. He obviously didn't want to find out what else I was capable of doing.

THE END

Dear Mr. Thister,

When I received your last rejection slip, it gave me the idea for this odd little tale. I hope, if nothing else, you get a laugh out of it.

Sincerely,

John Cranville

Dear Mr. Cranville:

This is a most interesting and unusual story. In fact, it makes me vaguely uneasy. No one would actually consider doing anything like this. Or would he? I think I will accept your tale as a change of pace for *Adventure Story Magazine*. If the enclosed contract is acceptable, please sign it and return it to me for countersigning.

By the way, who is your present agent? I want to avoid him, if possible.

Cautiously,

William Thister
Editor

This one was great fun—I saw it in my head like a movie.

NIGHT SONG

The conveyance rattled and thumped, swaying sickeningly as it pounded around the bends of the serpentine road. Gilels swallowed bile and tried to ignore the sharp corner of the basket poking into his thigh. He stared out the badly glazed window of the coach at the stream beside the road, winking like pewter in the last light of the day.

Though his stomach was in a state of uneasy truce with the greasy meal taken at the last stop, he was more worried about the condition of the musical instrument on top of the coach. He had supervised the tying down, and his strongest tugs could not dislodge it. Yet this had been a horribly long day of joggling. If he arrived at Senrival without that instrument...his chilled skin goose-pimpled at the thought.

They swayed around a sharp curve, sending him hard against the fat woman with the basket. All of the half-dozen riders in the coach were flung sideways to left, then to right.

When Gilels righted himself, he saw that they had turned away from the streamside, and he realized that the last of the twilight was gone. Now the coach sped in a puddle of light from its lanthorns along a narrow track walled by midnight forest.

He laid his head back against the hard cushion. Since the abrupt turn, the road seemed better, as seemed proper as they approached the principal city of Sextus. Even in such a backward country, on such a primitive world, that made sense. Now he was able to hold his head still, instead of having it bumped against the worn horsehide by the ruts in the road.

That gave him time to worry again about the grampion, upon which the success of his mission depended. He doubted strongly the effectiveness of "a capella" singing upon the disposition of a murderous daemon. And the Magister Cantorum would, he felt, accept no excuses for his failure (should he survive), no matter how ill-equipped he might be when he faced the potential devastator of the city of Senrival.

Once more the coach rounded a bend, and for the last time Gilels found himself uncomfortably intimate with his fat neighbor. Then the trees fell away, and a wide prospect of twinkling lights opened out on either hand. The Musiciam stared, entranced, at this city built, against all logic of his kind, beneath the open sky.

For a moment, agoraphobia gripped him. In his own world and those others his kind inhabited, habitations were inevitably dug deep beneath mountains or under ploughlands.

Safe, of course, and easy to warm and cool—yet the glittering display before him almost persuaded him that other ways might have their own positive points.

Pitch torches and oil lamps stood in standards or hung from poles along the street into which they plunged, the hooves of the horses ringing and clattering on cobblestones. Yet to his amazement, from time to time he saw a high-tech trondbim blazing blue-white brilliance upon the façades of buildings decorated with carvings in stone, carvings in wood, even carvings hammered into metal.

He realized, after a few rods, that most of those carvings represented Diophors, the resident daemon and periodical downfall of Senrival. He found that he still did not believe in such a creature. His rigidly logical training denied its possibility. If something did, indeed, destroy Senrival on a regular basis, it was a natural creature of nasty habits, rather than a daemon from the days of superstition.

They went through arcades lined with small shops. Even so late, throngs of shoppers surrounded them. They curved into a wide central plaza at last, and drew up before a stone doorway whose heavy doors opened onto the paved space.

Gilels sighed. Whatever came next, this hellish journey was over. Wherever he was sent from Sextus, he would travel via a proper Transmission. The art of travel, he found, had been lost by his kind, for they had lived with instantaneous movement from place to place for centuries.

The driver opened the door and let down the step. Gilels waited for his fellow sufferers to get their stiff legs and awkward bundles out of the way before he groaned and began to struggle out. Immediately, he looked up toward the spot where he had seen the grampion tied.

Mercifully, it was still there. The driver, at his elbow, asked, "Songmaster Gilels?"

The musician nodded. "Get down the grampion," he said. "It must go with me at once. The luggage can follow, but I must have that when I attend the Master Despot. Was word left here for me?"

"Indeed, Songmaster. The innkeeper met me with the message, when I got down from the box. When you are ready, follow that young man, and he will lead you to your quarters. You will be informed when to meet with the Master Despot." The message was rattled off so precisely that Gilels knew it was word-perfect. When a people were illiterate, their memories had to be amazingly accurate, and literacy was not a thing that the world of Sextus had cultivated.

The young man waiting for him seemed impatient, as Gilels supervised the lowering of the grampion. Once the case was in hand, the youth set off, and the Songmaster had to hurry to keep up with him, while a boy with a barrow brought his bags. He had no time to examine the instrument, and he prayed that it was still playable after its rough journey.

The case bumped his shoulder and his knee, as he hastened through a garden so cunningly arranged that even now, in winter, the hardy greenery made it still graceful and pleasant. Beyond was an elaborate doorway, where the youth turned to speak to him.

The face was young and filled with scorn, but before the clean-cut lips could open, Gilels found himself saying in amazement, "You are no young man! You are a girl!"

At that the lips opened, indeed. "Girl! A woman! Shereva Messenger! Woman's garb is unhandy for one who carries messages up and down the ways of the city. I am one of a trained guild, used for centuries to convey word from place to place. How like one of your arrogant kind to think less well of me because of my sex!"

"Less well of you? No, indeed. I was just surprised, for the innkeeper said you were a man. On the worlds my people inhabit, women and men work together without prejudice."

Her dark-rimmed blue eyes widened. "Truly? Without laughing at women who must work for their bread?" But then she remembered her duty and backed away, frowning.

"But there is no time for chatter. You have come, I was told, to save Senrival from her daemon. Such a promise seems to me the cruelest of lies, for tomorrow's dawn will see the city filled with corpses, as has happened every double hand-span of years since our kind has lived here."

Her expression was bitter, as she said, "My father died on the night of the daemon, but he sent my mother and sister and brother and me into the forest for safety. Most of those you see in the streets have done the same, offering themselves as tribute, but saving those who will carry on their families."

Gilels felt a twinge of pity. "Why do you stay? You must have been very young twenty years ago, when it happened last. Why do you not save yourself?"

Her head went up proudly. "I am a messenger. My sister and her young are safe, and my brother's family is with them. We two go to Diophors tonight, as our family's gift to our city. But I will carry out my duties to the last, and you are my duty for this night. Come after me to your quarters. When you are ready, I will lead you to the Master Despot."

They went up a curving stair, and she opened an ornate door. "I will wait in the courtyard," she said. "Do not delay. There is little time."

There was warm water for washing, for which Gilels was grateful. The shell-shaped tub beneath the large urn, heated by a charcoal brazier and fitted with a spigot, was already full. Once he had removed the grime of travel, he put on his best wing-sleeved coat and his silken tights.

Only then did he set up the grampion, fitting its pegs and keys into place. He tried the open notes, then the mutes, his fingers tentative.

Its tone was clear and true, which was wonderful after such an arduous trip. Though Gilels still did not understand why he could not have been Transported directly into Senrival, his irritation subsided as he ran a double scale. Yes, the instrument would do, and no "a capella" attempt would have to be made.

There came a rap on his door. That peremptory young woman was there, he knew, and he called, "Immediately!" She loaded the awkward instrument onto his back and opened the door. "Now show me the way."

* * * * * * *

The Master Despot received him in a modest study filled with mnemonic devices. Of all the refinements and conveniences that the Great Association had offered the people of Sextus, only that of literacy had been rejected, without argument or reasoning. At the time of recontact, nobody understood why, but now he had observed the people, the alertness and retentiveness of their minds, and he thought he understood. Literacy eroded memory, that was plain to see.

Now he set the grampion beside a curtained doorway leading

out into a garden. He set his right toe forward and swept back the wings of his coat in a graceful salute. The Despot smiled amid his luxuriant beard, only the waggling of the silken strands showing his amiability.

Gilels straightened. "I bring the concern of my people, my guild, and others who inhabit this arm of the galaxy," he began. "I am sent to deliver your city from the daemon Diophors tonight. Let us pray together that I am able to succeed."

"There is little time for niceties," remarked the Despot. "Diophors will appear through a crevice in the floor of the forest, five hundred meters from my garden wall, before the green moon rises past the ilex tree."

Gilels calculated frantically. Given the rate of rotation of the green moon, plus the fact that it was now already showing above the garden wall—egad! He had only about fifteen minutes to prepare for this strange encounter.

"What place is best for positioning my instrument?" he asked. His voice was unsteady, to his disgust, but Shereva Messenger kindly took no notice of that. She caught one end and motioned for him to lift the other.

"In the garden, so the people can see," she grunted, lifting.

He would have preferred a more distant site, but he followed her into the garden, where they set the instrument on grass, doubly green in the moonlight. Then he understood why: a wall had been removed from the garden, and beyond it, on a slight rise, were hundreds of people, waiting.

Most were men of middle age, though some women as young as Shereva were among them. Even a few children stood toward the front, staring at him with great curiosity.

Gilels, used to audiences, made a bow. Then he turned to tune the grampion. A delicate trill rippled beneath his fingers. A crescendo followed, with bass notes gonging into the air. He tried a treble tremolo. Everything was excellent.

Now the moon was tangled in the ilex tree, about to pull free of the upper branches. Gilels held his breath. Was he about to see a real daemon? He would not and could not believe that. But there was something there, something so terrible that a city had died many times on the night when the stars reached this precise configuration.

Beyond the wall separating the garden from the wood, a shimmer of scarlet began to glow. It grew in intensity to blinding brilliance, and Gilels closed his eyes extremely tightly. That triggered the signal implanted in his skull by the Magister Cantorum, sending the impulses of his internal sensors across the voids to the Schola

Cantorum.

When he opened his eyes again, he looked into five blazing orbs. It had to be a daemon. There were the ugly snout, the coils, the warts and knobbly hands with long discolored nails. They looked just like those in the ancient books he had studied before leaving Andios. But there was no time for staring. He must act, if he and all those watching were to survive.

His hands moved on the grampion, and a melody filled the air with sweetness. The eyes atop the wall dimmed a bit...but not enough. The maw, studded with rotted teeth, was opening. Gilels knew that once that poisoned breath poured forth, everyone in Senrival, including himself, was doomed.

He played more quickly, sending poignant notes into the green-tinged air. He joined his own voice with that of the instrument in the song his Magister had chosen as potent for this occasion.

The craggy mouth closed. The eyelids lowered over eyes that had paled to pink. Soothed and charmed by the music, Diophors forgot his hunger, attendant upon awakening from twenty years of sleep, and his five eyes dreamed across the garden. His terrible face lost its ferocity, as the music filled the alien mind of the creature.

Gilels felt the Field forming about him. He moved closer to the wall, away from the grampion, toward Diophors. When the Field had enveloped them both, he willed his monitors to act, and the Transmission began. He sang softly, all the way home to the Schola Cantorum.

* * * * * * *

Without any doubt, Diophors was the most popular exhibit ever donated to the Zoological Gardens. Behind one-way impermaglas shielding, the Daemon, the only surviving member of his species, slept in red-lit visibility for months at a time. At intervals, the computers of the Gardens arranged the subtle shifts and compulsions of artificial gravities, duplicating the twenty-year cycle of Sextus.

Then the daemon woke in his duplicate of the forest den, and artificial protein, animated by mechanical means, seemed to die and to decay, and the creature fed (wondering, it is probable, why he was not hungrier). The spectacle was dramatic, gruesome, and yet harmless, and the tourists, as well as the inhabitants of Andios, loved it.

On a plaque beneath the impermaglas wall, there was this inscription:

DIOPHORS, *daemonis horribilis*,

DONATED BY THE SCHOLA

CANTORUM THROUGH THE EFFORTS OF

SONGMASTER GILELS

Through the efforts of this dedicated Songmaster, the city of Senrival, on Sextus XXV, was delivered of a regularly occurring disaster, which in the generations since the colonization of that world has claimed nine hundred thousand lives. Sextus, in gratitude, has offered numbers of their Messengers, trained as dependable couriers with impeccable memories, for sensitive communications throughout our Association.

* * * * * * *

Gilels never tired of visiting that display, when he was at leisure, which was not often. And he always recalled, as he read the legend, the awed and joyful face of Shereva Messenger, when she was chosen as the first of those special members of her guild to travel among other worlds.

He was warmed, as he moved from world to world, singing away the troubles of their inhabitants, at the recollection of this most dangerous of his missions. The fact that he survived his journey in the coach, it always seemed to him, almost outweighed his capture of the daemon itself.

ABOUT THE AUTHOR

The author of seventy books, more than forty of them published commercially, **ARDATH MAYHAR** began her career in the early eighties with science fiction novels from Doubleday and TSR. Atheneum published several of her young adult and children's novels. Changing focus, she wrote westerns (as **Frank Cannon**) and mountain man novels (as **John Killdeer**), four prehistoric Indian books under her own name, and historical western *High Mountain Winter* under the byline **Frances Hurst**.

Recently she has been working with on-line publishers. *A Road of Stars* was her first original novel to appear in print-on-demand format. Many of her out-of-print titles are now available from e-publishers fictionwise.com and renebooks.com; many other novels and collections are being published by the Borgo Press Imprint of Wildside Press.

Now eighty, Mayhar was widowed in 1999, after forty-one years of marriage, and has four grown sons. She works at home, writing short fiction and nonfiction, and doing book doctoring professionally. Her web pages can be found at:

w2.netdot.com/ardathm/

and

http://ofearna.us/books/mayhar.html

www.ingramcontent.com/pod-product-compliance
Lightning Source LLC
Chambersburg PA
CBHW022152260626
47155CB00017B/1853